**Praise for #1 *New York Times* and
#1 *USA TODAY* bestselling author Robyn Carr**

"A touching romance that adds another chapter to Carr's engaging series that hovers at the borders of women's fiction and romance and is sure to appeal to fans of both."

—*Library Journal* on *A New Hope*

"Carr fills her seventh visit to Thunder Point with a charming cast of characters and a tender love story."

—*Publishers Weekly* on *One Wish*

"The captivating sixth installment of Carr's Thunder Point series...brings up big emotions."

—*Publishers Weekly* on *The Homecoming*

"In Carr's very capable hands, the Thunder Point saga continues to delight."

—*RT Book Reviews* on *The Promise*

"Sexy, funny, and intensely touching."

—*Library Journal* on *The Chance*

"A touch of danger and suspense make the latest in Carr's Thunder Point series a powerful read."

—*RT Book Reviews* on *The Hero*

"With her trademark mixture of humor, realistic conflict, and razor-sharp insights, Carr brings Thunder Point to vivid life."

—*Library Journal* on *The Newcomer*

"No one can do small-town life like Carr."

—*RT Book Reviews* on *The Wanderer*

"Carr has hit her stride with this captivating series."

—*Library Journal* on the Virgin River series

Also available from ROBYN CARR and MIRA Books

Thunder Point

WILDEST DREAMS
A NEW HOPE
ONE WISH
THE HOMECOMING
THE PROMISE
THE CHANCE
THE HERO
THE NEWCOMER
THE WANDERER

Virgin River

MY KIND OF CHRISTMAS
SUNRISE POINT
REDWOOD BEND
HIDDEN SUMMIT
BRING ME HOME FOR CHRISTMAS
HARVEST MOON
WILD MAN CREEK
PROMISE CANYON
MOONLIGHT ROAD
ANGEL'S PEAK
FORBIDDEN FALLS
PARADISE VALLEY
TEMPTATION RIDGE
SECOND CHANCE PASS
A VIRGIN RIVER CHRISTMAS
WHISPERING ROCK
SHELTER MOUNTAIN
VIRGIN RIVER

Grace Valley

DEEP IN THE VALLEY
JUST OVER THE MOUNTAIN
DOWN BY THE RIVER

Novels

FOUR FRIENDS
A SUMMER IN SONOMA
NEVER TOO LATE
RUNAWAY MISTRESS
BLUE SKIES
THE WEDDING PARTY
THE HOUSE ON OLIVE STREET

Look for Robyn Carr's next novel
available soon from MIRA Books

16

ROBYN CARR

BRING ME HOME *for* CHRISTMAS

Recycling programs for this product may not exist in your area.

ISBN-13: 978-0-7783-1763-0

Bring Me Home for Christmas

For questions and comments about the quality of this book, please contact us at CustomerService@Harlequin.com.

www.MIRABooks.com

Printed in U.S.A.

For Colleen Gleason, whose friendship
and encouragement mean the world to me.

BRING ME HOME *for* CHRISTMAS

One

Rich Timm drove into Virgin River a mere ten hours after leaving San Diego. He'd made excellent time because he tended to ignore little things like speed limits. And…he had been trapped in the Ford truck with his twin sister, Becca, all day and had had about enough.

As Becca gazed out the window at the town, she muttered, "Seriously?"

"What?" Rich said.

"*This* is the place Denny never wants to leave? It isn't exactly…you know…*quaint.*"

Rich pulled up to the only bar in town, right next to a truck he knew belonged to one of two other buddies from the Marines who were meeting him here. "Maybe that's not what he was looking for." Rich put the truck in Park. Before he turned off the ignition, he turned in his seat and said to his sister, "Since you wouldn't let me warn Denny you were coming along, promise me you won't make trouble."

"Rich," she said with a laugh. "Why would I make trouble?"

"Oh, I don't know," he said, rolling his eyes. "Because you're his ex-girlfriend? Because this is a guys' hunting trip and you're not a guy and everyone will have to take care of you?"

"No one has to take care of me," she said indignantly. Then she smiled very sweetly. "I'm anxious to meet your other friends. And to hunt—I'm anxious to hunt."

He scowled. "Right," he said. "You expect me to believe you're going to shoot a duck and pluck it?"

If I have to pluck it with my teeth to be convincing, she thought. "Of course! I'm a little more excited about fly-fishing, though. I can't wait to try that." She opened her door. "You about ready?"

He grunted. "Do not be a problem. Do not be a pain in my ass for a week!"

"Do not be a jerk," she countered.

Becca had arrived at Rich's town house at three in the morning, big suitcase and shotgun in hand. When he opened the door, wearing nothing but boxers, she said, "Guess what? I don't have anything to do this week, so I'm coming with you. I've never been duck hunting or fly-fishing."

"You're out of your mind, right?" he said, scratching his hair, which was crazy from bed. "Didn't you tell Mom and Dad you were going home with Doug for Thanksgiving?"

She shook her head. "That isn't going to work out and I don't want Mom and Dad to cancel their trip plans just so I'm not alone on Thanksgiving."

"Why isn't it going to work out?"

"Doug's way too busy—he's going all the way to the East Coast for two days. Come on, this is a great idea. A little last minute, but it'll be fun. Be a sport."

"And what about Denny?" he asked. "Your ex?"

She put a hand on her hip. "It's time we all moved on from that, don't you think? I have no hard feelings and I'm sure he doesn't. He probably has a girlfriend. This is a perfect opportunity to make sure it's all cool between us. I mean, really—since you guys are good friends and all… And it was a long time ago."

"Yeah, but it was brutal," Rich said, looking down at her suspiciously.

"We were young," she said with a shrug.

"And what does Doug think about this?" Rich asked.

"Doug isn't the jealous type. He told me to have a good time. Anyway, Doug is not your problem."

"I know," Rich said. "Apparently, *you're* my problem." He let her come into his town house.

"You better know what you're doing," he said. "If you screw up my hunting trip, you're going to pay."

Becca's decision really hadn't been as spur of the moment as she had pretended. A lot of planets had converged and she found herself planning, quickly. Rich had been talking about this hunting trip for weeks, with good old Denny—the guy she once thought she was going to marry. The guy who broke up with her three years ago. The guy she still thought about *way* too much. Then the elementary school where she taught shut down, due to financial issues they just couldn't resolve, and she found herself suddenly unemployed. And Doug, the law student she'd been seeing for the past year, asked her to look at engagement rings.

She would have had nothing to do besides look for work during the Thanksgiving holidays—a dismal prospect—and worry about the fact that Doug was probably leading up to a marriage proposal while the last guy was still on her mind. *All the time.*

She didn't get it. Why did she still think about Denny, dream about him? Was it just wanting what was out of reach, rather than appreciating what was right in front of her? When Denny broke up with her before going to Afghanistan, she had been devastated. By the time he looked her up two years later and suggested they give it another try, she had been furious and told him he was too late, she wasn't interested. Then she met Doug Carey a year ago, a good-looking, second-year law student, and her mother had been *so* relieved! Beverly Timm found Doug so much more appropriate for her daughter. Doug had it all. He was a good guy. Becca enjoyed spending time with him. He had a bright future. He came from a successful, financially secure family. He loved her. His family had their own *sailboat*! It made absolutely no sense to continue to think about Denny.

There was a time when Becca had dreamed of a Christmas proposal and a beautiful ring under the tree. Christmas was her favorite season—the sparkling lights, the carols, the time with her family. Now she feared it. She wanted to want to marry Doug Carey, but she just couldn't commit to him while this ghost haunted her. It would be so wrong. So unfair to both of them.

So she had decided. She was going to force Rich to take her with him to this Virgin River, the place Denny had chosen as his home. She'd hunt and fish and try to figure out why she just couldn't let go of the guy. She would see him again and come to the conclusion that it had been a crush, a first love between a couple of kids, that she had idealized in her mind. Then she'd go home to the perfect man, finally appreciating him as much as he deserved.

They would live happily ever after and the image of Denny would disappear.

She looked around the town once more as she went up the steps of the log-cabin bar where they were all meeting. "Seriously?" she said again under her breath. It was kind of a dumpy old town; the houses were small, a lot of them had peeling paint. There weren't even streetlights or sidewalks. Besides a little grocery store and the bar, there didn't appear to be any other businesses. What did these people do for entertainment? For fun? "Hunting and fishing," she reminded herself. "Whoopee."

Yeah, she was hopeful. Just a look at this backwoods little town was promising—she'd figure out what happened with Denny, where it all went so wrong and why. They'd been so different in the first place. Now she had to find a way to move on, so she could happily marry a man with a law degree and his own *sailboat*.

Denny Cutler had come to Virgin River in search of roots, and a year after stumbling into Jack's Bar, he was sure he'd found the place where he would live for the rest of his life. He had friends who were as tight as family. He also had a career, one he had never in his craziest dreams envisioned—he was a farmer! An associate in Jilly

Farms, an organic farm that promised to grow strong and profitable.

It had been Jack's idea that Denny reach out to a couple of his buddies, maybe from the Marine Corps, where he'd spent four years, and invite them to Virgin River for a little guy stuff—hunting, fishing, poker. Jilly Farms wasn't too busy in late fall and could spare him for a few days. He knew exactly which guys he wanted to invite. Troy, Dirk and Rich had been like brothers to him during his deployment to Iraq. Dirk Curtis and Troy were both reservists and lived near Sacramento. Rich Timm, also known as Big Richie or sometimes just Big, was from San Diego, where Denny grew up, though Denny hadn't met him until the Corps. Rich got out of the Marines after two years, finished college and was now an engineer who worked for the highway department in San Diego, building freeways and bridges. All three of these guys loved camping, hiking, fishing, hunting—anything a little rugged. They would love Virgin River.

There was only one downside to his friendship with Rich—he was Becca's twin brother. That's how Denny had met his old girlfriend, through Rich, while they were on leave together back in San Diego, years ago. After Denny and Becca broke up, the continued friendship put Denny a little too close to all available news about Becca.

Rich only passed along info if he asked, of course, which he couldn't seem to keep himself from doing, even though he wanted to forget her as thoroughly as she'd forgotten him.

When plans fell together for the four guys, it turned out Thanksgiving week was the best time for everyone. "Perfect," Jack said. "We've got Riordan cabins on the river and my guesthouse is available—plenty of room. We have duck hunting, fishing and Preacher always serves a big Thanksgiving dinner at the bar. The day after Thanksgiving, we go out into the woods to chop down a thirty-foot Christmas tree to put outside the bar—that's a circus you don't want to miss."

So the plans were set. Troy, Dirk and Rich were due to arrive on the Sunday before Thanksgiving and depart a week later.

Denny had had a few rough years before settling in Virgin River—his mother had died, he reentered the Corps and was deployed to Afghanistan, he broke up with Becca after they'd been together for over three years—but finally, at the age of twenty-five, things were finally falling into place for him. Life was good. He was happy.

Troy and Dirk arrived by four o'clock on Sunday afternoon. Denny was on hand at the bar to greet them and serve them up a beer, and both Jack and Preacher made a point to be around. Dirk and

Troy were going to stay in one of Luke Riordan's cabins, so Luke and Colin Riordan dropped by for a quick beer to be part of the welcoming party. Preacher had a hearty meal planned, but since it was the Sunday night before a big family holiday week like Thanksgiving, there weren't too many out-of-towners in the bar—just four hunters over in the corner at the table by the hearth, enjoying a pitcher of beer.

They practically had the place to themselves.

Finally the door to the bar opened and Big Richie stepped inside. He stood just inside the entrance wearing a look on his face that Denny could describe only as apologetic. Then she stepped inside, right behind him.

Becca!

What the hell? Denny stood behind the bar, next to Jack, his mouth hanging open. She lifted her chin and smiled at the gathering.

Rich gave a lame shrug.

God, she sure hadn't gotten any worse looking, Denny thought. Five-seven, slim, large blue eyes. Her sun-streaked hair was pulled back in a clip that left it flouncing in large, loose curls on the back of her head with little wisps around her face. She was tanned, of course. She was a beach bunny. The memory of how she looked in a very tiny bikini came instantly to Denny's mind, although those long legs and perfect butt sure did justice to a pair of jeans and boots.

He was in a complete daze. Except for the physical response. He was so glad he was standing behind the bar.

Smiling, she walked around her brother and approached the bar. She barely looked at Denny. "Hi," she said, putting out her hand first to Troy. "I'm Becca, Rich's sister. I hope I'm not intruding."

Dirk and Troy knew of Becca, but they'd never actually met her. Troy took her hand and a smile slid slowly across his face. "Not. At. All," he said smoothly.

She grinned at him as he hung on to her hand. "Bet you have a name," she said.

"Ah…yeah… I'll think of it in a second…"

"Troy," Denny said impatiently. "His name is *Troy.*"

"Nice to meet you, Troy." She offered her hand to Dirk.

"Dirk Curtis," he said. "Nice to finally meet you."

"Becca, what are you doing here?" Denny asked.

She lifted one shoulder and tilted her head. "Well, I guess it's going to be either duck hunting or fly-fishing—two things I've been dying to try. I need to expand my horizons a little bit. Thanks for including me."

"I *didn't* include you."

"Rich said it would probably be okay, and

thanks." She looked between Dirk and Troy. "You guys don't mind, do you?"

"It's a pleasure," Dirk said.

Troy leaned an elbow on the bar, his head on his hand. "I take it you don't hunt or fish?"

"She *surfs*," Denny said sharply, glowering.

"And I sail, among other things," she added pleasantly. "If you guys show me the hunting and fishing ropes, I'll be glad to teach you to surf—I'm much better at it than Rich, although he might be a slightly better sailor. Don't do anything different because I'm along—I'm just one of the guys on this trip. I promise not to get in the way."

"Right," Denny said.

"Seriously," she insisted, narrowing her eyes at him.

"You're going to be sorry you said that when one of these clowns decides to pee on a bush," he said snidely, lifting one eyebrow.

A bark of laughter came from Colin Riordan, which marked the first time Denny remembered there were others present. Just a second after Colin's laugh, a giant hand came down on his shoulder and Preacher said, "Give me a hand in the kitchen, would you, Den?"

He treated her to one final, withering glare before following the big cook into the kitchen. Once there, he found himself face-to-face with a man who could easily top him for fierce, intimidating stares. Preacher said, "What the *hell*, Dennis! Were you raised by apes?"

"She's my ex-girlfriend, all right?" Denny said by way of explanation.

"We got that," Preacher said, his hands on his hips, his bushy black eyebrows drawn together in a scowl. "And your excuse for acting like an ass is…?"

"It was complicated," he said. "My mom died, I closed up and wouldn't talk, shut Becca out when she wanted to help. Then, I rejoined the Corps and told her after the fact. About which she was very pissed. So I broke up with her before I deployed so she could date other guys while I was gone."

As he was finishing that tale, Jack entered the kitchen and got the last of it, but he didn't need the details. He'd actually heard the story before. Now Jack wore his upside-down, contemplative smile, nodding. "Makes perfect sense," he said.

"It does?" Denny asked.

"Of course. You can't stand to even see her shake hands with another guy in a public bar, so you cut her loose to date someone else. Oh, yeah. Brilliant."

"It was not a smart time in my life," he admitted. "After my two-year commitment, I went straight to her and apologized, asked if maybe we could try again."

"And she said?" Jack asked.

"I believe the direct quote was 'Dream on.' We argued a little bit and she told me I'd been replaced, that she'd probably be engaged in a year. That's when I decided to come up here. Start over."

"Well, don't look now, Denny, but your past has followed you. You have to go out there and apologize. Again."

"Wait a sec, she shouldn't have just dropped in like this, right on my—my—my whatever this is. She should've called. Or Big should've called!"

"You seem to be the only one put out by her appearance," Jack pointed out.

"Rich didn't look all that happy. And the other two? The only time they're not on the prowl looking for chicks is when they're asleep. I'm sure they're thrilled to meet Becca."

"Then if it bothers you, I suggest you keep an eye on things," Jack said.

Denny stole a glance at Preacher, who gave a nod.

"Starting with you having a word with Becca, see if you can sort things out enough to have a good week," Jack said. "You can't make everyone else miserable just because you have a bug up your ass about a girl. Call a truce or something. Whatever it takes." And with that, Jack returned to the bar.

What Denny really wanted to do was take off, out the back door.

No, not true, he thought. What he'd rather do was walk back into the bar, grab her and kiss the hell out of her. And beat the crap out of anyone who tried to get between him and her.

But he heard someone say *Dream on* inside his head. And the voice was hers.

"That went well," Becca said as soon as Denny stepped through the swinging door into the kitchen with Preacher. Jack quickly served Rich a beer and Becca a glass of wine before following Denny and Preacher.

Becca took a breath and said to Troy and Dirk, "In case you missed the weird, shocked look on Denny's face, we used to date."

"They know, Becca," Rich said. "We were all in Iraq together, remember?"

Troy was still leaning on his hand, elbow on the bar, gazing at her. "Believe me, I wasn't looking at Denny," he said.

"I'm probably the last person he expected to show up…."

"No," Rich said, irritably. "Luke Skywalker was the last person. You were second to last." He hefted his beer and took a long drink.

"We didn't part on the best of terms," she explained. "But that was a while ago and we both told Rich there were no hard feelings."

"Because that's what people *say*, Becca," Rich

explained impatiently. "I told you we should've called him first."

"Well, gee, it was last minute. Rich had been talking about this for weeks, I didn't have anything to do." She grinned. "I thought maybe some cold drizzle and the acrid smell of gunpowder might shake things up a little, be a nice change."

"Just so you know," Dirk said. "We have a pretty strong rule about another guy's girl. As in, no touching. Unless we're given a pass by the guy. You know?"

"Are you *kidding* me? Permission?" she asked. "Because that borders on icky."

Dirk just shrugged. "That's how it is with friends."

"Well, it's not an issue. He broke up with me. Over three years ago." Actually, she could easily figure out the number of days....

"That's probably a pass," Troy said. "Wouldn't you say, Dirk?"

"God," Rich said. "I'm going to need another beer! This *is* my sister! Even if she is a pain in my—"

Luke coughed. Colin laughed. "You starting to feel old?" Luke asked his brother.

"Elderly," Colin answered. "Much as I'd love to stay and watch this, I think I'd better hit the road. Happy hunting." He winked.

"Cabin number four, boys," Luke said. "It's unlocked. Jack or Denny will give you directions."

"Oh, are you Mr. Riordan?" Becca asked. To his nod, she asked, "Any chance there's another cabin out at your place that I could rent? Otherwise I have to stay with Rich, and God knows..." She shook her head and shuddered as if in revulsion.

"You bet," Luke said. "Try number two—also unlocked."

"Cool," she said.

"Very cool," Dirk said. "Thanks, man. See you around."

"Yeah, thanks," Troy said. "Nice meeting you guys. See you later."

And then Denny was back. The expression on his face wasn't much improved. It was starting to irritate her that he couldn't at least fake being happy to see her. Maybe being finally finished with him would be easier than she'd thought.

He walked around the bar and stood right in front of Becca. "I need to talk to you for a minute, Becca. All right?"

That made her a little nervous; it sounded like he might be getting ready to tell her when her bus was leaving for San Diego. She hoped her emotions didn't show. She tilted her head to one side, smiled into his brown eyes and said, "Sure. Shoot."

"Privately." He stepped back. "Come outside with me. It'll just take a second."

He turned and she followed. It wasn't even five-thirty, yet it was almost completely dark outside.

Though she could see there were space heaters on the porch, they weren't lit. She faced him, waited, shivering in the cold.

"I apologize," he said. "If I'd known you were coming, if I'd had time to get used to the idea, I would've been a lot more..."

"Civil?" she added for him, lifting both tawny eyebrows.

"Becca, this is a *hunting* trip!"

"I know that, Denny. Rich hasn't stopped talking about it for weeks."

"What are you *doing* here?"

She took a breath. "It was very last minute. I packed last night. When I showed up at his condo at three this morning to go with, Rich pitched a fit. I told him I needed a change, a break. He said it was a bad idea, because it was all guys, and I said I'd skip the getting drunk and smoking cigars part, that I'd get my own place to stay and, you know... I just wanted to get out of town. Too early to ski, too cold to surf without a wet suit."

"What about work?"

"Well... I got laid off. The private school where I've been teaching shut down. We'd seen it coming but it was still a shock. I'm going to substitute until I can land something permanent. But for right now, it's a holiday week, my parents are going out of town and I wanted something fun to do, to kind of offset being so bummed about losing my job."

He looked into her eyes for a long moment, then slowly reached for her left hand, pulling it out of her jacket pocket. "I don't see a ring," he said. "What about the boyfriend? He can't like the idea of you going on a guys' hunting trip?"

"He's tied up with finals and stuff," she said. "And he's going home to Cape Cod for Thanksgiving with his family."

"Finals?" Denny asked. "You're marrying a college kid?"

"Law student," she said. "And we're not engaged. Yet."

"But you're going to be engaged?"

"Probably. We've talked about it. We looked at rings. And stuff."

"Right," Denny said. "And he's okay with you going on a hunting trip with a bunch of guys, including your ex?"

"He trusts me," she said. And there was the little fact that she hadn't told him all the details. It wasn't that she couldn't, but she might've overestimated his casualness about this event. She'd probably keep the fact that her ex was also present to herself. After all, that was the whole point of the trip. She had to figure this thing out before Christmas.

She told Doug she was with her brother. Doug liked her brother.

"Okay, okay," Denny said, rubbing his hand

along the back of his neck. "All right, listen. If you insist you're going to do this stupid thing—"

"Careful," she warned, crossing her arms over her chest.

"Are you here to hunt, really?"

She narrowed her eyes. "Why else would I be here?"

"Do you even have a gun with you?"

She leaned toward him. "Yes," she hissed.

"Stick close to me. Or maybe Rich. We'll make sure you're safe and know what to do. With the gun, that is."

"I *know* what to do with the gun," she said indignantly. "I've never killed anything but skeet, but I know what to do. I'm in danger of getting hooked in the ear trying to fly-fish, but I'm a good shot."

"You've been shooting skeet?" he asked. Denny was a Marine marksman. He had a sniper ribbon. "Since when?"

Her dad had taught her, but she said, "The boyfriend." She wasn't really sure why she'd lied. So he wouldn't think she was just a loser who still wasn't over him? She'd have to think about that.

"Great. But there's a lot more to know than that. You staying with Rich? Out at Jack's?"

"No," she said, shaking her head. "Mr. Riordan has another cabin. I'll go out there. I don't share space with Rich—he's a slob."

"No," Denny said. "You can take my place—it's

just an efficiency, but it's right in town, just down the street. The landlord and landlady will look out for you if you need anything. You'll be safe there."

"It's not your job to keep me safe, Denny. And where will you be, if I'm in your place?"

"With the slob."

Two

When Becca was a nineteen-year-old college student at the University of Southern California, she began dating Denny, a Marine. He was at Camp Pendleton with her brother at the time. For a few blissful months, they saw each other every time Becca came home from USC for a weekend. She fell in love with him *immediately.* She spent the summer at home and every time Denny could get away from the base, they went to the beach and surfed or played volleyball, hiked into the mountains or biked along the coast, spending every possible minute together.

Rich and Denny went to Iraq together for a year and her emails to Denny were long, gushy and frequent—several a day. Her care packages were stuffed with lovingly collected treats. Then he came home from Iraq, exited the Corps, and for almost a year, life was heaven. When Becca was home from USC, they were inseparable. They had so much fun together. They could laugh for hours; they could make love for hours. They talked about getting married after Becca graduated with her teaching degree.

Then things got crazy. Denny's mom, Sue, who had been battling breast cancer for years, became very sick, very suddenly. At least Denny was home with her through her final battle. He was there for her when she died and Becca did everything she could think of to show her support, though because she was at school most of the time, she was limited to weekend visits and daily phone calls.

But Denny shut down. He grew distant, detached. Instead of leaning on her and accepting her comfort, he reenlisted in the Marine Corps without saying a word to her, knowing he'd be sent back to the war. And sure enough, he got orders for Afghanistan almost right away. Before he deployed, he said, "It's a hard world, Becca, and I don't want to worry about how you'll get by if something happens to me. Until I can get back home and get my head straight, let's just take a breather. We'll take another look at this in a year or so..."

"Are you *crazy*?" she asked him, choking on her tears. "Don't you know how much I *love* you?"

"Yes," he said. "And it's kind of heavy on me right now."

"But we've been together three years. We talked about getting married!"

"Yeah, I shouldn't have gotten so far ahead of myself," he said. "Go on, get to know other guys. Have a good time. You deserve it."

So he left—left the country and the relationship. She reached out a couple of times through Rich, whose friendship apparently wasn't too heavy for Denny, since they kept in touch. But Denny didn't respond to her.

It was a painful, lonely year. She'd never forget those late nights of sitting up until two, three, four in the morning to watch news coverage of the war because Afghanistan was twelve hours ahead of L.A. She didn't know a person could cry so much. She lost weight and there were dark circles under her eyes. She had no sense of humor and grew more lethargic by the day. Her grades dropped significantly, though she hung on so she could graduate. Her mother was beside herself with worry, and with anger toward Denny.

The painful truth was that Becca's life had been pretty easy until then, when she lost the man she'd thought was the love of her life. It was a horrible experience. If they'd been in touch so she could occasionally have that reassurance that he was all right, that he loved her, she would have gotten through it much better.

By the time Becca learned that Denny was

safely returned to the U.S., she was a newly minted second-grade teacher, and she'd managed to do a lot of thinking. The way he'd acted was irrational; she'd expected their relationship to be a team effort, a true partnership in which he could count on her in hard times and she could count on him.

She heard through Rich that Denny finished his two-year commitment at Camp Lejeune, but even though he was stateside again, he didn't get in touch with her. During that time, Becca came to some conclusions about the kind of relationship she needed. She wasn't sure she'd ever get to share her thoughts with Denny, but in fact she did. When Denny exited the Corps for the second time. Rich gave him the address for Becca's apartment and he went to see her.

"Okay," he said, "it was a stupid move, breaking up with you. But I was all torn up over my mom's death. If you're game, I'd like to try again."

"Game?" she repeated, stunned. Outraged. He'd dumped her and ignored her for two painful years and that's how he came back around? *"Game?"*

"Look, Becca, I can admit to being screwed up, all right?"

"There's no question about that, Denny," she said. "I'm teaching school now, you know. Second grade. Seven-year-olds. I love them—they're precious. One of my kids has Tourette's syndrome and some days are real hard for him. One of my little girls is recovering from six months of chemo after being diagnosed with leukemia. If we try again, fall in love again, get married and have a family, and one of *our* kids gets sick, will you bail? Will it be *too heavy* for you?"

"I admit, I was wrong…"

"Will you be wrong again? Leave to deal with whatever heartache it is alone? Leave me behind while you try to figure out your head?"

"I hope not," he had said.

She lifted her chin, blinked away her tears and said, "I haven't heard from you in two years. I have a guy in my life now who isn't going to bolt on me if times get hard."

"Really?" he asked. "Rich didn't say anything…"

"Rich hasn't met him yet. I'll probably be engaged in a year. I guess that means I'm not *game.* You might have to come up with something more compelling if you want a second chance."

She had been vindicated by the expression of shock and disbelief on his face. Did he really think he could screw up that bad, walk back into her life with some lame apology and wipe out the pain and loneliness she'd suffered for *two whole years*?

He did. He said, "Well, I really blew that one. I'm sorry, Becca. I'm an idiot and I'm sorry."

And then he had left. Again. Left her, left San Diego. Rich said he'd gone to some little town in

Northern California in search of his biological father and a new beginning.

She had lied about the other guy, about the imminent engagement, out of hurt and anger. So Becca, who hadn't been dating because she'd been grieving, said yes to a date with a guy she met on the beach—Doug Carey, down from UCLA Law School. And what she found was a guy who wasn't very complicated. He had a list of commendable qualities—brains, education, money, confidence and looks. The thought of being with him forever should have lit up Becca's world. Her mother, Beverly, was *thrilled.*

But it was as if Denny had left a hole in her heart. She knew she should dive at the chance to marry Doug, but instead, it scared her to death. She needed to get over that if she was ever to be happy again.

Now here they were, Denny and Becca, both twenty-five, six years older than the day they met. The past few years had been really rough. Then Rich started talking about a guys' hunting trip with Denny coming up, and she began to wonder—*is this a chance to face him and figure out why I can't let go?*

Then she was suddenly jobless. Doug was tied up at UCLA with finals and study and was flying home for a quick Thanksgiving with his family. He had invited her along, but her mind was made up—she wanted to go hunting with Rich. She didn't *exactly* lie to her mother, but she did say "Don't worry about me for Thanksgiving. Doug invited me to Cape Cod with him." So her parents had planned a last-minute trip to Cabo, since their kids would be away. Becca went to a sportsman's store for clothes and gear, packed a big suitcase, showed up on Rich's doorstep in the predawn and insisted on going along. *Once and for all, I'm confronting this!*

And here she and Denny stood, on the porch at Jack's Bar, staring each other down. Trying to get a grip on this strange reunion.

"We're going to have to go back in there, have a drink and some laughs, eat Preacher's dinner," Denny said to her. "We're going to have to call a truce. Let bygones be bygones. Whatever."

"Fine," she said. "I'm not the one acting like there's a problem."

"You took me by surprise," he said. "I shouldn't have been so rude. Sorry. But it was a guys' trip and you are definitely not a guy."

Well. At least he noticed that. Because she was noticing him—that square, unshaven jaw, crazy hair that looked so thick it should probably be thinned, dark brown eyes, wide shoulders. The way his jeans fit over his narrow hips and long legs. It made her feel warm. *Note to self, remember this reaction. There's no logical reason for this, but it's still happening. I feel him all over me. Damn it all.*

"I kind of insisted, and Rich thought it would be okay, if I wasn't any trouble. I can hold my own in outdoor sports."

"You pressured him," Denny said.

"I'm the oldest—he can't say no to me. I told him I really wanted a break and that I'd fit in fine."

"Yeah. Sure."

"Is this how you call a truce? By needling me and trying to make me feel like I'm invading your territory? The other guys seem to be okay with it."

"Look, Becca, we should have talked first, all right? Obviously there are some hard feelings between us."

She stuffed her hands back in her pockets. "Well, I was the one who got dumped and I'm not holding a grudge."

"I said I was sorry and you dumped me right back. You have to admit, I apologized."

She smirked and shook her head sadly. "That you did. That you did."

"What else could I have done?"

"Well, I wonder," she said. "Did it ever occur to you that you might have to do more than apologize? You could've tried twice, I guess. Or, hey—maybe even three times. You could've sent flowers or something. You could've tried to get the point across that you really were sorry and that you weren't out of your mind anymore. But you were on the next train out of San Diego. Now, I'm cold. I'm going back in by the fire. I'm going to drink my wine, have a good meal, laugh with my new friends. If you want to be miserable, have at it. I really couldn't care less." She turned and went back into the bar.

And Denny thought, *I could have changed everything with* flowers?

They had a little camaraderie over dinner; some reminiscing among the guys, some jokes. The subject of Denny and Becca was strictly avoided. Denny was just a little more quiet than usual, but no one seemed to notice. Probably because Becca was adorable, funny and just slightly flirtatious.

Denny wanted to shake her.

No one was more relieved than Denny when it was time for everyone to say good-night and retire to their respective rooms. This event was not shaping up the way he expected.

Troy and Dirk went off to their cabin by the river and Denny and Rich went with Becca down the street to Denny's efficiency over the Fitchs' garage. "I'll show Becca the room and pack a few things," Denny said. "I can give her my keys and leave her my truck just in case, but she won't need it."

"Sure," Rich said. "I'll wait here. But let's move it, huh? I've been up since before four...."

"Five minutes," he said, heading inside.

Becca was already halfway up the stairs, struggling with a very large suitcase. He took the stairs two at a time and said, "I'll get that."

"No, please. I insist on pulling my own weight."

"Come on, gimme," he said, grabbing the suitcase out of her hand.

He nearly toppled down the stairs. It weighed a ton. "Jesus," he swore. "What have you got in this thing?"

"Clothes. Warm clothes. A couple of jackets. Boots."

"And bricks?"

"I was doing fine," she said. "Let me have it."

"No, I've got it," he insisted. He winced as he hefted it, but he was not about to pull it up on its wheels, one step at a time, as she had been doing.

She skipped up the stairs ahead of him, getting out of his way, and waited at the top. "Thank you, Denny," she said. "Very thoughtful."

He opened the door.

"Oh." She laughed. "I was waiting for you to unlock it."

"Hardly anything is locked around here." He flipped on the light just inside the door and dropped her bag.

Denny went to the trunk at the foot of his bed and pulled out a military duffel. He went to the bathroom and got his shaving kit. While he was in there, he pulled out a clean towel for Becca, tossing his towel from the morning into the hamper. When he came out of the bathroom, she was standing in the middle of the room, checking it out. "There are clean sheets under the sink in the bathroom," he said.

She looked around the room with interest. "This is very…cute."

The bedspread was floral, the upholstery on the chair and ottoman was striped with some birds on it, the curtains yellow-and-white striped. The walls were yellow with white trim. "Mrs. Fitch decorated this room. She offered to butch it up a little but I told her not to bother. I've been looking around for something a little more…permanent. Larger."

"Permanent?" she asked.

"That's right," he said, opening the chest of drawers to find his thermal underwear. It was going to be cold, wet and miserable at 4:00 a.m.

"Rich said you were planning to stay here awhile."

"A long while," he said. "I like it here." He shoved the shaving kit, underwear, jeans and sweatshirt into the bag.

"You're not coming back to San Diego?" she asked.

He gave a shrug. "What for?" he asked.

"Won't you miss it? The sunshine and beach and wonderful weather?"

The look that came into his eyes was unmistakably sad. "There's a lot about San Diego I'll miss, Becca. But not the beach or the weather." He hefted the bag over one shoulder and grabbed the twelve-gauge shotgun that leaned up against the wall.

"Really, Denny? You'd never come back?"

"What would I go back to San Diego for? We're meeting at 4:00 a.m. at the bar tomorrow, Becca. Don't make us wait for you. Dress in camouflage. You brought camouflage, right?"

"Right," she said.

"See you in the morning," he said, going out the door.

"Whew," she said when the door closed. *This was a bad idea. He hates me!* Her next thought was, *If I hadn't come up here, I'd never have seen him again!*

After brushing her teeth, washing her face and putting on some warm pajamas, she crawled into bed. She hadn't bothered with the clean sheets, but she should have. She caught Denny's scent on the linens and she remembered it far too distinctly. It was that perfect combination from both of them—her flowery scent combined with his masculine musk. It was so long ago she was astonished she could still summon it in her mind, but it came back to her effortlessly.

A tear escaped. *They're going to come after*

me with a net, she thought. What if she was still in love with him? And he hated her? How the hell was she going to have a life?

This is going to be torture, she thought. *Pure torture.*

Denny and Rich were all ready at the bar at 4:00 a.m. when Troy and Dirk arrived. Denny had Jack's decoys and a duck boat in the back of Big Richie's truck, a couple of thermoses of coffee and a box of sandwiches Preacher had gotten ready the night before.

"Jack's from Sacramento and did a lot of hunting around there with his dad. He says you're going to find it even better up here," he told Troy and Dirk. "Colder, but better. He and Preacher prefer deer hunting, but they go out for a little fowl sometimes, so he showed me a great blind back in Trinity, not too far from here. You can follow us. We're going to meet one of the neighbors out there—Muriel St. Claire. She's a big waterfowl hunter and she's bringing at least one of her dogs. Where's Becca?"

"Right here," she said from behind them.

He turned to look at her and grinned. She had high rubber boots over her army-green jeans, wore a brown turtleneck under a camouflage vest and covered her golden hair with a khaki hat. Hah!

This was not a last-minute deal! “Where’s your gun?” he asked.

“I left it in Rich’s truck last night,” she said.

“You’re dressed perfect, Becca,” he pointed out to her.

“Why, thank you, Dennis. I looked up what to wear on Google.”

“Very smart,” he said. He knew his girl. Okay, she hadn’t been *his girl* in a long time, but she couldn’t have changed that much. She was into clothes in a big way; work or school clothes; going out to dinner clothes; club clothes, beach clothes, biking or hiking or skiing clothes. Very girlie things. Did she really expect him to believe she had rubber boots and a camouflage vest lying around waiting for her first duck-hunting excursion? So…she had an agenda. “Let’s go,” he said. “Becca, stick close to your brother. Ride with us.”

“Sure,” she said, jumping in the back of Rich’s extended cab.

Denny took the wheel on Rich’s truck, since he knew the way, and within thirty minutes they arrived at a marshy lake in a designated hunting area in Trinity County. It was still foggy in the predawn hours; there were probably ducks on the lake. They pulled up right behind a big dually truck. Standing beside it with a couple of Labs, one brown and one yellow, was Muriel. A few other trucks pulled off up ahead indicated other hunters.

Denny made the introductions. When Muriel shook Becca's hand, she said, "Nice to have another woman along. I'm almost always the only one!"

"Well, I'm a novice," Becca said. "I've never been duck hunting before. How long have you been hunting?"

"Since I was a girl," Muriel said. "I grew up on a farm around here. My dad taught me to hunt when I was about twelve, but I'd been tagging along for a few years before that. This is Luce," she said, introducing the chocolate Lab. "She's an expert. Buff is still iffy—sometimes he retrieves, sometimes he just goes for a swim." Muriel nodded at the rifle, still in the case. "I take it you shoot."

"Skeet," Becca said. "I'm not sure how I'll do with ducks."

"Ducks are bigger, but you don't set them off by yelling 'pull.' Just stay quiet, pay attention, try to be invisible. Damn fowl have excellent vision, I swear. Coffee? Danish?"

"Sure," she said. "That would be great."

Muriel opened the passenger side of her truck and poured Becca a cup. "We have a few minutes before we get in the weeds. Your boys are unloading their boat and setting up their decoys. Are you going in the boat?" she asked.

"I don't know," Becca said.

"One of the advantages to having a couple of

dogs, I can stay on dry land and they'll do the swimming."

"Doesn't look to me like there's enough room for everyone in that boat," Becca said. She sipped her coffee.

"I like this area," Muriel said. "Lots of natural blinds. I get comfy with my thermos and my dogs and wait for the ducks to come to me." She smiled. "What's your excuse for doing this?"

Becca gestured toward the men with her coffee cup. "See the big one? My twin, Richard. And the two guys carrying the boat to the water? Friends of Richie's from the Marine Corps. And the really cute one? Denny. We used to be together. We broke up about three years ago."

"Really?" Muriel said. "You and Denny?"

"We were just kids."

"Ah," she said. "You're not over him."

"I have a boyfriend," Becca said, but she didn't make eye contact with Muriel. "I think he's getting real serious, too."

"So, you're not over him," Muriel said again.

"It's not relevant. He's over me," she said.

Muriel sipped her coffee. "Gotcha," she finally said.

It was an hour before Becca realized who Muriel was—a well-known actress. She just didn't look the same without makeup, her hair covered with a stocking cap and hood. “I’m sorry, Muriel,” she said softly. “I didn’t know you were *that* Muriel!”

The woman just laughed softly.

“Is this how a famous actress spends her spare time?” Becca asked.

“I’m just a farm girl who learned to act, sweetheart.”

Becca was so happy to have Muriel to follow. She imitated her behavior, sitting still and silent in the bushes. Thank God there was another woman to cover for her when the time came to go behind a bush to pee; at that moment, she wished she really was one of the guys! And she stood guard while one of the best-known actresses in Hollywood squatted behind a bush. “Talk about something for my Facebook page,” Becca joked.

“Don’t even think about it, darling,” Muriel said with a smile that promised dire consequences and no sense of humor on that suggestion.

It drizzled on and off through the early morning and even though everyone had rain slickers, Becca felt damp to her bones. There were a couple of flushes of birds, a few shots fired, but it wasn’t until 10:00 a.m. that Muriel bagged a mallard. Luce went out for the duck, brought it back to her mistress, and Muriel praised her Lab proudly, tossing the dead bird into the back of her truck.

Becca hoped she didn’t hit anything. Though

she was every inch an athlete who could keep up with the boys, she *seriously* didn't want to touch a dead duck.

"What are you going to do with that duck?" Becca asked her.

"Eat it, hopefully."

"You're a cook, too?"

"Well, no. Not at all. I can barely slice cheese. But I very wisely found myself a guy who loves to cook and he's brilliant at it."

"And will you pluck it and gut it?" Becca asked.

"Well, I can, if it comes to that. But I think Walt will take over. He loves thinking he takes care of me." She smiled. "And I love promoting that idea. I like to train the dogs and shoot a lot more than I like handling the game."

"It's a relief to hear that. I was feeling a little out of place with the boys," Becca said.

Then they went back to sitting, silent and shivering, waiting for game. *What about this is fun, exactly?* Becca wondered. She heard soft masculine laughter now and then. What could possibly be entertaining them? The cold? The rain?

At a little before noon, Muriel decided she'd had enough, bid everyone goodbye and took her dogs home. A little while later, Becca took refuge in her brother's truck, drank more hot coffee and ate a sandwich. She turned on the truck to run the heater and within seconds Denny was there, telling her to kill the engine. The noise! She hadn't gotten even an ounce of heat, but she turned the ignition off. She decided the guys could have as much wet, cold fun as they could stand, she was done for the day. She couldn't feel her toes; her nose would never again be a normal color. At least it was a little warmer inside the truck, even without the heater. She leaned back and closed her eyes.

She wasn't sure how long she had dozed when the truck's door on the driver's side opened and caused her to wake. Smiling, Troy settled behind the wheel. "Just thought I'd grab a cup of coffee and a sandwich. You okay?"

"Fine. Just got cold and hungry. Time for a break."

He reached into the back of the extended cab, into the picnic box Preacher had packed, and pulled out a sandwich. "So, what do you think of duck hunting so far?"

"Honestly?" she asked. "A little on the, uh, boring side. Not to mention cold and wet."

He laughed and nodded in agreement. "Good weather for ducks, but not for us. I'd rather hunt on a clear day, but the cold doesn't bother me. And when you actually hit your target, that's when it's cool. And we like to eat our kill," he said, grinning, before taking a big bite of his sandwich.

"How caveman of you," she said. "Do you also like to pluck your kill?"

"We let our women do that," he teased. "We go out, club the beasts, drag them home and our women clean them, cook them and make our clothes out of their skins."

"And what tribe do you come from?" she asked, laughing at him. But he just chewed and his eyes twinkled. "Rich has mentioned you a hundred times, at least, but I don't know that much about you. Besides being a Marine reservist, how do you earn a living?" she asked him.

"I teach seventh-grade math. Geometry and pre-algebra."

"No kidding?" she asked, sitting straighter. "I teach!"

"I know. We have a lot in common."

"I wonder why Rich didn't tell me that," she said.

Troy laughed. "Let me guess—maybe it's not way up there on his list of important conversational topics. I haven't been teaching long. I did two years in the Corps, finished college, got called for Iraq again and came home to teach. I think I'll get in a good stretch at home now."

"But why the Marines? I mean, why *still* the Marines?"

He shrugged. "I love the Marine Corps."

"And if you get called again?"

"I'll go again," he said easily.

"And Dirk? Did I hear he worked construction…?"

"Heavy equipment operator—a crane. Just like his dad and his brother."

"No interest in college for him?"

Troy laughed. "I don't think so, no. It takes about three teachers' salaries to make one crane operator's."

"Now, see, that's just wrong. What's more important—the future of your children or the construction of a building?"

"You're not looking at it the way they do," he said. "It's not the building that's valued above the future of the children, it's the guys in the hard hats *under* the crane who count on a really good operator. Their lives depend on it. They would be the fathers."

"Teachers are underpaid," she pointed out to him.

"As are cops, firefighters, librarians and just about everyone who is a public servant. I don't know about you, but most of us don't teach because it'll make us rich."

"You do it for love?"

"I guess. And because I'm having fun!" Then he grinned handsomely. "Those kids just crack me up."

"Me, too," she admitted. "Mine are seven—what a hoot. I hear about teacher burnout all the time, but I'm still on the honeymoon. I look forward to every day. Well… I used to."

"Used to?" he asked.

"My school closed. I'm currently unemployed. When I get home, I'll see if I can sub while I'm sending around applications. It's not a great time to be job hunting. Not only is it a holiday season, but education funds have been cut, too."

"Bummer," he said. "I don't know why I've been lucky enough to hang on to my job while everyone else seems to be getting laid off or cut back on hours. But as Big Richie tells it, you'll probably just get married."

"Wow. That's pretty sexist. I hope I *also* get married."

"I stand corrected. Who's the lucky guy?" he asked.

"Good question. I've been seeing someone for the past year, but we're not engaged."

"Which allows you to go duck hunting with your ex?" he asked.

"Which allows me to go hunting with my *brother,*" she emphasized.

"And Denny," he said, taking another bite of his sandwich. "You must have a very understanding boyfriend."

"Well, he is, as a matter of fact. Denny and Rich have been friends for years—before and after we dated. It really doesn't have anything to do with me. And what about you? Girlfriend?"

"Sort of," he said with a shrug.

"Sort of?" she pushed. "Either you do or don't have a girlfriend."

"Whoa, whoa, whoa," Troy said before he had time to fully chew and swallow. He finished that task. "I don't have a steady girl at the moment. I date here and there. I'm talking dinner, movie, clubs sometimes, group things. Lately I've been seeing this girl who gives accident-adjustment estimates—I had a fortuitous little fender bender. She's not quite over the last guy, so we're taking it very slow. We've been out about four times—a couple of softball games with her friends, one Monday-night football at a sports bar with mine and a high school football game to watch her little brother play. I'm not committed and neither is she."

"And Dirk?" she asked.

"Same girl for about six months now. Diedre. An assistant manager of a bowling alley. Personally, I think Dirk might be down for the count. Diedre seems to be around all the time." He took a sip of his coffee. "Tell me more about the guy, Becca," he said. "Teacher? Like you?"

"Law student."

He laughed uncomfortably. "Stiff competition," he said.

"For who?" Becca asked, wondering if her cover had just been blown.

"Well, me, for starters."

"Are you making a pass?"

"I'm saying I wouldn't mind hearing you're open to the possibility." He touched her nose. Then he smiled and winked.

Three

Denny watched Troy and Becca in the front seat of the truck for about a half hour, drinking coffee, laughing, talking. He caught a little casual touching—Troy reached toward her face; she put a hand on his shoulder—stealing glances over his shoulder while he crouched in the blind. Dirk and Rich were in the boat, right in the midst of some shoreline reeds.

Finally Troy exited the truck, grabbed the shotgun that leaned against it and went back to his cozy little nest in the bushes at the water's edge. Every few minutes one of the guys would blow on a duck call, but other than that the only sound was the occasional rustle of leaves in the wind.

Then a flock of ducks burst from the narrow end of the lake and took flight. Shotguns blasted as all the hunters fired, but the flock escaped unscathed. Nothing dropped from the sky. Nothing.

Rich and Dirk brought the boat in and dragged it up on the bank, ready to take a little break while any fowl that remained nearby regrouped and recovered from the shock of gunfire.

"I think I'm done in," Denny said. He looked at his watch—it was barely after noon. "How about you guys?"

"I got a couple of hours in me," Rich said.

"I'm good. You gonna wimp out?" Troy asked.

"Might just," he said. "I'm going to help out in the bar tonight. I could use a shower before that. Looks like Becca's had about enough. Tell you what, I'll leave the thermoses and food in your truck, Dirk, and take Rich's truck back to town. I can give Becca a lift. When you boys are done, bring in the boat and the decoys, will you? And I'll see you at Jack's for dinner. How's that?"

Rich, Dirk and Troy looked back and forth between each other. Finally, Troy said, "Sure, Den. Okay."

"We'll do it again tomorrow. Maybe Becca will take a pass."

"Denny, Becca's no trouble," Troy said. "She's not asking to leave. She seems to be holding up fine. I bet she'd sit in the truck till dark, if that's how long we stay out."

"Yeah, probably," Denny admitted. "But there's no reason for her to do that, since I need to get back to town, shower and help Jack round up a good meal for you diehards. So I'll see you at Jack's."

"Sure," Troy said as the other two nodded.

Whew, that was close, Denny thought. Before anyone could decide to tag along, he headed for Rich's truck. He opened the back door and began to gather up thermoses and the food. Becca looked at him curiously. "I'm going to put this stuff in Dirk's truck. They want to hunt awhile longer. I'll take you back to town."

"You don't have to do that," she said. "I'm fine."

"Well, you're not hunting, so I'll take you back."

"I'm *fine*."

"You're just sitting in the truck."

"So? Am I bothering you? I can sit in Dirk's truck if you want to go."

"Becca," he said in exasperation, "let's just go back to town."

"I don't need to go back to town," she said. "But if you need company so *you* can go back to town, by all means. Let's go."

He frowned at her but held his tongue. Instead, he moved the coffee and sandwiches to Dirk's truck. When he was walking back, he noticed his friends standing on the bank of the lake, just watching him. He smiled at them and waved, then got in the truck and got the hell out of there before he had company.

They drove for about five minutes of stony silence before Becca said, "Well, that was a fast getaway, Denny. What's eating you?"

"Nothing's eating me, Rebecca!" he snapped. "I thought you were done hunting and so we'll leave!"

She just laughed softly and for some reason that lit a fire in him.

"Is something funny?" he asked. "I thought you said you had a serious guy in your life. It makes me wonder what he'd make of the way you cozied up to Troy." He glanced at her.

"You've completely lost your mind," she said.

"Wouldn't you say you're a little *overly* friendly?"

She shook her head. "No."

"If I were the guy, it would look that way to me," he said, totally amazed by how childish he sounded, even to himself.

"If you were the guy, you'd be studying for finals at UCLA and would've said, 'Have a good time and be careful.'"

"Must be a freaking god," Denny muttered.

"Jeez, what is up your butt?" she asked.

"I just thought a stand-up guy would get you out of what could be a bad situation. If you're practically engaged, you probably shouldn't be messing around with Troy."

She shook her head. "I wasn't. Unless you call having a cup of coffee and talking messing around.

If so, I mess around almost daily." She smiled indulgently. "I'm very loose that way."

"Damn it, Becca, don't you get what I'm saying?"

"No, Dennis, I'm completely lost. I don't know what your deal is. You almost act like you're jealous or something..."

"Don't be ridiculous," he said. "Why would I be jealous?"

"I can't imagine," she said.

"I guess I just don't get it, why you'd go hunting with a bunch of guys if you have a serious boyfriend. It makes no sense. Maybe I can do the guy a favor by a little intervention..."

"Intervention?" she asked, frowning.

"Well, you get a little flirty. And that's not smart."

She inhaled sharply, not sure if she was more offended by being called flirty or not smart. Her mouth formed a thin line, her nostrils flared, her eyes glittered and she said, "Stop the truck."

He looked over at her. "What?"

"I said, *stop the truck*!"

"This is a bad place to stop!"

"Stop anyway!" she yelled back.

There wasn't much of a shoulder, but he pulled over. The road was built up about three feet and ran between drenched fields that were probably lush with grain and corn in the summer. He stared at her.

"I made a big mistake here and I'm going to cut my losses," she said. "I thought if we spent a little time together, we might get some closure so we could both move on, but it's impossible if you're going to be such an ass! I'm going back to where we were hunting. I'll either sit with the guys or in the truck, but I'm not putting up with this bullshit anymore. I haven't heard a word from you in years. You have no right to judge me or my behavior." She opened the door.

"Becca, wait a sec," he said, reaching toward her.

"Seriously, if you had anything to say to me, you might've called or maybe shot me an email or—hey! You could've 'liked me' on fricking Facebook! But I haven't heard squat from you, so trust me, you have absolutely no right to even suggest who I talk to." She made a derisive sound. "Flirty," she muttered. "Of all the nerve."

"Becca, no—" he said, reaching out to her.

"Denny, *yes*!" And with that, she stepped out of the vehicle, forgot it was such a long step down from her brother's jacked-up truck, hit the very narrow shoulder with one booted foot, twisted her ankle, buckled, fell and rolled off that raised road and down to the mushy, muddy field below. And she did it all with a scream that included a very unladylike expletive.

In spite of himself, he laughed and lowered his head to the steering wheel. Well, he was an ass, like she said. And she never had listened. She was always full-steam ahead. He got out of the truck, walked around to her side and stood on the road, hands on his hips, looking down at her. She was sprawled, looking a little like she was ready to make a snow angel—in the mud. She glared up at him.

It was all he could do to keep from doubling over in hysterical laughter.

"I tried to stop you. I tried to tell you I'd take you back there..."

She blew a sputter of air through her lips to rid them of a splatter of mud. "Sure." Then she sat up. "Screw you."

"Come on," he said, trying to carefully slide down the bank to help her. "You're right and I was wrong. I have no right to tell you how to act or who to flirt with... I mean, talk to." He smiled, ready to duck if a mud clot came at him. "All right, let's just get you back to town so you can get out of those muddy clothes. I'm sorry, Becca," he said, unable to keep the laughter out of his voice as he looked at her. He reached a hand out to her. "Really, I'm—"

"Ah!" she cried, trying to stand. She grabbed her right leg. "Oh, *crap*!"

"What?" he said, jumping in the mud with her.

"Oh, God, I think I did something!" She reached for her ankle. "Damn, oh, *damn*! Oh, God!"

Denny crouched. "Maybe you sprained it," he said. "I can't look at it with the boot on. I have to get you up the hill and back to the truck. Then we'll look."

"On one leg?" she asked. Despite her sarcastic tone, tears of pain glistened in her eyes.

"Well, it would be easiest to just carry you." He reached out to pull her upright. "Just put the weight on your good leg."

"Denny..." she whimpered, giving in to the pain as she let him help her stand.

"It's okay, Becca, just lean on me." Once she was upright, balancing on her left leg, he wiped the tears with his thumb. "Over my shoulder, that's the best way."

"Noooo," she wailed.

"It's the best way for me to keep my balance getting up to the truck." He gave her a little smile. "You used to think it was fun."

She shook her head. "I used to think *you* were fun. I'm not sure I think so anymore."

He bent at the waist, put his shoulder in her midsection and folded her over his shoulder in a fireman's carry. "Try not to wiggle too much or you'll topple us both."

"Ugh," she said. "God, it *hurts*! What did I *do*?"

He took a few wobbling steps up the hill and said, "Watch your head," as he hefted her into the passenger seat. "Stay like this, legs dangling out.

Sit tight." He went to the truck bed, lifted Rich's tool storage bin and found a tool with a sharp edge.

When he came back to her, she pulled her knees up fearfully. "What are you going to do?"

"I'm going to cut off your rubber boot, Becca. You don't want me to pull it off—that would be awful. I'll get you a new pair."

"I don't care about the boots! I just don't want you to cut my leg off with that thing!"

"I'll be very careful," he promised.

"I've had a run of bad luck lately. Owwww!" she wailed as he carefully slid the slit boot off her foot.

Her foot dangled there at a very odd angle, pointing inward and limp. And it was already starting to swell. He lifted his eyes to hers. "Oh, man," he said. "That doesn't look too good."

Becca tried to hold back her tears all the way to the hospital and Denny tried to see how often he could apologize for being a total idiot. "I have no idea why I baited you like that," he said. "I really don't know. I think I'm still a little upside down that my old girlfriend is here with the guys."

"I don't even want to hear it," she said. "Where's the goddamn mute button?"

Denny laughed.

It was a long way across the mountains, through Virgin River and down the mountain to reach Valley Hospital. Denny lifted her carefully out of the truck and carried her into the E.R. From the odd angle of her foot, Denny suspected a break, and E.R. staff agreed with him. They contacted the on-call orthopedist to come to the hospital.

One of the nurses started an IV and Becca was given pain medication and a sedative, making her much more comfortable. While Denny held both her hands in both of his, the doctor gave her a shot of anesthetic right in her ankle. Then he gave it a sharp pull, setting it right. Becca half rose off the E.R. bed with a cry; Denny pulled her up against him, holding her tight until the pain subsided again.

"We're going to have to operate on this ankle, Becca," the doctor said. "It's a little too swollen right now, but we'll elevate it, put an ice pack on it and in a few hours we'll be able to do the surgery. You can stay overnight and go home in the morning."

"Operate?" she asked.

"A small plate and screws." He smiled. "You'll be good as new."

"I don't want to stay all night," she said. "I'm *miserable*!"

"I can appreciate that, but there's no alternative. What you really need is to go to a room where a nurse can get you out of those nasty clothes and get you washed up, into a hospital gown and comfortable. I'll come back in a few hours and we'll fix you up. You'll go home with a splint and crutches. I'm afraid you can't put any weight on it for six weeks—that's going to be the hard part."

She shifted her eyes to Denny. "Denny?" she said softly in a shaky voice.

"Easy, honey, you need to get taken care of. While you get cleaned up and put on some dry clothes, I'll call Jack's and make sure Big gets a message."

"Becca's going to need clean clothes to leave the hospital in," the doctor said. "Maybe you could do that while she's getting cleaned up and I take care of the ankle."

Denny lifted her chin and looked into her eyes. "Would you like me to do that, Becca? Get you some clothes? Leave a message for Big Richie that you're here?"

She nodded.

"I'll see you later," the doctor said, ducking out of the curtained cubicle.

"Becca, I'm sorry. You can add this to the list of things that are totally my fault. If there's room on the page, that is."

She just averted her eyes.

"Are you in a lot of pain right now?" he asked her. "I'll stay with you till you go to surgery, if you want. I can get your clothes then."

"It's okay," she said. "You can leave. Maybe

Rich could bring me some clothes in the morning and bring me back to Virgin River."

"I'll do it, Becca. I want to. And I'll bring back my own truck, which is a lot easier to get in and out of than Big's truck."

"Are we going to be able to get along?" she asked with a hiccup of emotion. "Because I'm just not in the mood for any more conflict."

He nodded. "Absolutely," he said. "I'll come back tonight…."

"That's all right, you don't have to—"

"How bad is it?"

She shook her head. "It's throbbing. But it feels far away, like it's someone else's foot."

A huff of laughter escaped him. He ran a finger along her jaw. "You really scared me with that foot, the way it looked."

"Scared *you*?" she asked, sinking back into her pillows.

A big orderly pulled back the curtain. "Ready to go for a ride, miss?"

"I hate to leave you," Denny said.

"Just go on. Tell Rich to absolutely not call our parents. Absolutely not."

"Don't you think they'd want to know?" Denny asked.

"I'm going to take care of that. And tell him I'm sorry about getting the inside of his truck all muddy. He worships that truck. He's going to marry that truck..."

"I'll clean it up," Denny said. "Try to rest."

Before heading to Virgin River, he went through Fortuna, stopped at a full-service gas station and had the truck cleaned up, inside and out. He drove out to Jack's guesthouse to retrieve his duffel and shaving kit, then went to his room above the Fitchs' garage and took a shower. Next, he opened Becca's suitcase and gathered some clothes to take to her. When his hands fell on her silky panties, they lingered there, remembering. God, how he had missed her! Then he folded her bra and panties inside a pair of jeans and a sweater, hiding her lingerie from view. Her camouflage vest was filthy, so he brought a jacket for her.

Then he went to Jack's. It was still before five, but the sun was setting and the place was starting to fill up with a few locals and some die-hard hunters and fishermen. Denny sat at the bar.

Jack came over. "Where's the rest of your posse?" he asked.

"I guess they'll be coming in anytime. I was bringing Becca back here this afternoon and she had a little accident. She fell getting out of her brother's jacked-up truck and twisted her ankle. Turns out it's broken. I took her to Valley Hospital for an X-ray, but the doctor says he needs to put a small plate and some screws in it. She has to stay overnight, but she'll be fine and can be released first thing in the morning." He looked down. "She's gonna be on crutches."

"Well," Jack said. "I always said, if they're running away, just kick their legs out from under them. That'll slow 'em down."

Denny scowled. "That's not funny."

"Not to you, maybe," he said with an amiable smile.

"She's in pain."

"I can imagine. Looks like you're feeling some pain, too. Need a beer?"

"Beer and a sandwich, if it's not too much trouble."

"Sure you don't want some of Preacher's dinner? Stew. Hard rolls. Cake."

"As soon as I tell Big where his sister is, I'm heading back to the hospital. She's fine, but she might wake up and not want to be alone."

Jack served him up a draft. "Any chance she could wake up and not want to be with you?"

"Ah, yeah," Denny admitted sheepishly. "Always a chance of that. But it's a chance I'm going to have to take." Right then the door to the bar opened and his buddies came in. "Jack, would you make that sandwich to go?"

"You bet, kid," he said.

Denny stood up from the bar. "Any luck?" he asked them.

"Nothing," Rich said. "But we reserved a couple of ducks for tomorrow."

"About tomorrow," Denny said. "I think you're going to be on your own. I'll be tied up. Rich, Becca fell." And then he explained as best he could, leaving out anything that would implicate him. "Your truck is outside, but I'm going to take her some clothes at the hospital. She's probably asleep, but I'm going to sit with her so I can bring her back to town as soon as they discharge her. I told her I'd be there for her in case she wakes up during the night."

"She did that by falling?" Rich asked.

"Well…by jumping out of the truck. She must've hit it just right. The doctor said it's not real bad, but a procedure is necessary and she'll be on crutches for six weeks."

"I should probably go," Rich said, yanking off his cap and running a hand through his hair. "My mother's going to kill me."

"She said not to call your parents."

"Because they're headed for Mexico in the morning," Rich said. "Bet that's why Becca doesn't want to call them. So my mother can kill me when she gets back. She expects me to look out for my sister."

"Don't worry about it," Denny said. "I feel responsible—she was with me. I told her I was going to let you know what's going on and bring her some clothes and she said okay. She's expecting me to come back for her and I want to."

"And then?" Rich said.

Denny shrugged. "I'll get her comfortable in my room over the garage and wait on her hand and foot while you guys hunt." He clapped a hand on Rich's shoulder. "No offense, buddy, but she doesn't want you to take care of her."

"My mother's going to kill me," he said again.

"Becca'll be okay. She's gonna get a splint that's almost like a cast."

Jack brought a wrapped sandwich out of the kitchen and put it on the bar. "Here you go, Denny." Then he looked at the three young hunters. "Serve you boys up something?"

"Starting with a cold draft," Dirk said.

"Tall and cold," Rich seconded.

"By all means," Troy said.

"Sorry about the inconvenience, guys," Denny said. "Jack, you're okay with the boys using the boat and decoys, right? And put whatever they need on my tab—they're my guests, even if I'm not the best host."

"I'll take care of your boys," Jack said. "Been a while since Preach and I took advantage of a bunch of greenhorns at poker. I can help out there. Hope you guys brought some money."

"Yeah, that's what you think, gunny," Dirk said. "I'm going to take your money, and I'll hunt tomorrow, but I'm not getting up at four. There weren't any more ducks at dawn than there were at noon."

"I second that," Rich said.

Denny picked up his sandwich. "I should get back to Valley Hospital. Who knows? Maybe they'll let her out sooner."

"Go for it," Jack said. "Tell her we all hope she's doing all right."

"Thanks." He headed out of the bar.

He was barely down the steps when he heard, "Denny." He turned around to find Troy standing on the porch. "Total accident?" Troy asked him.

"Yeah, what else?"

"You said you felt responsible. And you haven't been real happy about her being here," he said.

"Look, it really threw me off, all right, her being here. And I tried to stop her, warn her, before she jumped out of the truck—we were stopped on a raised road by a muddy field and she fell..."

"You were stopped?" Troy asked.

"Talking. That's all. We had some things to get straight so we could enjoy the rest of the week. You know I'd never let anything happen to her if I could prevent it."

"I've never known you to be mean to a woman."

"No, you never have and you never will. Really, I should get going..."

"Were you telling the truth when you said she wants you back at the hospital?" Troy asked.

Denny stiffened. "She said I didn't have to. She said she didn't need anyone to be there, but I said I wanted to."

"Listen," Troy said, stepping closer to the edge of the porch. "You gotta be careful with her. I get the idea you have issues with the ex-girlfriend. You get real pissed off around her and that's not going to work."

"Are you giving me advice about how to treat my—" He stopped and cleared his throat. "Hey, I feel bad enough that she fell without you telling me how to act."

Troy frowned at him. "You should work this out, Denny. Without the drama. Without all the attitude."

The fact that Troy was absolutely right didn't go down easy. "Maybe I'll get you to script that out for me later, since you're such an expert."

Troy touched his cap. "Give Becca my best. Tell her if there's anything I can do, just let me know."

"You bet," Denny said. And he thought, *Don't worry, man. I got this covered.*

Four

The throbbing ache in her ankle roused Becca. That and the fact that she had to pee. She groaned and Denny was beside her instantly.

"What are you doing here?" she asked. "It's almost midnight."

"Sleeping in the chair in case you need me," he said, brushing her hair back from her cheek. "Um, I had to sort of lie for them to let me stay."

She narrowed her eyes. "Lie, *how*?"

"I was pretty sure ex-boyfriend wouldn't qualify, so I told them I was your fiancé."

"But I told you to just send Rich in the morning. Didn't I tell you that?"

"Well, you said I *could* send Rich. You said I didn't have to come back, but I wanted to. Just in case. Is it terrible? The ankle?"

"I think the pain shot's wearing off. Did you tell Rich what happened?"

"Sort of. I didn't exactly tell him I figure it was my fault for pissing you off. He said your mother is going to kill him for letting that happen to you and I told him you didn't want him to call your folks. He said you probably didn't want to ruin their trip to Mexico, since you're okay."

"My mother," she said with a groan. "Oh, man…"

"What?"

"I didn't tell my mother I was coming up here."

"You didn't? Why not?"

"I didn't want to deal with her," she said, and winced.

He tilted his head. "Because…?"

"Because she adores Doug. Because she wouldn't have approved of me going on a hunting trip with a bunch of guys that included you, even if Rich was part of the group."

"Aw, Becca…"

She laughed a little bit. "Well, I'm old enough to make my own travel plans. Right? Maybe I'll just explain when I get home…."

"I could've told him you wanted him here, but I didn't," Denny said. "He's planning to play poker tonight and hunt tomorrow, anyway…."

"Good old Rich. He means well, but he can be clueless. Loveable, but clueless."

Denny sat on the edge of her bed. He touched

the ice pack. "You need a new one—this is almost warm. Can I look?"

"Knock yourself out," she invited. "There's nothing to see."

He lifted the dead ice pack. "Nice bandage," he said optimistically.

"It's a splint," she said. "It's gauze, plaster and an ACE wrap. They'll take it off to remove the stitches in about ten days."

"Jeez, Becca." He carefully put the useless ice pack back on her raised, ace-wrapped ankle. "Listen, can I ask you something?"

She gave a shrug. "What?"

"Did you really have a desire to go hunting?"

"Oh, gimme a break," she said. "What do you *really* want to ask me? Like, did I come up here to see you?"

"Okay, maybe that crossed my mind. Did you?"

"Not exactly," she said. "Here's the deal. Rich started talking about this guy-trip a few weeks ago—he was so jazzed. Then I lost my job. Then I thought, what the heck, I've never done anything like hunting but I have handled a shotgun and like shooting skeet. But I knew if I asked Rich, he'd tell me no. And if I even mentioned it to my mother, she'd freak out—she is in *love* with Doug. So I planned to give Rich no time to refuse."

"And Rich agreed?" he asked.

"I didn't give him much choice. And honestly, I

thought maybe enough time had passed that maybe we could at least be friendly toward each other. For all I knew, you were with someone now. Then when I saw how mad you were that I'd shown up, I started thinking something else."

"Something else?"

"Yeah, Denny. Something like maybe we'd better get this settled between us and move on. You and Rich are good friends. We're going to bump into each other sometimes. We broke up angry, too angry to even be friends. I don't know about you, but I'm twenty-five and not interested in carrying around grudges till I'm forty-five. I just want to be happy. It didn't work out for us, that's the way it goes, let's at least be friends and get on with life."

"We might need a little practice at that—you have a broken ankle because we weren't getting on with life real well."

"Yes, and it's midnight and my pain shot is wearing off and it hurts like hell. And I have to go to the bathroom."

Even in the dim light of the room, Becca could see him pale and it almost made her smile, pain and all. *Ha-ha, Denny! Bet you didn't think I'd need something like that!*

"Okay," he said bravely. "Do I carry you to the bathroom or do I get a bedpan? What should I do?"

She gave him a small, tolerant half smile. "You

get the nurse. I need something for the pain and a little help with the bathroom."

He looked so relieved, and he let out his breath slowly. "Okay. Be right back."

"You might want to hurry," she advised.

"Right," he said, heading out the door.

Very interesting, Becca thought. He's either sleeping in the chair out of guilt or a feeling of obligation or interest. She would undoubtedly find out which before too long. What she would do about it was one of the great mysteries of the universe.

The doctor offered to call Becca's parents before the surgery, but she said it was unnecessary. She was twenty-five, with her own medical coverage. She blessed her luck! She could deal with her mother later. Her mother was going to have a very strong reaction to Becca spending the holiday with Denny rather than Doug. Maybe a little time on the beach in Cabo san Lucas would mellow her out. Or maybe she could tell her mother when they were all back in San Diego and the whole thing was resolved.

"You don't want your fiancé to help you to the bathroom?" the night nurse asked her.

"No," she said. "He's not that kind of fiancé."

"Oh?" the nurse asked.

"We've been separated for a while," Becca said.

"By...by the Marines. He did a tour in Afghanistan."

"Oh, honey."

"I'd just prefer to be at my best," Becca said.

So Denny stood outside the hospital room while Becca had a pain pill, a bathroom break, a new ice pack applied and a midnight snack brought to her, because she'd been more interested in sleep than food following her surgical procedure. It was nearly 1:00 a.m. when Denny came back into the room. "Denny, you can go home. This isn't necessary."

"You never know," he said. "You might just need me."

I needed you so much, she thought. *But you were so far away!*

"They give you this little call button in case you need anyone," she told him.

"I'm here, just the same," he said. And then he retreated to his chair. It looked like a comfortable chair for sitting, but not for spending the night. And then she thought how he might have slept in Afghanistan, on the rocky desert floor, with no love at home to look forward to. Why he would choose that over her was so far beyond her understanding.

She watched him out of the slits of her sleepy eyes for a few moments before her pain pill took over, then she came awake to the sounds of morning.

* * *

About the time breakfast was delivered, Denny stretched and stood from his chair. "How're you feeling?" he asked her.

He had that early-morning, scruffy growth of brown beard, sleepy eyes and the body of a Greek god. *If I didn't have a broken ankle, I could so jump your bones!* Her next thought was, *What is the* matter *with me? He dumped me and Doug wants me!* And she couldn't really say that Denny was that much more hot than Doug. Doug was hot in a totally sophisticated Cape Cod kind of way.... She looked at him and wondered, is the pain pill exaggerating his handsomeness? But she said, "I'm doing okay. I had a pain pill. I might be a little loopy."

"That's probably good."

"Want a bite of my French toast?"

"Nah, that's okay. Maybe I'll walk down to the cafeteria and grab some coffee, if you think you'll be okay."

"I'm okay. Go." And she almost said, *But don't shave.*

Before her breakfast was done, the orthopedist was there. It was barely seven. He tossed off the ice pack. "You're good to go. I'll have the ortho tech fit you with crutches and show you how to use them. The nurse will brief you on instructions and problem signs and I'll see you in ten days to get the stitches out. Call me if you have pain. Aside from some aching and throbbing now and then, your discomfort should be minimal. Most important things—no weight on it and keep it elevated as much as possible for a week to ten days."

"Um, I don't live here," she said. "I live in San Diego. I rode up with my brother to do some hunting. Duck hunting." She rolled her eyes. "Very dangerous sport. We'll drive back next Sunday—in five days."

The doctor got a kind of stunned look on his face. "Becca, do you have any friends here? Or family? Because you're going to be just fine, but you shouldn't travel. Not right away, anyway. And not that distance."

"What?" she said, shocked. *"What?"*

"Just because your ankle is all put back together doesn't mean the injury's not serious," the doctor said. "And San Diego isn't exactly down the street—San Diego is a long, long drive. It would even be a very long flight! You'd risk dangerous swelling, maybe blood clots, other complications. You have to remain mostly immobile, leg elevated—you don't want to swell under that splint. I don't really advise dangling that leg for more than an hour at a time for the rest of the week. Oh, you can get around as necessary on crutches, but you can't put any weight on this ankle and you can't sit in a car or plane for hours."

"But what if I traveled with the leg elevated?" she asked. "Like if I sat in the backseat of the cab with my leg on the console between the front bucket seats?"

"Hmm," he said. "Well, if you could manage that, it would be better. But not for a week, and even then you shouldn't travel more than three to four hours a day, and you should stop overnight. The best scenario is for you to stay close and see me in ten days to two weeks to take off the splint and remove the stitches before you head home. The ankle might bother you for a few days—you might need pain medication. I want you to really think about it."

Her eyes filled with tears. "I don't have anywhere to go. I have no family here…."

"And the young man who was here all night?"

"A…friend… I don't know. I don't think that would work out."

"Think about your options over the next day or two."

"Okay," she said.

While she was measured for crutches, she thought hard. It might be best just to take her chances. Or maybe she could tell her mother the truth and have her come to get her. Her mother would *want* to come and get her—so she could carry on for days about how insane it was to come to Virgin River in search of a solution to the Denny/Doug dilemma.

Didn't that make her feel nauseous....

By the time the tech wheeled her back to her hospital room, Denny had finally returned with a large paper cup filled with coffee.

"Hey," he said, standing from his chair. "You're looking pretty good!"

"Thanks," she said somberly.

The tech put the brakes on the wheelchair. "Want me to send the nurse down to help you get into your clothes?" he asked, looking at her face and Denny's.

"Please," she said.

When he left the room, Denny sat again so he could be at her eye level. "You in pain, Becca?"

"Oh, just a little uncomfortable. Not as bad as you'd think it would be."

"Are you so upset? It looks like you've been crying."

"Denny, I'm afraid I'm stuck here for a week at least. The doctor said I shouldn't travel, especially not a long trip. I have to elevate the leg, I can't have it dangling during a long car ride or even a long flight. I could get blood clots or other bad things."

"Then you'll keep it elevated," he said.

"Denny, it's going to be real hard to get around, to get cleaned up and dressed and all that. And I appreciate all you're doing, but no offense, the idea of sitting in that room above the garage without even a TV while you guys hunt and fish and play poker… It sounds awful."

He let out a little huff of laughter. "Becca, I won't do that to you. I'll help you. I'll make sure you have everything you need. I won't leave you all alone. I promise. And when you can travel again, I'll take you home. Why wouldn't I do that for you?" He reached out and wiped a little tear off her cheek. "How long did the doctor say before you can travel safely?"

"Ten days or so. He wants to see me again before I go."

"So I'll make sure you're taken care of, and then I'll take you home."

While the nurse was helping her into the clothes Denny brought her, Becca started to wonder about a few things—like who would help her bathe and dress once she left the hospital? She couldn't undress in front of Denny. Not now. Not under these circumstances. What a stupid mess.

"Uh-oh," the nurse said. "Okay, these jeans won't work. However, I think I can open the right leg in the seam a little bit, so you can stitch it back up later, when the splint has been taken off. I have a seam-ripper at the nurses' station for just this thing! Sit tight."

This is going to be an interesting challenge,

Becca thought. A broken ankle grounding her was about the furthest thing from her plans.

When the nurse came back, Becca said, "I bet I'm going to need one of those seam-ripper things. All I brought with me was jeans."

"You can pick one up anywhere they sell sewing supplies," she said. "And if you don't want to sacrifice your jeans, have your boyfriend run by Target or Wal-Mart and grab a couple of loose-fitting sweat suits. After the doctor takes the splint off to remove the stitches, he'll give you a soft, protective boot or shoe that you can take off for bathing and dressing. No need to rip up all your jeans. Borrow a pair of your boyfriend's socks—pull one over your splint to cover your toes. It's winter out there, girl!"

"Right," Becca said. "Um, exactly how am I supposed to, you know, shower?"

"Well, for the rest of this week, I recommend a sink full of water and a washcloth. That's really the safest method. Put a towel across the toilet cover, sit down on it, wash up."

"And my hair?" she asked with a little catch in her voice. She couldn't believe she was about to cry, but the idea of greasy, flat, smelly hair just about brought her to her knees. She'd always been so fastidious!

"Stick your head in a deep sink and shampoo. Or, kneel beside the tub and use the tub spigot—

just don't stand on the foot. For today, want me to braid it for you?"

"I'll do it," she said, taking the offered comb and working it through her long hair. Little bits of mud were still coming off. When she got all the tangles out, she began to work her fingers through her hair, putting it in a quick and neat French braid.

"Wow, you're good at that," the nurse said. "You're going to find that for the next few days, just washing up can wear you out. Some of that's the effects of anesthesia. You've had an injury and your body is spending lots of energy trying to heal. Start with your hair—it doesn't have to be shampooed every day. Rest a bit, then tackle the sponge bath. Next week, try a bath, hanging your right leg out of the tub. I know you probably prefer a shower but balancing on one leg to keep weight off your injured ankle is not only going to be difficult, it's risky. Plus, your leg needs to stay completely dry."

"And if I want to take a shower?"

"You can pull a small trash bag over the splint and tape it to your leg with surgical tape. Or you can wrap a bunch of self-adhesive saran around it. It's amazing stuff—stick's right to the skin. But my advice is to take a tub bath and hang your leg out. Trust me about not getting it wet." She wrinkled her nose. "Not a good idea at all. It'll itch and stink."

"Really?"

"Really. This is going to feel clumsy at first, so

just remember to take your time and do it in stages. Your balance is going to get better. But, Becca, if you put weight on that ankle, you could do some serious damage. Go slowly."

"I'm used to being very active. I can't imagine that washing my hair would make me tired," Becca said.

"Your body is working on mending that bone. Give it a chance. You need good nutrition and rest. Be nice to yourself." She smiled.

"Yes," she said. "Right."

The nurse gave her arm a stroke. "We put splints and casts on in the E.R. and send people right home all the time. You'll be fine. And let people help. It's okay."

On the drive back to Virgin River from the hospital, Denny said, "I gave Jack and Preacher a call while you were getting your crutches and I think we have a plan. A good plan. I'm taking you to Preacher and Paige's house—it's attached to the bar, but a totally private residence. You'll be comfortable there. You can lie down in their room if you feel like sleeping and I'll be around to make sure you have anything you need. I know you don't want to be left all alone all day and you also don't want to be locked in a room with me all day—but at least you'll be right next to Jack's in case you feel like company. You know, like your brother and

Troy and Dirk. Plus, at Preacher's you'll have a little privacy and a TV for when you feel like being left alone. Chris, their seven-year-old, is in school and Dana, their two-year-old, stays real close to Paige and Preacher. You can put your foot up and I'll bring you meals from the kitchen. Or, if you want to come to the bar, we can put your right foot up on a chair—your choice."

"But, Denny, I don't even know them!" she said.

"That doesn't matter. It was Preacher's idea. In the evenings, I'll take you back to my room. Those stairs—you're not ready to be going up and down those stairs, so I'll carry you up there. Jack is loaning me a nice big blow-up mattress. I'll sleep there with you at night so if you need anything, I'll be right there. Like if you need a drink of water or help getting to the bathroom…"

"Oh. My. God," she muttered.

Denny laughed at her. "I'll be sure to close the door. Come on, Becca, I'm not going to embarrass you. Would you rather have Big Richie help you to the bathroom?"

"Really, I want to die right now."

He laughed again. "You'll be fine. It'll take you about five minutes to feel at home with Paige and Preacher."

I want my mother, she thought with an internal cry.

Her relationship with her mother was great,

really. Her mother comforted her when she was down, praised her when she did well, laughed with her in happy times…and had an opinion about everything. Like most mothers and daughters, when it was good, it was very good and when it was bad it was horrid. For the past couple of years, Beverly's opinion was that Denny wasn't worth the tears and Doug had saved her life. Before that whole breakup with Denny, Beverly had loved him. He was Rich's best friend and Becca's boyfriend—double the pleasure. But then…

"I don't like that you're not telling your parents about me being here," Denny said. "Particularly your mother. I know she's probably pissed off at me, but you should still be honest with her."

Becca's head snapped around to look at him. Was he now reading her mind?

"But it's not up to me," he said. "We can take care of you."

"We?" she asked.

"Me. Mostly me. But there's also Jack and his wife, Mel—she's the local nurse practitioner and town midwife. There's Paige and Preacher, my boss, Jillian, and her sister, Kelly. Lots of real nice people who want to help out if they can." He glanced over at her. "These people are my family, Becca."

"But you haven't even been here that long."

"About a year. Becca, did they give you some pain pills or something?"

"Uh-huh, I had one just before we left the hospital. You'd be surprised how much my leg hurts, too, but the doctor said it's going to let up. Listen, I get that you're trying real hard but the thing that worries me...if you're going to be all pissy and angry with me, I'd rather just make Rich stay with me...."

"Believe me, Becca, I learned my lesson on that. Besides," he said softly, "I don't want to fight with you. I just want to help."

Five

To Becca's surprise, there was a welcoming party at Jack's. Jack and Preacher were there, of course, but Becca hadn't expected their wives. She recognized Paige from her first night at the bar and knew the other woman must be Mel, Jack's wife, because Jack had his arm around her. And Rich, Dirk and Troy were there, too.

Denny carried her into the bar. Rich immediately separated himself from the group and said, "Here, gimme that fat old load." Holding his hands out for Becca, he added, "Just one of the guys, huh, Becca?"

Mel said to Paige, "Isn't it amazing how you can always pick out the brother?"

Denny obliged, transferring her into Rich's capable, if rude, arms. "I'll go get the crutches."

"Thanks a lot, Rich," she said. "You're so sensitive and gentle."

He hefted her in his arms and said to Jack, "Where do you want this."

Becca whacked him in the head.

Mel came forward and put out her hand. "Hi, Becca, I'm Mel Sheridan. Please don't worry about a thing—we've got you covered. Denny's a good friend and his friends are our friends. Would you like to sit in the bar for a while, maybe have a sandwich and soda? Or are you ready for a little privacy and rest?"

"I don't know," she said honestly. "One thing I should do is make a phone call, and my cell doesn't seem to work here."

"Very few people can get good cell coverage in the mountains," Paige Middleton said. "But calling home is not a problem—we have unlimited long distance. You can make a call from my house anytime. Want to start right now?"

"Yes," she said. "Richard, follow Mrs. Middleton!"

Paige led them through the kitchen and right into her living room. She patted the sofa. The cordless phone was beside it on the table. Rich put her down. "You all right?" he asked her.

"You care?"

"Well, sure, Becca. But you totally screwed up duck hunting."

"Bite me."

Paige cleared her throat. "I have a boy and a

girl—is this what I have to look forward to? Never mind. Can I get you something to drink? A soda? Water?"

Becca sat on the cushy leather couch in the spacious living room in Paige's house, her leg propped up on the ottoman. Curled up at the other end of the couch on his very own doggy blanket was a black-and-white border collie, whom Paige introduced as Comet. The dog gave her a wag and a lick and then went to his corner like a good boy.

Paige brought her a glass of water and told her to take her time on the phone. She thought for a moment before dialing. To her surprise, there was an answer.

"This is Doug Carey."

She jumped in surprise. "Doug?"

"Becca?" he asked.

"I didn't expect you to answer. I was composing a message to leave you. Where are you?"

"At the airport. I got an earlier flight and, since you're not around, I'm heading out today. You did get a refund on your ticket, didn't you?"

She'd never even bought the ticket out East. Of course, Doug wanted to buy the ticket, but she insisted. "A credit," she lied. "I have a year to use it on any destination." She made herself a promise—when this was over and she was home, reassured and waiting for that engagement ring under the tree, she'd tell him everything. "Do you have a second to talk?"

"We'll be boarding in about ten," he said. "Go ahead."

"Well, I've had a little accident," she said. "Nothing to worry about, but I broke my ankle and have a splint. I'll be on crutches for six weeks."

"Becca," he said in a disapproving tone.

"I jumped out of my brother's truck and landed wrong. So much for hunting and fishing."

"Get a ride to the nearest airport and use that credit. Meet me in Boston, I'll drive you to Cape Cod...."

"Well, here's the thing. I'm stranded. Can't travel. Can't even drive home with Rich on Sunday. I have to get the splint taken off and the ankle checked by the doctor."

"Why can't you travel?"

"Aside from the fact that I can't manage my luggage on crutches, you mean?"

"Becca, that's what five dollar bills are for—skycaps."

"Oh," she said. "Of course." Doug Carey didn't schlepp bags. "Well, the main reason is that my leg has to be elevated so it doesn't swell. And it would be very bad if it swelled under the splint. And I guess the danger of blood clots if I'm on a long flight or drive is a factor. Best to just wait for the all clear."

"And then?"

"Well, I guess then I'll get a flight home. Me and my five dollar bills..."

He actually laughed. "Only you, Becca."

"Yeah," she said. "What a klutz, huh?" *Only a surfing champion with wicked good balance!* "Listen, on the off chance you get some wild, insane urge to speak to my mother, please do not call her and tell her about this."

"Why?" he asked.

"Because she and Dad went to Mexico for the holiday and I don't want them to worry or come back early. Just don't."

"It never occurred to me, but point taken. Dare I hope you got this out of your system?"

"This?" she asked.

"Hunting and fishing," he said. "Will you be off crutches by Christmas?"

"Very close, but I'll be cleared to travel much sooner than that."

"Good. Because I just picked up a great Napa package we can use around Christmas—a vineyard tour. It was supposed to be a surprise, but since I won't see you, I'm telling you now."

Right then, Denny came into the room, carrying her crutches. He gave her a smile and pointed at them. She pointed at the floor by the couch.

And suddenly, even though one of them was in the room and one hundreds of miles away at an airport, she could see both men as if they were standing beside each other. Denny was wearing jeans, boots, a plaid shirt with rolled-up sleeves and looked like a woodsman, while she knew Doug would be in dress slacks with a cashmere sweater, carrying his leather jacket in preparation for the cold Boston winter. The lumberjack next to the metrosexual.

"How does that sound, babe?" Doug went on.

"Great. Nice. Fun."

"I have a list of all the tasting rooms—we'll go over it before we even head that way. Decide exactly which vineyards appeal to us most."

"Sure," she said.

Denny put down the crutches and began to leave the room, heading back for the bar.

"There's my call—we're boarding. I love you, babe," he said.

"Have a safe trip."

"Becca. I said, I love you."

"Love you, too," she said. But she said it quietly.

Not quietly enough. Denny paused, stiffened just slightly, then continued on. And she thought, *Crap. I'm screwed.*

Becca relaxed on the sofa for a while before she grabbed up her crutches and made her way to the bathroom. She managed just fine. A little slow, maybe, but she never put weight on her foot and didn't fall, either. Surfing was better than skiing or ballet for balance.

Suddenly, she realized Doug never asked her where she was staying. Never asked if she needed him. His most immediate concern was whether she'd be able to travel when he wanted to take his Napa tour… She had a premonition of what life was going to be like—it was going to revolve around Doug. Of course. He was the busy one, the important one.

She sighed. Might be a good idea to cut her losses and shoot for spinsterhood.

She headed back into the bar. It was more crowded now than it was around the dinner hour. Troy separated himself from his friends and held out a chair at a table near the fire for her. She sat down gratefully and he quickly lifted her leg up onto a second chair, then leaned the crutches against the wall right behind her. "Thanks," she said. "That's more work than you'd think."

He sat down at the table. A quick glance around told her Denny was not in the room. "Where's Denny? Did he leave?"

"Out back," Troy said, pointing toward the window. "I take it he spends a lot of time helping out around here."

She turned and looked out the window. The day was bright and cold and Denny was splitting logs on a tree trunk, stacking up a nice pile of wood for the fireplace. She wondered if he was working off that "I love you" he'd overheard.

"He said these people are his family," Becca remarked, watching Denny heft that ax and bring it down. He didn't wear a jacket and the broadness of his shoulders made her long to be in his arms again. For just a little while. But the best view by far was that perfect butt. She believed he had a better butt than she did.

"So I hear," Troy said. "How's it feeling? The ankle?"

She looked back at him and gave him a thin smile. "Not so bad. You know what feels worst of all? I haven't put any makeup on in about twenty-four hours. And I think there might still be mud in my hair."

"You don't need makeup, Becca," he said. "You look great for someone who took a dive out of Big Richie's truck."

She laughed in spite of herself. "I guess I was in a hurry…."

Rich and Dirk wandered over to the table and pulled out chairs. "If you're feeling all right, we're going to get in a little hunting after lunch," Rich said.

She narrowed her eyes at her brother. "By all means," she said.

Denny came in the side door with an armload of split logs for the fire. "Don't worry, Becca, I'll stick around." He crouched beside the hearth to stack the wood, ready for the fire.

"No, you should go. I'll be fine. Especially if Mrs. Middleton doesn't mind if I sit in her living room and watch TV."

"She's already offered full use of her house, so I'm sure she won't mind, but I'll ask. She's making up sandwiches right now. What would you like to drink?"

"How hard is it to get hot chocolate?" Becca asked.

"It is not hard," Jack called from behind the bar. "Anything we can do for the infirm!"

"Your friend Jack is a comedian," Becca said. When she glanced at Jack, he was smiling appreciatively.

Within minutes the table was served, family style. A platter of sandwiches, a bowl of chips, a pitcher of cola and mugs, and Becca's hot chocolate, along with Paige's assurance that Becca was more than welcome to her couch and ottoman. They all crowded in; with Becca needing that extra chair to elevate her leg, it was a tight squeeze. And of course the ribbing began, starting with the lengths Becca would go to to get out of hunting, followed by the fact that she'd have to stay in Virgin River for over a week before being cleared to travel back home.

But soon, they were all pushing back chairs and standing to leave. All except Denny.

"For real, Denny, you can go. I can get around on my crutches."

"I don't know," he said, frowning, shaking his head. "I told you I'd be around if you needed anything."

"Well, I don't think I'm ready to take on a flight of stairs, but otherwise I can manage, certainly for a few hours. I'm going to go back to the Middletons' living room and zone out to *Oprah* or something."

"Well..." he said, thinking. "We'll go out in two trucks and I can come back early. You wouldn't be on your own that long."

"I'll be fine," she said. "I don't want to be a drag. This is your hunting party and I ruined it."

"No, you didn't, Becca. It was an accident."

"Just go," she said.

"If you're sure?"

"Go," she said again.

He gave her a little smile, then stacked up the plates on the table and walked them back to the kitchen. As he passed back through the bar, he said, "Paige said help yourself to the sofa, or if you're tired and you want to lie down, their bedroom is on the ground floor and you're welcome to it."

Tired? She might die of boredom, but she wasn't tired at all. She just smiled and nodded, waving him out the door. Becca was used to a very active lifestyle—chasing seven-year-olds combined with lots of sports from surfing to skiing. The last time she watched *Oprah*, she was home sick with the flu. The time before that, she was home sick with a broken heart.

She pulled herself up and with her crutches, hobbled through the kitchen door. Inside, busy with lunch and cleanup, was the Middleton family—Paige rolling out dough for pies, Preacher—or John, as Paige called him—scraping plates and filling the dishwasher, and little Dana in her high chair, messing around with Play-Doh.

"Are you absolutely sure?" Becca asked when Paige smiled at her.

"Absolutely. There are some DVDs if there's nothing on TV that interests you. Check out the bookcase—you might not be interested in John's military history but I have some fun stuff there. And please don't hesitate to use the phone or our bed, for that matter, if you want to lie down for a proper nap. When I'm done here, I'm going to put Dana down for her nap. She needs a good two hours to be pleasant for dinner!"

"Will the TV bother her?" Becca asked.

"Not in the least. She's a great little napper."

"Thanks. I really appreciate this. Denny doesn't have a TV or anything in his little apartment. He probably doesn't spend too much time there."

Paige laughed. "He's a very busy guy. Not only does he work for the farm and around here, he's always offering to help anyone who needs something."

This time when Becca walked into the Middleton house from the kitchen entrance, she noticed how perfect it was designed. She walked through a spacious laundry room that undoubtedly serviced the bar and the family. To her left was a kitchen that was more of a serving center, complete with cupboards, dishwasher, refrigerator, sink, countertops and a pass-through to a dining room. But there were no stoves or ovens because the bar kitchen was just steps away. Just opposite the serving station and dining room was the master bedroom and bath, and beyond that the great room, complete with entertainment center, fireplace, locked gun rack and open staircase that led to a loft. The kids' rooms must be up there—she could see a few toys scattered around. There was a door to the backyard from the great room. She peeked outside and saw a wooden jungle gym, slide and sandbox. To the far right, more behind the bar than the house, was a big brick barbecue and some picnic tables.

She paused in front of the bookcase in the entertainment center and found some old friends—Jill Shalvis, Kristan Higgins, Deanna Raybourn, Toni Blake. She pulled one out, tossed it across the room and followed it, causing the sleepy Comet to jump in surprise. "Sorry," she said to the dog. The remote was easier—it was right on the side table. She got her leg propped up on the ottoman, gave Comet an apologetic pat on the head, turned on the TV to an afternoon talk show with the volume down, book in her lap, and thought again about what Paige had said. *Denny's a pretty busy guy. He helps anyone who asks....*

He had a full-time job, even if he did say the farm wasn't too busy this time of year. And he helped Jack around the bar all the time—that was probably a part-time job. And that was the Denny she had known and missed—the guy who was the friend you could depend on if you needed something.

He wasn't going to be available to entertain her all the time, to keep her busy and her mind off the fact that she was bored out of her skull. She leaned back against the leather couch cushions and thought yet again, *Oh, man, this is going to be so tedious!* What was she supposed to do for two weeks? Watch daytime TV and reread her favorite romances? Nap? How in the world was she supposed to nap? She wasn't the least bit tired. All she'd done for twenty-four hours was sit around with her foot up!

And that was the last conscious thought she had for a while. When she opened her eyes again, she blinked a couple of times. It was a different talk show and she had slumped down on the couch. There was a kid sitting on the sofa next to her. His backpack was on the floor and he was petting his dog.

"Did I wake you up?" he asked. "Because my mom said to be quiet."

"No. No, not at all," she said, pushing herself upright a little.

"I think you got a little drool there on your mouth."

"Oh, Jesus," she said, wiping her mouth. Sure enough.

"Oh, that's okay. My mom does that all the time."

"Does she? I bet you're Chris."

"Yup. And you're Becca. What kind of name is Becca?"

"Short for Rebecca," she said. "Are you just getting home from school?"

"Yup. And I have chores and homework. I'm not allowed to have TV on after school till the chores and homework are done."

Becca fished around the couch until she came up with the remote and flicked off the TV. "That's very smart of your mom. Mind if I ask about the chores? Like what kind?"

"I get the trash together, but my dad takes it out because the Dumpster is too tall for me. Sometimes I fold the napkins for the bar and when no one is sleeping on the couch, I run the vacuum around—Comet's hairy. I have to let Comet out—I did that part already. My bed's made—I did it this morning before the bus came. But I always look at my homework first, before the chores. Except Comet—he really needs to get outside right away."

Becca liked that. "What kind of homework?"

"Math, spelling and reading. I worked on the spelling on the bus a little, but everyone was rowdy so I'm gonna have to do it again. I have to use my whole brain for the math. And I'm already good at reading."

She smiled at him. "How old are you?"

"Seven. I'm in second grade."

"Boy, do I have a surprise for you," she said. "I'm a second-grade teacher."

"In real life?" he asked.

"In real life. In my pretend life I'm a girl with a broken ankle."

"From jumping out of the truck without looking where you were going?" he asked.

"Something like that."

"Denny came back from hunting with a dead duck. He gave it to my dad and went down to his place for a shower. After he looked at you sleeping. He said if you woke up to tell you he'd be back when he smelled better."

Her first thought was that he'd seen her *drooling*. "Nice," she said.

"So he's like your boyfriend or something?"

Becca thought about this for two seconds or less before changing the subject. "Since I'm a teacher and everything, want me to work on your homework with you? We could do math or spelling or you could read to me."

"I like to read to myself, but I could use a little help with the math. We're doing multiplying, which is like adding over and over and over."

"In second grade?"

"Some of us got ahead of ourselves."

"Totally. Where do you normally do your homework?"

"At the table over there."

"Let's go."

"You gonna use your crutches and everything?"

"Uh-huh," she said, dragging herself to her feet. "I have to put my leg up on a chair, so can I have the end, please?"

"Oh, yeah. Sure. You gonna do it by yourself?"

She balanced on her crutches. "Wait till you see how good I am at this." She swung her way across the room, pulled out a couple of chairs, got situated and hoisted her leg up. "Ready for math!"

"You act like you like homework or something," he said.

"Well, being a teacher and all…"

"Yeah. You prob'ly can't get enough of it, huh?"

"There you go. Show me your books, Chris. I want to see what you're working on."

"Sure," he said, unloading his books onto the dining table. "Try not to get too excited about this—it's work."

She laughed at him. "You know how I learned my multiplication tables? We had to write them out a hundred times when we got in trouble. But for me, it was fourth grade, not second. I think maybe you're a wizard or something."

"Well, I don't want to write 'em a hundred times, no offense."

"I understand completely. But it really works. Not that it's what I'd call pleasant. Ah," she said, opening his math book. "You're working at fourth-grade math, just as I thought. Very progressive. You should be proud of yourself."

"Well, I would be, except, it's a lot harder to get an A on this math than at second-grade math."

He was so right! It would be years before he'd appreciate having a teacher who had moved him along at his pace.

A half hour later, with Chris's books spread around the table, Denny stuck his head in from the hall. "How you feeling, Becca?"

"Okay. You got a duck?"

"I got a duck. That lake was crazy with ducks this afternoon. Can I get you anything? Want a cola or hot chocolate or anything?"

"Cola would be good. Chris, do you get a snack after school?"

"I had it already. I get milk and whatever cookies my dad made. Today was peanut butter."

"Hey, Denny. Can you snag me a milk-and-cookie snack? After all, I'm working on homework!"

Six

Becca wondered if it was weird that a little time with a seven-year-old put her right, but it did. And before they were done with homework, Dana was up from her nap and sat at the big dining table for a little while to color; Becca colored with her. For some of the time Paige sat on the sofa in the great room with a big pile of freshly laundered kids' clothes that she folded and stacked in the basket to be carried upstairs to their bedrooms.

All this time, Denny was helping out behind the bar. When the folding and coloring and homework were done, Dana and Chris moved to the kitchen. Paige and John had worked all afternoon on dinner; now it was down to serving. Chris would have his dinner at the kitchen work island, while Dana had hers in the high chair. "When you run a restaurant, it's hard to sit down together as a family," Paige told Becca. "But we manage sometimes. When Denny helps serve and bus, the kids and I get a table in the bar, usually with Jack's wife and kids. And every Sunday is reserved for a family meal at our own table—we have our family meal at two in the afternoon and Jack and his family have theirs at three-thirty. It's harder for the Sheridans—Mel being a midwife and all. We have to be flexible."

"It must be a challenge sometimes," Becca said.

"Somehow it works," she said, shaking her head and laughing.

Becca left the Middleton's residence and went into the bar as the dinner hour approached. The bar was starting to fill up with hunters and locals. She found a table and no sooner had she gotten settled than her brother and his friends came in. They were exuberant; they had dead ducks in the back of the truck. Becca laughed as she secretly measured the merits of broken bones.

Denny was busy behind the bar, but only for a few minutes after his pals returned from hunting. He made sure his party was served, then sat with them. Since Becca hadn't had a pain pill since morning, she thought a beer might serve her just as well, so she asked for a mug and poured one from the pitcher Denny brought.

The hunting party of Marines relaxed with their beer and reminisced about Iraq, about mutual friends, about what they'd been doing for the past few years, and she enjoyed it thoroughly. Men, she knew, weren't too good about keeping in touch with each other. There were the occasional emails or phone calls, but it took a gathering like this to really put them in touch again. And these were men who had served in a war together, who'd kept each other's backs, who had stood watch while their buddies slept on the desert floor in a faraway land.

They poked and jabbed at each other, made fun, and no one escaped. There were a few toasts to comrades past and one very solemn remembrance of a man named Swany—she made a mental note to ask Denny or Rich about him later.

It seemed they all but forgot she was there and this was very much to her liking. She sat at the end of the table with her foot up on the opposite chair, while Denny and Rich sat on one side and Troy and Dirk on the other. She was able to be an observer, taking in their easy rapport, their humor and even gallantry as they spoke up for each other, praising small acts of bravery in the field.

"That Seth—he couldn't walk and chew gum at the same time. Didn't you carry him, Troy, about two miles after he blew out his knee in Baghdad?" Denny asked.

"Yeah, it was me, and I've had trouble with my knee ever since."

"I offered to take him," Rich said. "I think you were looking for a medal or something."

"And all I got was a bad knee. Seth, though—he's fine."

Denny served them a salmon and wild rice dinner, a culinary event that had the boys talking about fishing as opposed to duck hunting the next day. They had all come with empty coolers, prepared to take their trophies home to impress either girlfriends or mothers.

When Denny cleared the dinner plates away, the bar was taking on a slightly different atmosphere. The locals had cleared out and there were only a few out-of-towners, either fishermen or hunters. Jack wandered over to their group, pulled another table up close and sat down with them. He asked the guys about their hunting. A few minutes later, Preacher came out of the kitchen, checked to make sure their few patrons were fine, then went behind the bar to pour a couple of shots, which he carried to the table Jack had pulled up.

There was a little grousing about last night's poker—apparently Jack had taken complete advantage of the younger guys and Preacher had folded before becoming a victim.

Talk among the men wandered back to the Marine Corps, how it had been in the old days, how it was now. The few patrons who had lingered wandered off and it was just them—Jack and Preacher and Denny's hunting party. The bar was dim and cozy, the fire was warm, the mood was one of friendship, camaraderie and mutual respect. Becca was feeling more comfortable and at home than she had since arriving. She was feeling less alone than she had in a long time.

"What time do we go out to the river?" Dirk asked.

"It's close and dawn is later—seven is good," Denny said. "Salmon's up now and it's good fishing. They're moving upriver to spawn."

"Salmon's bleak in Sacramento right now," Troy said. "I'm looking for something huge. Like that," he said, gesturing to the mounted thirty-pounder over the bar.

"Becca, you feel okay?" Rich suddenly asked her.

"Sure," she said. "Why?"

"You haven't kept your mouth shut this long since the day you were born," he pointed out.

"I said the salmon dinner was amazing!"

"You usually have a lot more to say," he said. "About everything."

Denny laughed before he said, "You about ready for bed, Becca?"

The entire gathering, including Jack, sent up a great round of whoops and laughter. Becca actually blushed.

"You know what I mean," Denny said, more

to the men than to Becca. "I'm sleeping on an air mattress so I can be handy if she needs anything."

"Becca, even though it might make Dirk jealous, I could do air-mattress duty tonight if you'd rather," Troy said with a teasing grin. "You know, since Denny broke your ankle and everything…"

"Jealous?" Dirk protested loudly, giving Troy a shove.

"Now boys," she said. "We all know it wasn't Denny's fault and he's been very thoughtful. So shut up and back off."

"Whatever you say," Troy said, holding up his palms toward her.

Rich stood to his full six foot two, gave his trousers a yank upward and pulled his jacket off the back of his chair. He draped it around Becca's shoulders and said, "Come on, gimpy. I'll drive you home. Then you're on your own."

"I better go with or he'll leave her at the bottom of the stairs," Denny said, getting to his feet. "Jack, you need me for anything? I can get Becca settled and come right back…."

"Nah, we're good here. We don't need you. Aren't we good, Preach?"

"Good," Preacher said, standing.

The gathering dispersed with plans to meet in the morning for fishing. Rich drove Becca home and carried her up the stairs to Denny's room while Denny followed with the crutches.

And then, there they were. Alone.

Denny stood just inside the door, looking across the room at her. He had obviously taken care of inflating the air mattress earlier; it was lying on the floor at the foot of the bed, a pillow and blanket tossed on top. Although her crutches held her up, she sank to the bed, bone tired again.

"Do you need a little help to get ready for bed, Becca?"

She shook her head. "No, but if you wouldn't mind lifting that suitcase onto the bed, I'd sure appreciate it. I can't figure out how to kneel on the floor."

"You got it," he said, accommodating her at once. "Do you have warm pajamas? Because I have sweats and stuff..."

"I have it covered," she said. She immediately began digging around in her big suitcase.

"I'll clean out a couple of drawers," he said. "Top drawers, so you don't have to worry about lifting the suitcase or kneeling."

"Don't go to any trouble," she said. Pajamas tucked under her arm, she stood from the bed. "Do you need the bathroom?"

"No, go ahead. Take your time. Here, let me carry those in for you. Need anything else in here?"

"That small cosmetic bag there would help—toothbrush and stuff."

"Got it," he said. "Leave this in the bathroom, if you want."

"Thanks," she said. "I hate needing help."

He grinned at her. "But I like helping, so we're okay so far."

And then he backed out, pulling the door closed.

Becca sighed. She certainly had herself in a situation. All alone with the man she considered to be her long-lost love, and getting ready to brush her teeth and don her flannels. Over her bandaged foot. Ah yes, this was the moment every woman dreamed of.

After washing up and getting into her pajamas, tucking her clothes under her arms to toss back into the suitcase, she exited the bathroom. Denny stood beside his air mattress. He wore a pair of sweats that were slung low on his hips, his chest bare, and she got the impression he was still a bit overdressed for bed. *Way* overdressed. Becca was momentarily paralyzed. Yes, this was the Denny she remembered, yet so much more. She had fallen in love with a boy; this version was all man. He seemed taller and broader; his arms and shoulders were so muscled, his belly ripped. There was now a mat of hair on his chest, when before there was some brown fur surrounding his nipples and disappearing into his waistband. And he had that scruffy unshaved look again. The guy had so much testosterone running through his bloodstream he could produce a beard in eight hours.

She wanted him. She wanted to throw herself on him and kiss him until her panties melted off. She wanted to lick him like a lollipop.

"You okay, Becca?"

She shook herself and dumped her clothes in her suitcase. "I can't figure out what makes me so tired..." she said, pulling back the floral bedspread.

He lifted the suitcase back onto the floor, away from the bed so neither of them would trip on it. "Injuries will do that to you. I broke a couple of bones in Afghanistan and I could barely drag myself around."

She was frozen in place. "You were *wounded*?" she asked.

"Not exactly. Motor-vehicle accident two days before I was scheduled out." He laughed and ran a hand around the back of his neck. "Couldn't happen eleven months before, but two days. What luck, huh? Jump in there. Put a pillow under the ankle."

"Are you going to tuck me in?" she asked.

"You object?" he asked, lifting one sexy brow and giving her a half smile.

She slid into bed, grabbed one of the pillows to prop up her ankle and let him pull the covers over her.

"You want the light on for reading or anything?" he asked.

"No. Do you?"

"Nope, I'm ready for lights out if you are."

"Ready," she said.

"I'm going to leave the bathroom light on and pull the door mostly closed, just in case you wake up in the night."

"Thanks."

And then all was quiet and almost completely dark. They were both very still in their respective beds, his on the floor at the foot of hers. There wasn't so much as a rustle of bedding, a cough or a snore. Finally she said, "Denny?"

"Hmm?"

"You guys—you and Rich and Dirk and Troy—you're good friends."

"Yup."

"I don't remember even hearing about Dirk and Troy till you and Rich came home."

"Aw, you know… Guys don't talk that much about guy friends. We were all together in Iraq. Me and Rich were just kids. Troy and Dirk are a couple of years older. There were a bunch of us who were like brothers over there. Six years ago, the conflict was still young and exciting and scary. We stay in touch. Phone and email—I borrow Preacher's computer sometimes. When I went to Afghanistan, Troy was called up for another tour in Iraq."

"You guys toasted a lot of friends… There was one toast to Swany…"

He was quiet for a long moment that seemed to stretch out in the dark. Finally he said, "Eric Swanlund. Gunny. He was killed by a sniper. We never saw it coming. Great loss. He had a wife and couple of little kids."

"In Iraq?" she asked.

"Uh-huh. I wasn't with Dirk, Rich and Troy anywhere else…."

"But…but we were still together then," she said. "That was before we broke up. You never mentioned…"

"Becca, I tried not to tell you things that would just make you worry—things I couldn't control, anyway. Not my mom, either. I didn't tell her anything that might cost her sleep. Anyway, we guys hung tight. We talked about it till we wore it out."

She was quiet, contemplating this. Then very softly, she said, "I never even thought of that—that you wouldn't tell me things…."

"We were young then," he said. "I didn't want to scare you."

"It was only a few years ago!"

"I know," he replied in a low voice. "Amazing what a couple of wars and some hard times will do to grow you up."

"What does that mean? Does that mean that if

you were sent over there now, that if I were your girlfriend now, you'd talk to me about it?"

He took a breath and let it out. "Becca, I thought I was doing you a favor by not saying too much about Iraq while I was there. We couldn't be in touch that much, you and me, and most of the guys didn't want to worry their wives or girls, so I figured that was the way to go. I'm not going back... but if I went now, I might do a lot of things differently."

"Like?"

"When I did my first hitch in the Corps, it was hard but good. These guys and some others—they were like my brothers. For an only child with no extended family, that meant something. I had you at home, my mom, my brothers in the Corps and I felt like I belonged to something. I knew right away I didn't want a military career, but I didn't regret a second of it. So when my mom died, all I could think of was to go back to a place I understood, where there would be brothers. Family. I had no idea it wouldn't be the same."

"I would've been your family if you'd have let me...."

"Yeah, I know that now. I'm not going to make excuses, Becca, but I was so screwed up right about then, I couldn't have made a smart decision for a million dollars. That second deployment sucked. We weren't a tight squad, it was miserable and felt futile and I regretted every second. Instead of feeling like I was back where I belonged, I felt like I was in jail."

"You could've answered my emails. You could've written. You could've—"

"*Should* have," he corrected. "You can say it. I knew right away I should have been in touch, but I didn't have the guts. After I'd been out of touch for months, I just wanted to finish my commitment, get out of the Corps and go home so I could look you in the eye and try to explain. I didn't want to write a letter and ask you to forgive me and then wait for me. Becca, what made perfect sense to me when I was signing up for the second time made no sense at all when I got to Afghanistan. Seriously, it was a bad idea. It cost me. When I got back to you, I was too late."

"What would you have explained?" she tossed out into the darkness. After all, when he *did* finally show up, she hadn't given him a second of her attention. She had been so angry, it had been hard not to throw things!

But he didn't answer. They both just lay in their respective beds. Then there was a little movement from his side of the room and she saw his shadow, then his silhouette as he leaned over her. He gently sat on the edge of her bed. He brushed away the strands of hair that had escaped her braid. "When

I decided to go back in the Corps, I'd just learned something that left me really confused."

"What, Denny?"

He took a breath. "Right before my mom died, she told me my dad wasn't really my dad. My real father was some other guy she hadn't seen or heard from in over twenty years. Then she died. For some reason, that news messed me up, made me feel more orphaned than ever. I couldn't believe how confused I felt. How alone I was."

She could see him shrug in the darkness.

"Because of the way I felt when I was in the Corps with Big Richie and the boys, I just went back to the recruiter and signed up and took the oath."

"But what about me?" she asked in a whisper. "Did you feel alone even though you had me?"

"You were *all* I had—I didn't have anyone *but* you. But you were stretched kinda thin, babe. You had a family, a sorority, a college, a surfing team, a lot of friends…and you lived and went to school in another city. I had to have something I could attach to, something bigger than me, something that felt important. I really needed to be needed. That's one thing about the Marine Corps—they can make you feel like you're doing something important." He laughed, but it was a hollow sound. "Talk about feeling needed…"

"You know, if you'd just told me that before…"

"I had a real hard time making any sense to myself, much less someone else. Then when I got orders for Afghanistan, I couldn't let you go through what I just went through burying my mom. I couldn't think about you missing me or being lonely or, worst case, being grief stricken. So I talked myself into the idea that we'd break up for a year. I didn't like the idea but I figured if you had your freedom, even went out with a few guys, I could live with that if it kept you safe from being all ripped up about me. What I didn't figure on was you being so furious at the whole idea you'd never want to see me again."

"I didn't say that," she said. "I never said that!"

"Not before I left. But after I got back."

"Well, by then I *was* that furious. I'd just spent the whole year you were in Afghanistan staying up all night, every night, watching news reports on the war. I'd written you and emailed you and…"

"I didn't have internet access very often, but I still have the letters. By the time I was back in the States, I had to work through a couple of injuries before I could get away so I could talk to you face-to-face, to try to explain."

"You waited too long," she said, shaking her head.

"I know, Becca. I never said you had any fault in it. I was completely screwed up. I made so many mistakes. I'm really sorry I hurt you. It's no excuse, but I was twenty-two. And I'd barely gotten back from Iraq when my mom took a turn for the worse. When I look back on all that, it's like a fog. I don't even remember it very well. I'm kind of surprised I didn't step in front of a bus or something, I was such a total idiot. But I'm sorry, really sorry. And…"

She gave him plenty of time to finish and when he didn't, she pushed a little. "And…?"

"Thanks for letting me try to explain now. I know it'll never make much sense, but thanks…"

"But that business about your father?" she asked.

"Yet another misunderstanding, but I don't think it was a mistake. See, my mom told me Jack Sheridan was my father, not the man we lived with till I was about seven. So I came up here to find him. It turned out my mom wasn't telling the truth about that. I think she wanted to give me a gift before she died, a man to look up to instead of the one I had, the one who not only never married my mom but never supported me after he left. So I came up here to find Jack."

"Oh, Denny…"

"You don't have to feel sorry for me. It worked out. For a little while, we thought we were father and son and we got close. But the thing is, once we realized it wasn't that way, it didn't change anything. We're still just as tight, and that's what

I learned—sometimes you make your family. One of the best days of my life was when I found Jack and the rest of this town. It's the closest thing to family I've ever had. They rely on me. It feels good." He stroked her forehead. "You should get some sleep." And then he leaned down and kissed her forehead right before moving to his mattress on the floor.

The room was bathed in darkness, a silent, black womb in which they both kept their thoughts private. Becca had no idea what Denny might be thinking, but she was remembering the boy she'd loved. He was such a beautiful and happy young man, so energetic and positive and supportive. He had joined the Corps the same time as her brother, and for the same reasons—both of them were very physical, very patriotic and there was the little incidental fact that neither of them was sure what to do with the rest of their lives. The Corps toughened them up, educated them in ways they hadn't expected, and as Denny said, gave them vital attachments.

Rich came home, ready for college, ready for the challenge—he majored in engineering. Rich was such a big goof it was hard to imagine him as adept in mathematics, but he was. He had excelled. Denny still hadn't been sure what he wanted and before he could consider his options, his mother took a turn for the worse. His only real choice was to take care of her; there was no one else. All this time, Becca was at USC finishing her teaching degree, hoping to do her student teaching at home in San Diego; she talked to him daily and saw him almost every weekend.

Almost.

He was right—she had had many commitments. She was busy, had friends, activities, responsibilities, family. It was just Denny and his mom; he had a job at Home Depot, part-time so he had plenty of free time for his mother. Sue was either having cancer treatments or home on the sofa, weak and ill, waiting for her son to take her to the clinic or warm up some soup for her. And finally there had been hospice.

He must have been so lonely.

So afraid…

Becca was naturally a very nurturing person, one of the reasons she sought teaching as a career and wanted a family of her own, so of course she empathized with her boyfriend. She thought even he would admit she was sensitive, sweetly and lovingly checking on him, making herself available to him…

By long distance. When she wasn't in class. When she wasn't studying or at a sorority function. When she was home on some weekends and not busy with her family or friends or surfing with her old team.

But her mother checked on Denny and Sue regularly—at least once a week! And of course, when Sue died, Becca and her entire family were there at the funeral.

He must have felt so alone....

There were silent tears that wet her pillow; she was very careful not to let him hear her cry. He took all the blame for being wrong, for being so screwed up that he reenlisted, when he could have thrown some of the blame on the busy coed girlfriend who was just as absent.

Becca just began understanding something that even Denny hadn't understood at the time. He had been isolated, depressed and reached out for the only thing that made him feel useful and valuable—the military. So without giving it much thought, he went.

Of course, everything might've been different. He could have told her he needed her and asked her to leave college and the sorority and come home to him...

Oh, brother, she thought. What a reach that was! First of all, Denny was too proud, too strong. Second, and shamefully, she wouldn't have done it. She would have called him twice as much maybe, but only to tell him she loved him and to hang in there. Because she was in her senior year!

They were twenty-two. Only twenty-two.

So, twenty-five didn't make a wise old sage, but

she'd grown up a little. She'd suffered through the pain of loss, for one thing. There was the despair of constant worry and the agony of rejection. It had wreaked havoc on her appearance from sleeplessness and loss of appetite. She cried at the drop of a hat. Her rich social life lost its luster and she grew isolated, too.

Then she'd lived on her own and supported herself for three years—it had been tougher than she thought it would be for a brand-new teacher. She'd been through a couple of challenging situations, not the least of which was an ex-boyfriend she was still in love with so far out of her reach.

And along came Doug. When she met him and found herself laughing, enjoying a date, finally having a lover's arms around her again, she thought maybe her life wasn't over, after all. And although Doug was always under pressure, being a law student, his life was one-dimensional. He was uncomplicated. There hadn't been any wars or close losses in his past, and maybe on some level she liked that.

But she couldn't go any further with Doug until she smoothed out some of the kinks in what had been an emotional ride with Denny. Maybe now they could, since there was a bit of maturity, a little understanding and a whole lot more honesty. Knowing what she knew, maybe they could reach out to each other at least in friendship. Once, a long time ago, when they were just kids, they hadn't just been lovers. They'd been such good friends.

She'd grieved that as much as anything.

Seven

The sound of Denny moving around the room woke her before the sunlight. She heard the shower, the water in the sink, the toilet. Then he came to the bed and gently touched her cheek. "I'm sorry to have to wake you," he whispered. "After you get some breakfast, you can nap the day away in Preacher's house if you want to. But I feel like I should take the boys out to the river. After all, I asked them to come."

"Hmm, go ahead. I'll be fine."

"Becca, I don't want to even think about you trying the stairs."

"Don't worry. If you write down the number, I'll call the bar and see if Jack or Preacher can help me down." She touched his cheek and gave him a sleepy smile. "That way, I can have my morning grooming without you standing right outside the bathroom door. Okay?"

"You promise? You'll call the bar for help?"

"Sure," she said, lying through her teeth. She had absolutely no intention of calling anyone. But she did have a plan. "Can I make a long-distance call from that phone?"

He hesitated for just a second. "No problem," he said.

"Thanks. Go on. Have fun. Let me sleep some more."

She rolled over and heard Denny leave the apartment. She sighed gratefully. She felt disgusting and in dire need of a fluff and buff. She'd had only sponge baths since falling into the mud hole. Her hair felt itchy and greasy and she'd had only one change of clothes.

When she was completely sure he wasn't coming back, she pulled herself out of bed. She hopped over to the door and threw the dead bolt. Then went back to the bed where she sat on the edge for balance and stripped down to her panties. She was planning a good scrub and reassembly.

She started by figuring out how to kneel. With her hands on the rim of the tub, she lowered herself carefully, first onto the knee of the splinted foot. Then the other knee. Painless. Then she started the water and prepared to wash her hair. Ahhh… scrubbing her scalp felt like pure heaven.

Next came a real bath. Despite the discharge nurse's recommendation that she make do with sponge baths out of the sink for a week, she was overdue for a good soak. Keeping her wrapped ankle dry while getting in wasn't that easy, but she used her head—she lowered herself into the tub before there was too much water, which kept the splash manageable. Likewise, she had to let most of the water out before attempting to leave the tub.

She felt like a new woman!

She had to use her blow-dryer and apply her makeup while seated on the bed—although her balance was exceptional, she didn't trust herself to stand on one leg for more than a minute at a time. Next, she had to find a sharp knife in one of Denny's kitchen drawers to use to open a seam in her jeans—the only way she'd get into them.

Finally, she donned jeans, one boot, one of Denny's socks pulled over her splint to keep her toes warm, a turtleneck and bright purple sweater, then sat on the bed beside the phone. She thought for just a moment before dialing Doug's cell number. She punched in the private-caller code first. The last thing she needed was for Doug to call this number and have Denny answer!

You have reached the cell phone of Doug Carey. Please leave a message and I'll get back to you.

She actually sighed in relief. She cleared her throat. "Hi, Doug. Just checking in. We had to get off the phone so quickly yesterday because you were getting on the plane that I didn't have a chance to tell you there's hardly any cell-phone reception around here. I can use the phone at the restaurant sometimes and you can leave a message on my cell and I'll pick it up when I have a signal… But I'm fine and I'll call when I can. Have fun with your family!"

She realized she hadn't said the obligatory *I love you* before hanging up.

"Oops," she said to no one.

With a sigh, she pulled on her jacket and looped the strap of her purse over her arm. She used the crutches to get out the door, then stood at the top of the stairs and looked down at the long, frightening descent.

Then she sat down on the top step. She slid her crutches down and carefully lowered her butt to the next step. And the next. And the next.

And she laughed.

She even practiced going up a few steps using the same method.

There was no reason to risk falling and breaking the other leg. If she could stay upright while riding a twenty-foot wave, traveling twenty miles an hour, she could get up and down these stairs without doing further damage.

Yup, she thought. *I don't need no steenking babysitter!*

Jack's Bar was only a couple of short blocks from Denny's little efficiency. Under any other circumstances, that might've felt like miles on a pair of crutches, but Becca was so pleased with herself she didn't feel tired at all. When she faced the porch at Jack's and the three steps up, she gave them careful consideration before taking them one slow step at a time.

Another victory! When she made it inside, she was wearing a smile brighter than the sun.

"Hey," Jack said from behind the bar. "I was expecting a call from you! Denny said you'd need a little help getting down the stairs."

She hefted herself onto a bar stool, lifting her leg onto the one right beside her. "Hah! Fooled him, didn't I?"

"Becca," he said, putting a coffee cup in front of her. "You shouldn't take chances. What if you'd gotten hurt? I mean, more hurt."

"Jack, I didn't take any chances," she said. "I was very careful and went down the stairs on my butt." She grinned and tapped her cup. "Oh, please, coffee. I was so busy getting cleaned up—in *private*—that I never even looked through Denny's cupboards for coffee!"

He chuckled at her and poured. "How's it working out with your new roommate?"

She took a sip of the steaming coffee. "Poor Denny," she said. "If it wasn't bad enough I crashed his party, then I became his invalid to take care of because he feels at least partially responsible. What a load, huh?"

"Why does he feel responsible?" Jack asked.

"He was picking at me, so I told him to pull over and I…" She made a face. "I jumped out without looking."

Jack frowned. "He shouldn't be doing that—picking and arguing. If I do that with Mel, it never goes the way I think it will. Big mistake."

"*You* do that?" she asked.

"Been known to, yeah."

"I'm amazed," she said. "You really don't seem like that kind of guy."

"Because I'm ninety-five percent sweetheart and five percent asshole." He smiled, pushing the cream and sugar toward her.

"This coffee is so wonderful, I don't even need the cream and sugar, but that's how I usually fix it. Spoon, please?"

He put a spoon and napkin on the bar for her. "That's how I trapped Mel—the coffee. I'm only particular about a few things, and coffee is one of them. She was on her way out of town. She couldn't wait to make this little one-horse town a memory, but she wasn't leaving without a cup of coffee."

She grinned at him. "And she stayed for the coffee?" she asked, dressing her cup.

"No, kiddo. The coffee distracted her just long

enough for me to make my move. In the end, she stayed for me." He smiled right back at her.

Becca looked around and realized she was the only one in the bar. "Where is everyone?"

"It's after nine-thirty, Becca. My breakfast crowd is early. Plus, it's the day before Thanksgiving—people are busy. I bet you're hungry."

"I'm starving! You have no idea what an ordeal a hair wash, bath, dressing and walking a couple of blocks can be."

"Preacher was making omelets earlier. He always has bacon and sausage. What would you like?"

"I usually just have cereal, but I think I need some protein. Would you ask him to just break up a little sausage in the eggs and make a small omelet? Maybe a tiny bit of cheese?"

"I'll ask, but I warn you, it's very hard for Preacher to think small. Stay tuned," he said, heading for the kitchen.

It was just a few minutes when Paige carried a plate with an omelet on it out to the bar. Jack was right, Preacher wasn't good at making anything small. "Wow," she said when Paige put it in front of her.

"It's wonderful, you'll see. I have to make a run into Fortuna this morning. Can I pick up anything for you?"

"Oh, I hate to ask favors…" Becca said, taking a second bite of a fantastic omelet.

Paige leaned on the bar, facing her. "What do you need?"

"Well, if you're anywhere near a store that sells sewing supplies, I need a seam ripper." She lifted the leg with the cast and opened jeans. "I used a sharp knife this morning, but I can see the advantage of having the right equipment. Before I slice off a finger or something."

"I'll not only be near that kind of store, I'll be in one. I'm going to buy construction paper, glue and craft stuff. The kids all get out a little early today because of the holiday and we're going to make some table favors for Thanksgiving dinner. The bar is usually quiet on Wednesday night before the holiday, so Jack and John can handle dinner alone. There are a bunch of town kids who want to make stuff for their tables."

Becca's fork paused in midair. "Don't they do crafts at school to bring home?"

"Not so much," Paige said. "They do have Thanksgiving stories, an assembly program and they make stuff for the school bulletin boards, but nothing for our tables. And we'll have a nice, big crowd here tomorrow. Of course, other people have big family gatherings, too, so we're meeting in the church basement. It's fun for the kids."

Becca put down her fork. "Can I come?"

"Shopping?"

"Yes, that. But can I come do crafts? Paige,

that's my specialty, sort of." She ran her fingers through her hair. "Oh, man, I wish I had my stuff! You just don't know how much stuff I have—patterns and instruction books and stencils, all kinds of supplies. You know, money's been so tight, lots of teachers just go buy stuff for the class. I used to hit up my surfing team for donations for supplies and once word spread, I had everyone from my mom's ladies golf group to the neighborhood firefighters buying stuff for my kids. When the elementary school where I was teaching shut down, they let me keep all the things I had donated or bought myself."

Paige was frowning. "Didn't I understand that you're not supposed to travel? It's a good half hour, one way, to Fortuna."

"Do you have a console between the front seats in your car? I can sit in the back and elevate my leg by putting it on the console."

"You'd be sitting beside Dana, the road queen. She loves to go anywhere. She puts her jacket on every morning and says 'We go now?'"

Becca laughed. "Even better. Love a road queen!" She shoveled some of her omelet into her mouth. "When are you going?"

Paige shook her head. "Finish your breakfast. The kids won't be home till around two. We have lots of time."

"Oh, this will be *great*," she said. Finally, she thought—something she was actually good at!

Although Paige argued with her, Becca couldn't help herself. She had great ideas for Thanksgiving projects for kids. She bought terra-cotta flowerpots, black felt and artificial mums for pilgrim-hat centerpieces; she found stencils for construction-paper turkeys; she knew how to make cornucopias out of paper plates and string, and decorative gourds from crumpled-up colored tissue paper. Then there was the standard turkey out of a handprint. Actually, that was the tip of the iceberg—she had a million craft ideas. But she didn't want to overwhelm the kids. She was absolutely in her element.

"I see you've mastered pushing around a shopping cart while on crutches," Paige said. "What a woman!"

There were a couple of other women helping out with the crafts—Denny's landlady, Jo Fitch, and the pastor's wife, Ellie Kincaid. By two-fifteen, she was meeting the children in the basement of the church. Ellie's kids, Danielle and Trevor, were nine and five. Danielle's little friend, Megan Thickson, was only eight and hung pretty close to her; she seemed awful shy. Megan's little brother, Jeremy, played with Trevor.

The first order of business was an after-school

snack—these kids had had a long day. Jo and Ellie served up milk and chocolate chip cookies. Mel Sheridan brought her kids, though they were too young to do anything constructive—they sat at a table with Dana and colored on a large roll of butcher paper. Of course, there was Christopher and about six other kids who regularly attended Sunday school there and played with each other around the neighborhood.

Becca showed them how to glue precut black felt to the flowerpots, making them look like pilgrim hats. The older kids turned them out like little factories. She cut the colorful construction paper for the younger ones so they could glue the tail feathers on the paper turkeys. And she worked on constructing the horns of plenty from paper plates, then showed the older girls—Danielle and Megan—how to crumple tissue paper into the shape of gourds. Because Megan seemed so shy, Becca spent a little extra time showing her the ropes, trying to make conversation.

"Aren't you supposed to be keeping your leg elevated?" Jo Fitch asked her.

"I forget, but it feels okay."

"Forget less," Jo said. "You don't want trouble." She pushed a chair next to Becca so she could put her leg up.

"How did you break it?" Megan asked her very softly.

"Oh, I was careless. I jumped out of my brother's big old truck without looking first and twisted it funny. It turns out I'm lucky. It could've been worse. But I did have surgery and have a couple of screws holding it together!"

"My dad had surgery, too," she said.

"Oh? Is he all right now?"

Megan shrugged and concentrated on her tissue-paper gourds. "Yeah. Except he doesn't have his job."

"Oh?" Becca asked. "What was his job?"

"Logger. He cut down the really big trees. He fell and got hurt and ran out of ability and they won't hire him back."

"Ability?" Becca asked. "Ran out of ability?"

"You know. What they pay you to live because you're hurt."

"Ah, yes, I remember," Becca said. *Disability.* She wouldn't correct the child. It was obviously an emotional issue. "But is he healed?"

She shrugged. "I guess. Except for his quiet spells. And his arm."

"His arm is hurt?"

"Not exactly," Megan said. "It ain't there. But it don't hurt, he said."

"Oh," she said. Sure. What guy wouldn't have quiet spells, hurt on the job, left disabled, out of disability pay, no job? "Do you have brothers and sisters?"

"Three brothers. I'm oldest." She pointed to the table Christopher occupied. "Jeremy is next oldest. He's in first grade."

"I bet you have tons of responsibility around the house."

"Some. My mom has a job now, so we all have more chores."

"And will you have to help fix the Thanksgiving dinner tomorrow?" Becca asked.

Megan turned her large, sad brown eyes up to Becca's and said, "I don't know. My dad said he ain't interested in no town turkey."

Becca was completely baffled. "What's a town turkey?"

"It's the one you get from Jack and the church because you can't buy your own."

Here was something Becca hadn't exactly run up against in her school; it was a charter school and it was quite expensive. They gave out a few scholarships, but they didn't go to children who lived on the brink of poverty, but rather to the kids whose folks earned a living, just not enough of a living to put their kids in an expensive private school. Her kids didn't need a charity basket to have a Thanksgiving dinner.

She had another epiphany. Just like her stable and secure family life, she'd had a job in a safe zone. Oh, she'd had some challenges, but if she were a teacher in a town like this, there would be a much broader cross section of students who ranged from well-off to quite the opposite.

"Well, I hope you and your mom fix it up and I hope the good smells change his mind, because you know what? I bet a town turkey tastes every bit as good as the kind you go out and buy. And your decorations will make it smell even better!" She put an arm around Megan's shoulders and pulled her close. "Hopefully this will pass and your dad will find a job. I'm crossing my fingers for your family."

Megan smiled then. "I think you're nice. I'm glad you moved here."

"Oh, I'm just visiting for a little while. I'll be going home to San Diego soon. But one of the best parts of my visit so far is meeting you."

"Me, too," Megan said quietly.

It seemed like the time flew, yet it had been almost three hours. At five, parents started showing up to collect their kids and their crafts. When Becca saw a woman in a pink waitress uniform giving Megan a hug and helping her into her coat, she assumed that was her mother. She hobbled over and said, "Hi, I'm Becca. I worked on some crafts with Megan. She's such a sweet girl."

The woman's smile, as well as her eyes, were tired. "So nice to meet you. I'm Lorraine Thickson. Nice of you to help out."

"I had fun. I've been so bored, grounded with

this splint on my leg. Once I met the kids, things really perked up for me." She put her arm around Megan's shoulders. "And this one is special. Thank you for coming today, Megan."

"She rides the bus home with Danielle. Since my kids are about the same age as the pastor's kids, they stay either at the church or the pastor's house until I'm off work," Lorraine said. "You can't imagine how much it helps."

"Maybe I'll see you again before I leave, Megan. The doctor wants me to hang around a couple of weeks."

"Okay," she said shyly.

Little by little, the basement of the church emptied of children as they left with their parents. Becca started gathering up construction paper and other art supplies, when Jo Fitch came over to her and said, "No, no, no, Miss Becca. You're supposed to be resting, keeping the leg up. We'll handle cleanup. You were a fantastic help and we so appreciate it."

"Will you be doing anything else with the kids? Because while my brother and his friends are hunting, I'm just sitting around."

"The Christmas tree goes up this weekend," Jo said. "We don't exactly plan activities, but it's such an event, almost everyone in town turns out. Stick around the bar and you can't miss the action. You'll love it."

* * *

The fishermen beat Becca back to the bar, and they had returned victorious. In their coolers, packed in ice, were four big, healthy, robust salmon ranging in size from six to sixteen pounds. All four sweaty, grimy, grinning guys were enjoying a pitcher at a table in front of the fire.

"Ducks and fish—you must be in heaven," she said, joining them at their table.

Denny immediately pulled up an extra chair to elevate her leg. "Not bad. I think we had a good take."

"And what's it going to be tomorrow?" she asked. "Duck or fish?"

"I think it's turkey tomorrow. Then on Friday, it's wood." He pushed a beer toward her.

"Wood?" she asked, lifting her beer.

"The Friday after Thanksgiving we go into the woods and find a tree worthy of what passes for the town square—the parking lot between Jack's and the church. It has to be about thirty feet."

"And who does this?"

"Only the most manly of men," Jack shouted from behind the bar.

"Yeah," the fishermen called out, lifting their ale toward him.

"Oh, brother," she said, sipping her beer.

"Tomorrow morning, we have to stay out of the way so Preacher can concentrate on cooking. Big holiday dinners get him all revved up," Denny said. "So, after breakfast we're going out to the river for a little while, do a little more fishing. We'll take you with us. You can stay in the truck with a thermos of hot cocoa or something."

"That's okay. I can borrow a book from Paige and just stay in your room...."

He grinned at her. "You should come, Becca. It's fun to watch. And Jack says a lot of men are told to get out of the house on Thanksgiving morning so their wives can cook. The river could be full of action."

"Well..."

"You'll come. It's settled."

They ate beef-and-barley soup with soft, warm bread and apple pie for dinner. Then Becca did borrow that book, but only for something to read before sleep. Jack and Preacher closed up a little early, but Denny had his own set of keys and after getting Becca safely up the stairs to his apartment, he went back to the bar for some cards with his boys. Becca didn't feel the least bit left out. If there was anything that seemed less intriguing than watching men fish, it was watching them play poker. What she hadn't been prepared for was how much the kids had worn her out. Before this broken ankle, she could match the little ones for energy, but she was asleep before turning a half dozen pages on her borrowed paperback.

She had no idea when Denny returned to the room, but the sun was lighting the sky when he woke her.

"I made some coffee," he said. "You can take your time getting dressed. I have to run out to the Riordan cabins to pick up the boys for breakfast."

"Huh?" she asked, sitting up a little.

He ran a hand over the top of his head. "Preacher took 'em all out to the cabins. Your brother bunked in with them so Preacher wouldn't have to drive all over the mountains. Fortunately, I could walk home."

"But why did Preacher have to drive…"

"There was some serious drinking going on."

She sat up in bed. "But couldn't you have driven them?" she stupidly asked.

"No. We were pretty much equally drunk. Now we can check that one off—Got Drunk With Friends. I have a headache."

"And you want to go fishing?"

"Don't want to so much as *have* to. You never let a stupid night interrupt your plans for the next day. He who gives in is wearing panties…"

She put her hand over her mouth but giggled just the same.

"Enjoy your coffee, get dressed, and I'll come back for you."

"Sure," she said. But what she thought was, *I'll get myself down the stairs!* She took a brief sponge bath, promising herself a legitimate grooming before sitting down to the turkey dinner later. Then she dressed warmly and made her way down the street to the bar, beating Denny and the boys there. When she got inside, she saw only a few men, who appeared to be finishing their breakfast, and Preacher, who was behind the bar. "Morning," she said. "I heard you were commissioned to drive late last night."

"Wasn't all that late," he said with a shrug. "They're young candy-asses. Don't know anything about pacing themselves." Then he actually smiled and Becca realized for the first time that a smile was unusual for this big man unless something amused him a great deal.

"Not very busy this morning?"

"Not on Thanksgiving. We stay open regular hours, but there isn't usually much business. Anyone who wanders in here after two in the afternoon is forced to join us for turkey. No one pays or leaves my bar hungry on this day."

She smiled at him. "That doesn't surprise me. Where's Jack?"

"He'll come in a little later. The kids will nap and play in my house while we're getting ready for a big crowd out here."

"Do you need me to help?" she asked.

Again the smile. "No, Becca. I think I need you

to have some breakfast. I hear you're going out to the river with them."

"Denny insists."

"You won't regret it. Let me bring you something to eat. Eggs, just about any way you want. Cereal. Toast. Bacon. I'm not making pancakes today…."

"A couple of eggs, scrambled, bacon, toast. And thank you."

Before her breakfast was even delivered, the guys—minus Denny—came in, seemingly none the worse for their night of drinking. They were scruffy as hell; apparently no one thought it prudent to clean up before getting in the river. It made sense on a practical level, but she wrinkled her nose at her brother.

"What?" Rich said.

"After fishing, before Thanksgiving dinner, give yourself a good once-over, please."

"See, this is the trouble with having girls on a fishing-hunting trip," Rich complained.

Preacher was just delivering Becca's eggs. "There will be women at the table today," he said. "Do exactly what she says. Smell lots better. Eggs?" he asked them.

"Thanks," came three replies.

Then Denny burst through the door. He saw Becca sitting at the bar, eating her breakfast, and let out his breath. "You did it again," he said.

She nodded, chewing a mouthful of eggs. “On my butt. Perfectly safe. Have some breakfast.”

He leaned close to her. “I wish you’d just let me help.”

“I will,” she said softly. “When I need something, I’ll ask.”

Eight

When they got to the river, Becca was completely surprised by how engrossing she found the whole experience. There were seven men already standing along the river, waders held up by suspenders. They didn't acknowledge the newcomers at first, but eventually each one gave a rather solemn nod toward them. They were completely absorbed in their sport. Their art.

Fly-fishing was a beautiful thing to watch. Their lines soared in arcs and S shapes, in high curves or powerful torpedo-like shots over the water. As they plied their lines and multicolored flies, salmon fled upstream, sometimes clearing the water, sometimes jumping up small waterfalls. She saw a couple as they were caught, good-size fish.

But that wasn't the only thing that enchanted

her. The wide river as it flowed between towering pines backed by rising mountains… It was stunning. The landscape appeared both dangerous and breathtaking. The river was awesome in its beauty and the trees were enormous. The sounds were enthralling; all she could hear was the whirring of reels, rushing of the river and splashing of fish. Large fish.

Of the four young Marines, Denny was the best at this art. She couldn't take her eyes off him. Not only his mastery fascinated her, but his physique and confidence. She hadn't remembered him well enough, she decided. Either that, or he'd grown much taller and broader. And this skill with the rod and reel—he'd never mentioned fly-fishing when they were together. This must have come from Jack, the man who was almost his father.

He was so beautiful. So at home up to his knees in water, sending those colorful flies over the river. She loved watching the play of muscles across his back, in his shoulders. And then there was that perfect booty. Oh, my, that body… That was the body that taught her about sex, that showed her how to have pleasure and how to give it.

She shivered.

She stayed mostly in the truck, her leg elevated, but from time to time she couldn't resist and carefully got out just so she could breathe the air, get the full view, stand closer to the river to hear the sounds. The men were quiet, while the whirring, rushing and occasional splashing provided the background music. They didn't even shout at a catch but rather made low congratulatory sounds. The man nearest the one with the catch might step closer and offer the net in assist, but that was all. It was a quiet, solitary, peaceful, plentiful sport.

She loved it. She wished she could learn it. If her ankle weren't broken, she'd be out there trying to master that beautiful cast.

This was what Denny had wanted to share with his friends, and it was worthy. This was magnificent. Rich and lush.

After a few hours on the river, everyone dispersed. She went with Denny. She wouldn't allow him to lift her up the stairs but she did accept his help. She was afraid that after her full morning of gazing at him, if he carried her she might just lose control and start kissing his neck.

They took their turns in the bathroom, getting cleaned up for dinner. She insisted on showing him her method for getting down. By his expression, she could tell he went along with it grudgingly.

Then the holiday proceeded, so different from her usual experience. Although Becca and Rich each had their own places in San Diego, they spent Thanksgiving at their parents' house, just the four of them. Dinner at Jack's was a gathering of friends and neighbors. The TV was turned off, the tables were pushed together and all the little decorations Chris helped to make adorned a long table. Becca not only enjoyed meeting a few couples from town, but she was, unsurprisingly, a magnet to the kids and spent a lot of time reading stories to Mel and Jack's little ones, as well as Dana. Chris was too old to be read to, of course, but that didn't keep him from hanging real close.

There were twenty people, including the kids, who sat down to a delicious Thanksgiving dinner. Afterward, rather than poker and cigars, Denny and his friends, along with Jack and Preacher, indulged in several cribbage games, while the women sat around the fire and gossiped.

"How do you normally spend the holiday, Becca?" Mel Sheridan asked her.

"At my parents' house. While the guys have a whole day of football, that's when my mom and I get a start on our favorite holiday movies—*It's A Wonderful Life* and some of the Bing Crosby classics like *Holiday Inn.* My mom loves Christmas, and so do I. We start celebrating right after Thanksgiving. This year will be so different for them. When my mom found out Rich and I would be out of town, she informed my dad that he was taking her to Cabo, where they'd golf and lounge around the beach. He's probably recording the football games for later." She looked at her watch.

She'd have to call her mother before Rich went back to San Diego. She dreaded it.

"We're going to have to do the holiday classics." Paige said. "It's been years since I've watched some of those great old films. Let's pick a time to get some of the women together for movies! It'll get us in the Christmas spirit."

"I'm in," Mel said. "Especially if we can get the guys to watch the kids. How about you, Becca?"

"If I'm here," she said with a shrug.

"How long do you think you'll stay?"

"I'm not sure. We'll see what the doctor says next week."

Mel grinned at her. "I think there's more to this broken ankle than meets the eye."

"I beg your pardon, I'll have you know I have screws in my joint!"

"And an ex-boyfriend in your crosshairs," Mel said.

"Purely a coincidence. I have a boyfriend. He lives in L.A., but we've been exclusive for a year. But if I'm here, I'd love to watch movies with you."

A bit later, while Mel was gathering up her kids for home and Paige was settling hers into bed, Becca used the phone to leave another message for Doug. "Hope you had a great Thanksgiving, sweetie. We had a town gathering at the bar and, you know what? It was really fun. I'm going to head for bed now and I'll try you again tomorrow."

She didn't even wonder why he wasn't picking up. She was relieved.

That's when she began to know the truth about why she came to Virgin River. To find what she'd lost with her first love.

The cutting of the Virgin River Christmas tree was an all-day affair that involved way more spectators than actual woodsmen. First, there was the hunting for the tree—a thirty-foot fir high in the mountains. Becca watched from the truck the entire time. Then there was the cutting down. She would've expected that to take seconds, but it took a very long time and involved pulleys and ropes and chain saws. Next came the netting and dragging of the tree along barely visible old logging roads. Only big pickups with four-wheel-drive ventured back into the thickest part of the forest.

Once the tree was dragged as far as a main road, a local builder, Paul Haggerty, and his crew met it with a big flatbed truck and their hydraulic gear to lift it and haul it the rest of the way. By the time the tree made it to Virgin River, it was dark, but half the town seemed to be present to look at their catch, so to speak. There was lots of "oohing" and "aahing" going on.

On Saturday, the tree was erected—a process that took many hands and more of Paul Haggerty's equipment and men.

"The first time we brought a tree this size into town, it was just Jack, Preacher and Mike Valenzuela standing it up," Mel told Becca. "During the night, it fell down. Thankfully not on the bar!"

Becca sat on Jack's porch between Mel and Paige. They all held hot drinks. Her eyes grew large at the prospect of that huge tree falling on the bar. She couldn't run, after all. "Should we move?" she asked.

Mel just laughed. "I think now that Paul's on board with this project, we're in pretty good hands. And I think your brother and his friends are kind of enjoying this. Too bad they won't see it completely decorated."

"That must take a long time," Becca said.

"A day or day and a half, and at least one cherry picker," Mel told her.

It was past noon before that tree was upright and stable. Mel and Paige were back and forth to the porch, taking children in and outside. By afternoon, a couple of cherry pickers had arrived and the stringing of the lights commenced.

Becca was surprised she wasn't frozen to the bone, but she couldn't stand to miss a second of this process. And neither could anyone else! Townsfolk came and went throughout the day, everyone with a new opinion about the tree. By then, night was falling, although it was only about five, and Jack and Denny were fastening up the last of the lights.

Cars and trucks were pulling into town. Becca gave a wave to Noah Kincaid and his family. Connie and Ron walked across the street from The Corner Store. Lorraine Thickson arrived in a beat-up old pickup with a passel of kids somehow stuffed into it. No husband and father, she noticed. Becca sat up a little straighter as she saw Denny in the cherry-picker basket, going *up up up* to the top of the huge tree. Mel and Paige came back outside; their kids ran into the street. Everyone seemed to sense that the culmination was near.

Denny fussed with the top of the tree, then the cherry picker lowered him to the ground again. Jack must have connected the electricity, because the tree came alive! Lights twinkled all over the giant fir and on the very top was a star that positively brightened the sky! There was a collective "aww" in the crowd and as the night grew dark and the lights bright, there was silence. People seemed motionless.

Then magic happened—a gentle snow began to fall.

"Unbelievable," Becca whispered to no one. "Amazing." She felt her eyes watering from the sheer beauty of the moment. Then the tree went dark and, after her eyes adjusted a bit, she noticed people beginning to disperse.

Suddenly Denny was beside her, scooting his chair close. "You okay?" he asked.

"Sure," she said, wiping at her eyes. "It was just so emotional—seeing all the work done and so many people turn out."

"It's far from done. There are ornaments and trim still to do. The official lighting is tomorrow night, after the rest of it's decorated. It takes half the town to get it done." He grabbed her hand and squeezed it. "You're going to love it. Too bad the boys can't stay for that."

That evening Preacher served up a fantastic pot of turkey soup and it seemed to Becca there were more than the usual number of people stopping by the bar, probably curious about the tree. The temperature dropped and the snow fell gently and she loved the sound of people stomping the snow off their boots on the front porch. Dinner was barely over when Rich pulled his chair closer to hers.

"You sure this is what you want me to do, Becca? Leave you here and go home?"

For a second, she wore a shocked expression. How had she managed not to think about Rich and his buddies leaving? Now that he was, she felt oddly vulnerable. But determined. "I'll be fine," she said.

"If you need me to stay and bring you home at the end of the week, I'll stay. I'll call in to work, tell them you were hurt and I'm stuck here with you."

She shook her head. "You know I'll be fine with Denny. He would never do anything to hurt me. He said he'll drive me home."

"Well, that's just it, Becca. He'd never do anything on *purpose,* but you two were like oil and water there for a while. It didn't work too well for you and Denny. You were real..." He hung his head briefly. "While he was in the sandbox, you were hurting all over the place. I felt like it was kind of my fault—I was the one who hooked you up in the first place." He squeezed her hand tenderly, something Rich *never* did. "I don't want to see you go through something like that again."

"Wow," she said in a whisper. "I didn't think you even noticed."

"I didn't say anything," he said, shrugging, "because I didn't know what to say, for one thing. I didn't know how to make it better. And I couldn't say anything to Denny until he got back from Afghanistan—you don't go telling a fighting Marine his at-home life is all a wreck. But yeah, I noticed. And then you started to get a little better..."

She smiled at him. "A little, huh?"

"You went from being crushed to being pissed. It was an improvement."

"Aww. Our problems had nothing to do with you. It wasn't your fault. Then I met Doug and—"

"Here's the thing, Becca. You have to tell Mom and Dad where you are and who's taking responsibility for you. And you have to tell them how you got here—that I didn't have much of a choice."

She stiffened indignantly. "Excuse me, but I'm taking responsibility for myself. Denny's giving me a place to stay, but I'm twenty-five and I'm—"

He was shaking his head. "I'm leaving you and going home because Denny said he'd look out for you. I know you're all grown up, but he's your ex. And you know how Mom feels about your ex. You have to tell her. And you have to do it tomorrow, because when she asks me about you, I'm not going to lie to her. I kind of feel like she can still ground me or take away my truck or something."

That made her grin. Really, Rich's relationship with that truck was funny.

"Okay. I was going to, anyway."

"Have you told Doug?"

"Mostly," she said with a shrug. "I told him I was hunting with you…."

Rich sucked in his breath. "Okay, I don't want to know any more about this. You kept it from Mom and Dad, you kept the important parts from Doug, Denny's the one I'm leaving in charge…" He groaned.

"I'm going to tell everyone everything, but right now, I'm still here because I have a broken ankle."

"At least promise to call Mom. Before I get home and she puts the screws to me."

"For goodness' sake, you're twenty-five! You build bridges! Why are you so nervous about our mother?"

"I don't know," he said, shaking his head. "I hate it when she's pissed at me." He ran a big meaty hand over his face. "You sure you're going to be all right if I leave you?"

She nodded. "I'm sure. I think this worked out just the way it's supposed to."

"And your ankle doesn't hurt too much anymore?" he asked.

She shook her head.

"Okay, one more thing, Becca. If anything happens and you need me, will you call me?"

"Huh? Richie, you never act like this!"

"Yeah," he said, running a hand around the back of his neck. "I know you think you're the boss, the big sister, but it really bothers me to see you upset. I do care about you, you know." He grimaced. "Don't tell anyone I said that."

She put her fingers over her mouth to cover her laugh.

"If you're sure, I gotta go. I'm leaving early in the morning—I have work on Monday."

"Yeah. Go," she said. "And hey, Rich? Thanks. That was a real nice brother-thing to do."

"Yeah? Well, don't get used to it." He stood up. "Call me if you have a problem. Okay?"

"Okay."

"Jack and Preacher said they'd be looking out for you, too."

"Thanks."

He leaned down and gave her a kiss on the forehead. "See ya in a week or so."

"Drive carefully."

Because Rich needed to be on the road by about 4:00 a.m. to make the drive to San Diego in just one long day, he left the bar early. Dirk and Troy didn't have as far to go the next day—Sacramento was approximately a five-hour drive. Denny made sure Becca was settled in his apartment, then drove out to the Riordan cabins to hang out with his friends.

Becca had been asleep awhile when he finally came in. It was almost midnight. She kept her eyes squeezed shut while he undressed in the semidark. She was afraid a mere glimpse of him undressed might blow her mind. She held stock-still while he rustled around on his blow-up mattress. Seemed like he flipped around for a long time before she said, "Everything all right, Denny?"

"Huh?"

"You sound real restless," she said. "You okay?"

"Just getting comfortable," he said.

"Why don't I sleep on that thing tonight so you can get a good night's sleep in your own bed," she offered.

"I'll be fine in a second. This bed is good."

"I don't mind at all...."

"Shh," he said. "Go back to sleep."

But she was completely conscious of his presence. She inhaled deeply; she could smell him and he was divine. She wanted to put her arms around him, hold him, kiss him, taste him... She had missed him so.

Becca had absolutely no idea where they might go from this point, but one thing was glaringly obvious to her—she had to come clean with Doug. She wouldn't cheat; she wouldn't mislead. And she couldn't leave Doug believing they were quickly moving toward a permanent commitment when, in fact, she was trying to figure out what her relationship was with her ex-boyfriend.

Which meant there were going to be two very uncomfortable phone calls in the morning.

Becca dreamed about the day she met Denny. On a weekend pass from Camp Pendleton, Rich brought Denny over for dinner with their parents. Becca was home from college for the weekend.

They locked eyes and that was just about it. He grinned at her and she smiled at him. Rich said,

"Oh, crap! I should have known something like this would happen!"

From that moment on, if they were in the same room, they were touching. They abandoned Rich and went off to be alone together. They talked on the phone daily, sometimes several times a day. There was passion between them almost instantly. They talked about everything in life; they could go from hysterical laughter to serious heat in seconds.

When they made love for the first time, it was perfect. That first time they were a little clumsy, but utterly intoxicated with each other's bodies. By the time they'd made love a few times, they were absolute experts. Denny taught her about men; he told her nothing was easier than satisfying a guy, so encouraged her to help him concentrate on pleasing her. He put her at ease; he inspired her trust. While she felt inexperienced and awkward, he treated her like a goddess. Every time they made love was better than the time before.

She woke up at dawn, her eyes misting over with memories, with longing.

She heard the shower running in the little efficiency and was grateful. She needed a little time to compose herself. By the time he came out of the bathroom, she was ready to face him. She did have to concentrate to keep from staring at his naked chest.

"Want me to take you to breakfast with Dirk and Troy?" he asked.

"Are they leaving right away?"

"We planned to meet at Jack's for breakfast first."

"Why don't you go ahead while I dress. I think I'd better make a couple of phone calls before sliding down the stairs."

He pulled on his sweater, boots and jacket. "If you want help, call Jack's and I'll come back for you."

"Thanks," she said with a wan smile.

He frowned slightly. "You okay, Becca?"

"I'll be down shortly." She turned the bedside clock toward her. It was still early on Sunday morning—with any luck, she wouldn't have to just leave voice mails. "Go on now. Let me get going."

Once he'd gone, she dove right in. She called her mother's cell phone first. "Hey," she said when Beverly Timm answered. "How was Cabo?"

"How *is* Cabo, you mean. Glorious! It's the best idea I've had in years! We're going to be on our way to the airport in a couple of hours, home by late afternoon. And how is Cape Cod?"

"Well, that's why I'm calling. At the last minute, I changed my mind and I came to Virgin River with Rich. To hunt."

"You what?" Beverly asked, sounding genuinely confused.

"Okay, I didn't change my mind about Cape Cod at the very last minute, but almost. I wanted to see Denny."

Dead silence answered her, so she hurried on.

"I had the sense that Doug was getting serious," Becca said. "I needed to be sure this was resolved somehow, this traumatic thing between me and Denny. I knew it wouldn't be fair to either me or Doug to try to move ahead with our relationship if there was unfinished business. I had to know."

"Resolved? What does that mean?"

"I'm not sure," Becca said. "In the past? No hard feelings? Over and time to finally really move on? I don't know, Mom. I just know that, even though I was with Doug, I still found myself wondering what happened between me and Denny. I don't want that. I don't want to wonder."

"And, did you go up to that little town and throw yourself at him?" Beverly asked somewhat bitterly.

"Not at all. However, I did throw myself out of Rich's truck and break my ankle. I have a splint and crutches. In fact, I had a surgical procedure and then a splint. And now Rich is on his way home, while I'm stuck here for another week. Denny said he'd drive me home after the doctor takes the stitches out."

Silence again. "All right, let me get this right," Beverly finally said. "You went to Virgin River to see Denny, while we thought you were with Doug, and now you have a broken ankle and can't come home with your brother?"

"Well, Rich does have to work tomorrow. He couldn't hang around any longer."

"Becca, for the love of God! What are you thinking?"

She took a breath. "I'm thinking, this is the rest of my life. I'm not taking any chances. I'm not going to spend years wondering or brooding over a man who abandoned me and I'm not going to move forward with a man I'm not sure is the right one for me. That's what I'm thinking. That some things have to be *complete*."

"And is this thing with Denny *complete*?" her mother asked, her voice heavy with sarcasm.

"I will tell you this—we've made a little progress. I now understand some of the things he was going through when he left for Afghanistan. Things I never would have known if I hadn't made this trip."

"And does he understand some of the things he put *you* through?"

"What's more important to me, Mom, is that we all get past the hurts so we can go forward."

"But, Becca, you're too different," Beverly said. "You were never really right for each other. You come from completely different backgrounds and families. You and Doug seem such a good fit—your families are similar, you have both parents and siblings, you both went to college, you have similar interests. And unless there's something you haven't told me, Doug has never treated you badly. I knew right away that Doug was much more appropriate for you."

"You've used that word before, I think. *Appropriate.*"

"The minute I met him, I knew—this is more the type of man I expected you to attract. To marry. You have similar goals. His family is stable. Successful."

"Funny. Doug said something very similar...."

"See there?" Beverly said.

"He said, 'Becca, you're the kind of woman who looks like the wife of a lawyer.'"

"There you go. Really, there should be no question. You've been with Doug for a year! You and Denny broke up a long time ago. Why didn't you just come home with Rich?" she asked.

"Because the doctor was against the idea," she said. "Too long a drive, danger of swelling under the splint or even blood clots. I'll see the doctor on Friday. Denny said he'd drive me home, but of course, I can always catch a flight."

"And you're staying where?"

"In Denny's apartment."

"Oh, my God," she said weakly.

Becca laughed in spite of herself. "It's one-room over a garage, an efficiency. He's letting me use it."

"And where is he staying? Never mind, I don't want to know. Becca, this is a huge mistake. Doug might never understand! Who would expect him to?"

"Mom, I didn't do this so that Doug could understand. I did this in hopes that I might finally understand. Like I said, this is the rest of my life. I intend to be sure."

Nine

Oddly enough, that conversation with her mother made telling Doug what she was doing all that much easier. She couldn't count the number of times Beverly had openly said, with great relief, *He's so much more right for you!* But today was the first time she put that statement with Doug's. *You're the right kind of woman to be married to a lawyer or even a senator.*

Doug was a very careful planner. He'd been aiming for his father's legal firm since he started in pre-law. He chose his fraternity carefully; he wanted the right political connections to be strong. He came from good Northeastern stock. He had aspirations to make a lot of money in law and perhaps enter politics. Yes, he'd been good to her. But she couldn't shake the notion that he might be choosing his future wife like a man might chose a horse.

He answered sleepily. "I woke you," she said.

"It's pretty early," he said.

"Well, I had to use the phone when I could. I need to talk to you about something very important—can you think straight? Doug, Rich left this morning and I'm still here, on my crutches."

"Uh-huh," he said, and yawned.

"Here's what I didn't tell you but I have to tell you now—and I'm sorry it's over the phone. Believe me, if it weren't for the broken ankle, I'd be talking to you face-to-face. What I didn't tell you is, one of the reasons I decided to come with Rich is because my ex-boyfriend, the one I broke up with three years ago, is here."

He yawned again. "Very funny, Becca."

"No, Doug. I'm not joking. See, I began to get the feeling you and I were getting serious. Moving real close to that forever territory. You've been talking about marriage and graduating from law school and moving back East and—"

"Eventually," he said. "But we agreed that possibility is right out there, after law school. What's he got to do with us?"

"Not with us, Doug. With me. I hadn't seen him in a long time, but so many times I wondered what really happened. When I looked back on the whole thing, I was never really sure if I was just an idiot who didn't get it or if we were two people who'd never been right for each other in the first place. And I needed to be sure before moving forward with you."

"That's ridiculous," he said. "Didn't not hearing from him in years give you a hint? That's your answer, right there."

"But I did hear from him. I told you that," she said. "He came back from the Marines and asked for another chance, but I was so angry, I sent him away. That was right before I met you. Listen, I know this is asking a lot, for you to understand this, but I have to figure out a few things about the past before I can make a smart decision about the future. If there's even one small question… Ten years from now, I don't want to find myself a wife and mother, asking myself if I did the right thing. I don't know if men do this, but sometimes women will romanticize the one that got away, the one they can't have, and it can stir up all kinds of trouble. All I want to know is that our breakup, painful as it was, was absolutely the right thing to do."

He gave a bark of laughter. *"Women,"* he said derisively. "So, you've been there for a week. That should've given you plenty of time to answer that one small question. Were you right to send him away? What's it going to be, Becca?"

"Doug, I've learned that we were pretty confused and screwed up. I think I understand how we ended up hurting each other so badly. His mother's death really took its toll. Unlike you and me, he didn't have any other family anywhere and—"

"So," he said, cutting her off. "You two are putting it back together now?"

"No, we've only talked about what happened to him. We haven't even gotten around to what happened to me. And I told him I have a boyfriend."

"He must find it pretty interesting that you're there, with him, and not with your boyfriend," Doug said. "This is asking a little much, don't you think?"

She sighed. "It is, I realize that. But before we make some kind of commitment, this old relationship needs to be dealt with. It wasn't a crush, Doug. It was very serious."

"No," he said. "No, I'm not going along with this. I'm not sitting still while you have some fling to see if you picked the right guy. Either you find a way to get out of that stupid little town and back home or we're done. Done, Becca! Because this is completely inappropriate!"

Appropriate. Wow, that word kept popping up. But it wasn't the right word in this context. What her mother meant and what Doug meant is this wasn't very comfortable. They weren't exactly having their way. But it was probably not only appropriate but also sensible to be sure you loved the man who was getting ready to ask you to marry him.

"Well, gee, Doug, I guess that would answer a

question I hadn't even asked myself. Tell you what, let's both think about that."

"I want you to come home," he said.

"Home for me is San Diego," she said. "You live in L.A. What you mean to say is you want me out of here."

"Same thing. You're playing with fire here. I'm not putting up with this."

She thought for a moment. She had created this challenge, after all. An awful lot to ask of a boyfriend. "I guess I have to say I understand, Doug. And I'm sorry. This old relationship still feels strangely unfinished. I have to work this out. Bye."

She hung up.

And felt like a dog.

She'd done what she had to do, but she'd done it all wrong. Her original plan was to spend the week around Denny and figure something out about herself. Because it wasn't really about whether Denny wanted her. If she still couldn't let go, she had to break it off with Doug. It wasn't fair to him. But then she broke her ankle and things began to change…get a little more complicated…

The phone rang and she realized she hadn't concealed the number when she called Doug; it had shown up on his caller ID. "Hello?"

"I told my *mother* I was going to pop the question!" Doug said angrily. "I told my *mother* that you'd be with us at Christmas to get to know the whole family, to say yes, to talk about the wedding! You're making me look like a damn fool!"

She frowned. She had suspected a ring was coming soon, but he hadn't mentioned them spending Christmas with his family. In fact, he hadn't *asked* her. "Doug, we talked about spending Christmas together, but I assumed it would be with my family, since you were home at Thanksgiving. And why would I need to talk to *your* mother about a wedding?"

"Why would we get married in San Diego if we're going to live in Boston or Cape Cod? Now what am I supposed to say? That you went back to your old boyfriend? Some loser who barely made it out of high school?"

"Whew," she said. "I think maybe it's a good thing this came up now. I knew something was holding me back, but I wasn't sure what. Now at least I know, it wasn't Denny. I'm sorry I didn't see it sooner, Doug. I guess this is goodbye."

She hung up again. But this time she didn't have regrets. This time she thought maybe she'd barely dodged a bullet.

She'd always thought of him as uncomplicated, because he was. There weren't a lot of options with Doug. Because he had plans.

Becca made it down to the bar before Troy and Dirk left and she was able to say goodbye. She tried to hide her awkward emotions, but her life had just taken a leap. Truthfully, she came up here because she wasn't sure she was ready to accept a marriage proposal, but she hadn't really predicted she'd end things with Doug the way she had.

On a last-minute invitation from Paige after the guys left, she wandered over to the church but rather than attending the service, she spent her time with the little ones in the church nursery. She was no good for chasing them around but she was great at reading to them or sitting on the floor to stack blocks or roll balls with them.

She had lunch at the bar with several regulars, including Denny, but he was unusually quiet. He seemed a bit distant, which probably kept him from noticing she was a little reserved herself. He asked if she could manage on her own for a couple of hours while he checked in at Jilly's farm. His week with his friends had probably left a lot to be done out there. "Sure. Of course," she said. "Please, do whatever you need to do—I'm totally fine."

Right after he left, all hell broke loose.

"Becca, your mother's on the phone," Paige said. "She wants to speak to you."

"My mother?"

"Go ahead and take it in our great room—we're all either in the kitchen or outside helping decorate the tree. You'll have some privacy."

"My mother?" she said again. "Called *here*?"

"She sounds a little upset."

When she got to the phone and said hello, her mother launched into her. "Have you completely lost your mind?"

She sat down heavily. "I'm not sure. What are we talking about?"

"You broke up with Doug for *Denny*? Do you have any idea what you've done to yourself? What you've sacrificed for a foolish young man who treated you so badly?"

"Stop," Becca said. "I didn't do that. I told Doug exactly what I told you—that it was important for me to get a handle on the past before I could deal with the future. And how in the world do you know this? And how did you find this number?"

"Doug called me, thank God. There's still time, Becca. He's upset, but he'll come around. You have to call him, apologize, tell him you weren't thinking—"

"How did you find me here?"

"I called the number Doug gave me, but there was no answer. Your brother *finally* answered his cell and said I might try this number."

"Aren't you supposed to be on an airplane right about now?" Becca asked.

"Yes! I'll be boarding soon! Are you listening to me?"

"Yes. I hear you loud and clear," she said. "But I don't think you're listening to me. I—"

"You're throwing away the opportunity of a lifetime! I'd never have to worry about you again if you were married to Doug! You can't possibly be giving all that up for Denny! What does *he* have?"

A five-year-old Nissan truck. A bunch of good friends. A couple of jobs he enjoys. A life that makes him happy.

"You should get on your plane, Mom," she said. "I'm not talking to you about this. This is between me and Doug. Or…it *was* between me and Doug."

"Becca, don't be foolish!"

"Mother, I'm saying goodbye. I'll call you in a couple of days. I'm sorry you're disappointed, but you should know, I'm very relieved. I don't want to marry Doug Carey."

"Life isn't some little Cinderella story, Becca. It takes more than the right size slipper to be happy—it takes security! It takes—"

She was cut off by a beep.

"I have to hang up on you, Mother. There's another call coming on this line and it's not my phone. I'll call in a couple of days when we're both calmer." And then she clicked off. "Middletons," she answered.

"Becca, is that you?" Doug asked.

"How did *you* get this number?" she asked.

"From your brother."

The reasons to kill Big Richie were stacking up.

"I was angry," Doug said. "You caught me off

guard and I was angry. I never expected it. I had no idea you were still hung up on the ex. We'll work it out. You come back home, I'll take the weekend off and spend it with you, we'll talk things over and we'll get it sorted out."

"If I change my mind, I'll call you, but I don't think that's going to happen."

"Becca, we've been together for a *year*!"

"I know. I know. And I really wanted it to work, but no matter how hard I tried, it just wasn't. I just wasn't feeling it, Doug. I had too many doubts. And I'm glad to know that before I was in too deep. Really, I am sorry. I am. You're a great guy, a great catch. The right woman is just waiting for you to find her."

"You just need some time to think this through! You can't really be this stupid!"

She sighed, not even offended. She remembered how clumsy it felt each time she said *I love you*. "You need someone who is totally, completely and uncompromisingly in love with you. Doug, I'm sorry. I wanted it to be me, but it's not."

She disconnected.

The phone immediately rang. She looked at the caller ID and there he was. Big Richie. "I'm going to *kill* you!"

"What? It's not like this is *my* fault!"

"You gave out this number—to Mother and Doug! Are you crazy? Do you just plain hate me?"

"It's true, then? You broke up with Doug?"

"Surprised me as much as you," she said. "It wasn't what I intended to do, but I thought I had to tell him I was here with Denny… Well, not *with* him, but that I hoped while I was here I'd figure out… Oh, never mind, I'm tired of trying to explain this. Bottom line, I learned something important, and just in time. I don't love Doug. I don't think I ever did."

"So," Rich said, "you pretty much just lied to me about wanting to go hunting."

"Yeah, sorry about that. Although, I *was* kind of curious about hunting and I think I'd actually like to learn fly-fishing. You know I caught that big sailfish deep-sea fishing and—"

"Becca!" he yelled.

"What?"

"What's going to happen now?"

"I have absolutely no idea," she said, rubbing her temples. "Mother's furious with me for giving up a lawyer, Doug is furious with me for even thinking about giving him up and I'm stuck in Virgin River with a guy I used to love, who seems to be pretty distant right now. And you're giving out any number where I might be found!"

"I never saw you with Doug," Rich said.

"What are you talking about? You saw me with him all the time. You like Doug."

"Yeah, he's okay. I'm not sure I liked him for you."

"Huh?"

"It just didn't seem… I don't know. Maybe I was still hung up on you and my best friend or something. I couldn't see you with Doug."

"Now, that's interesting. Especially since I wouldn't consider you sensitive. Or intuitive. Or even conscious, most of the time."

"Try not to insult the only person on your side, Becca."

"Then try to tell me why. If you like Doug, why don't you like him for me?"

"Not sure," Big Richie said. "Maybe it was that stick he has up his ass…"

She laughed in spite of herself. "The *major important contacts through my fraternity* stick?"

"Possibly," Rich said, laughing.

"Or could it be the *you'd give me up for a guy with only a high school education* shtick?"

"Did he say that?" Rich asked. "I bet he actually said that, didn't he?"

"He actually did," Becca confirmed.

"See, that's the thing about Doug. He can be cool. He can be fun. And he can be a real dick. Every once in a while, he has a hard time holding his dickness down."

She laughed again. "I think this is the closest I've ever felt to you."

"We're the same age," he informed her soberly. "I never had anyone special. I had a lot of girls I thought might get special, but they didn't. I saw you all lit up once because you were totally caught… I didn't know what it was at the time. Then I saw it gone and I started to get it. Then I saw you with Doug and it just wasn't there. He had all the stuff that was going to make him a winner. But he didn't have any of the stuff that lit you up."

"Richie," she said, touched and almost teary.

"Until everyone started freaking out, I thought you'd play it safe. Find a way to go for the lawyer, shtick or not. Problem is… I have no idea where Denny stands. You could be looking for the right one as long as me."

"That's okay. That makes more sense than playing it safe."

"And, Becca?"

"Yes?"

"You ever lie to me and trick me like that again, you're gonna pay!"

After everyone who felt they had a stake in her love life had called, Becca spent most of the afternoon outside watching the rest of the tree trimming, an occupation that required a lot of volunteers and plenty of time in the cherry pickers. From her spot on the porch at Jack's bar, she had another look at the town. The tree was surrounded by people—

children and adults—all smiling, laughing, running around. A few who she assumed lived right on the street, held steaming mugs in their mitten-covered hands.

Had she called the town dumpy? In one week, it had taken on the appearance of a friendly, welcoming, unpretentious town. It was simple and kind of sweet. And that tree—a town project—was awesome. Finally done, it was trimmed with red, white and blue balls, laminated military unit badges and strung with gold tinsel. It was gorgeous in daylight; it would be magnificent lit against the night sky.

Denny returned at dinnertime and they were together for some of Preacher's stew and for the grand, official Christmas tree lighting, after which there was some tree-side caroling. Lots of people stopped into the bar to warm their bones against the snow. Denny spent much of that time behind the bar and even she could see he was kept extremely busy. Too busy to spend much time with her.

He hadn't talked a lot during dinner. Becca wanted to believe it was because he'd had to say goodbye to his buddies, friends he hadn't seen in a while and wouldn't see again until who knew when. After the way he acted last night, all restless and having a hard time sleeping, she had started to worry that he'd had serious second thoughts about being stuck with her for another week.

It was typical of her to be direct, to come right out with her concerns or questions. But there was one thing she remembered about her former relationship with Denny—she couldn't ask him what was wrong more than twice at the very most.

So she let it ride, even when he escorted her home at around eight o'clock, then went back to Jack's to help out until closing.

With a heavy sigh, she treated herself to a bath, unplugged Denny's phone just in case, then crawled into bed with her borrowed book. By the time Denny came back at a little after ten, she had nodded off, light still lit, opened book in her lap. She snapped awake at the sound of the closing door.

"Sorry," he said. "I woke you."

"It's all right. I just fell asleep reading. You can turn the light off if you want to. Or leave it on, I don't care."

He just shuffled inside the door for a moment. "Doesn't matter," he said. He took off his jacket and hung it on the peg just inside the door. Then he sat in the only chair in the room, rested his elbows on his knees, clasped his hands together and hung his head.

"Oh, for Pete's sake!" she said suddenly. "What

is bugging you? You want me to sleep on the air mattress? Because I'd be happy to!"

He lifted his head instantly. "No, no. We're good." He stood, went to his storage chest and reached inside to pull out some clothes. Then he headed for the bathroom, closing the door behind him.

She heard the shower running and she sank down in the bed. "Maybe he's got a girlfriend," she muttered to herself. "Maybe that's it. I'm in the way." She put her book on the table beside the bed and turned over, presenting her back toward the bathroom door. It was a *very* long shower. Yes, she thought. Very likely there was a girl around here somewhere and now that his friends were gone, he'd like to get back to her. Just because things hadn't worked out for Becca didn't mean Denny's life had been standing still. She'd sent him packing and he had been trying to jump-start a new life up here in the mountains.

It seemed a long time before he was back in the room, and she purposely didn't turn to look at him.

"Becca?" he asked softly.

"Hmm?"

"You ready for the light to be off now?"

"Sure," she said. *Tomorrow I am going to find the right moment to bring it up, to talk to him about whatever it is that is making him act so uncomfortable around me.*

He rummaged around, putting his clothes away, turning off the light beside her bed, crawling onto his air-mattress bed, then flopping around like a fish on the dock. She sighed heavily, not sure she was going to make it till the right moment tomorrow. She listened to his mattress gymnastics for another ten minutes, when the light beside her bed suddenly flicked on. Startled, she rolled over to look up at him.

"Look, I think I'm just going to head out to Jack's. If you think you'll be all right here by yourself."

She raised up in bed. "Jack's?"

"His guesthouse. You could probably, ah, use the privacy…."

"What the hell is going on with you? We didn't have a problem all week and all of a sudden something is eating you. And it's not letting you sleep! And it's about me! Is there a girlfriend? Do you have a girlfriend and you can't find a way to just tell me you want to spend time with her?"

He frowned in complete confusion, those beautiful expressive brows drawing together. "Girlfriend?"

"Well, I can't for my life figure out what's wrong with you!"

"Girlfriend?" he said again. He sat very gently on the edge of her bed. "Becca, there's no girlfriend. I'm finding it kind of… Well, it's hard to be alone with you."

"You were alone with me all week!"

"Yeah, but the guys were all here. Once I knew they'd all be gone, that I wouldn't have to look Rich in the eye in the morning… That's when it started to get really…*hard*," he said, emphasizing the word with agony.

"What's hard?" she asked. She reached out and touched his arm. "My God, you're *freezing*!"

He took a deep breath. "Cold shower, Becca."

"What for?" she asked, genuinely stumped. He rolled his eyes and she realized exactly what was hard. "Oh! But *why*?"

"Because, Becca… Are you going to make me say it?"

She pushed herself up in the bed a little bit. "I think you'd better, because I had myself convinced you had a girlfriend and you were feeling guilty about spending all this time with me."

"It's *you*, Becca. I'm miserable being alone with you and your broken ankle and knowing I can't get too close or I might just lose my mind. Knowing I'd have to face the guys every morning—that kind of kept my head on straight. But they're gone, it's just you and me. You, me and your *boyfriend*! And I don't think I can be alone here with you. Okay?"

Her blue eyes were wide and her lips parted

slightly as she stared at him. Finally she said, "Seriously?"

He glanced away. "I'll just go out to Jack's," he said, standing.

She grabbed his ice-cold hand. "You don't have to go to Jack's."

"Yeah, I do. Because I'm afraid even if I can fall asleep, I'll walk in my sleep and you'll have your hands full in the middle of the night."

She laughed softly. "I don't want you to leave. Especially for that reason."

"Aren't you listening? I haven't felt this out of control in years. I took a twenty-minute cold shower and still…"

Her eyes wandered downward and there it was, the evidence of his misery. A very obvious erection straining against the sweatpants he slept in. "Oh, my," she said, smiling at him. "You don't want to go out in the cold with that. You could hurt yourself."

"Funny," he said. "You have a broken ankle! Not to mention what's-his-name."

She shook her head. "No more what's-his-name."

"Huh?"

"I didn't exactly plan it, but when I called him today, I broke it off." She shook her head again. "It wasn't right, Denny. I'm not meant to be with him. And he's really not meant to be with me."

"Why?" he asked in a breath.

"To start with, I had way too many doubts." She shrugged. "Now I realize it never did feel quite right."

He reached out and smoothed her hair back along her temple. "Are you okay?" he asked.

"I'm better," she said. "I talked to my brother today. He was surprised, but even Rich said he just couldn't see me with him… With Doug. Imagine that? Rich."

Denny laughed briefly. "Rich Timm?" he asked.

"The same. Anyway, that's that."

Denny got a kind of bedazzled look in his eyes. "You still have a broken ankle…"

"Yes," she said, pulling him toward her. She put his hand to her mouth and kissed his palm. "Try to be careful of that, will you?"

He resisted for a second, studying her face. Thinking. Considering. "Whoa boy," he said. "You're sure?"

And she nodded.

Ten

Denny put his cold hands on her, framing her face, sliding his fingers into her hair. He leaned down to kiss her, briefly at first. Then his mouth was harder against hers. He tongued open her lips and she opened to him willingly. Oh, God, the taste! That was the taste she remembered and loved. He kissed her senseless for a moment and then one knee came up onto the bed, then the second, then he was straddling her. His lips were on her mouth, her cheek, her ear, her neck. She drank him in; his breathing grew ragged and excited.

She laughed right into his open mouth.

"Funny?" he asked, pulling away a little bit.

"You are soooo cold."

"That won't last long..." He went after her again, pulling her mouth hard against his; his tongue explored and he groaned from someplace deep inside.

For her, it felt at once like coming home and a whole new experience.

He felt her small, warm hands slip under his T-shirt and caress his chest and back. "My God, you're even cold under here."

"Warm me up," he said, his voice soft and husky. "You know what to do…."

She lifted up the T-shirt. "I think you'll warm up faster without this."

He pulled away from her just long enough to rip his shirt over his head. He was back to devouring her with kisses, but she'd managed a look at him, at his wide chest with that soft mat of hair and his flat belly.

While he kissed her, she caressed his back and slid her small hands under the waistband of his sweats to feel his hard butt. He worked on the buttons of her pajamas, taking his sweet time, and she found herself wishing she'd had the foresight to bring something sexier than warm jammies to Virgin River.

Finally he spread the pajama top and just stared at her. "Becca," he said in a whisper. "Ah, Becca, you have the most beautiful body in the world."

Her hands ran over his chest. "See?" she said softly. "You're warmer already…"

He pulled back the bedcovers and knelt between her legs. His hands were hot now, hot on her breasts, covering them and pressing them together. He kissed his way down her neck, across her collarbone and onto her chest, finally pulling a nipple into his mouth. The sensation caused her to arch against him, and while he suckled, he pressed himself against her. Her hand slipping around to the front beneath his sweats, she reached for him, grabbing that most proud member in her hand. He shuddered. "God," he said. "Oh, man… Baby, I'm going to make you feel so good."

Her moan was music to his ears. She pressed her pelvis against him, hungry. Eager. He sucked harder. His fingers slipped under the waistband of her pj bottoms and he began to slide them down. "You have to help me with this, baby. We have to be careful of your ankle…."

"Nice and slow, Denny. We don't want to have to explain anything embarrassing to the doctor."

He chuckled wickedly, happily, slowly pulling down the pajamas. "You embarrassed, honey?"

"Not at all," she said, lifting her butt and letting them slide. She kicked the good leg out and waited patiently while he pulled the other over her splint.

"Yeah, we can do this." Then he stopped and concentrated on her face. "You sure, Becca?"

She smiled and nodded. "Are you kidding? Of course I'm sure. You?"

He didn't answer, he just fell into her kiss again, covering her open mouth with his, pulling her tongue into his mouth and tasting her. His fingers moved lower to tease her, to test her, to see if she was getting ready for him. She was going to drown him; he almost lost it right there. His groan was so deep and low, he felt it rumble through him.

"Becca, baby, I don't think I can wait for you."

She tugged his sweats down to his thighs, then urged him toward her.

She was panting, arching, lifting against him. The size of him thrilled her. Then she moved his hand so that he was stroking her in the right place, getting her hotter. Closer. It was all a part of their sexual memory, the things they had learned about each other, not forgotten even after years of separation. And her moan turned into a whimper as she led him to her.

He pressed himself gently against her, just barely entering a little bit, then stopped and looked deeply into her eyes before pushing on. "I still love you, baby. I never stopped loving you…."

"Oh, Denny, I missed you so much…."

A small smile found his lips right before he drove it home. Ah, he'd been here before! His world went into a spin. Everything he was feeling, he knew he would feel with her. He watched her face. She bit her lower lip, moaned softly. Her hands found the hard muscles of his butt and pulled him more deeply into her. Then she lifted against him, held him tight inside her and everything clenched until her toes curled. "Oh, God, oh, God, oh, God…." she cried.

"That's my girl," he said. And that was all the endearment he could muster before he rode her hard, throbbing with his own pleasure. He didn't think it would ever end, and by the time the climax ebbed, he was weak. Breathing hard, he rested his face against her neck, giving her soft kisses while he held her, feeling her lips against his cheek.

"See?" she whispered. "You're not cold anymore."

He chuckled. He felt a little trickle against his face and when he pulled back to look at her, he found tears wetting her cheeks. He wiped them away with his fingers. "Honey, you're crying. I went crazy… Did I hurt you? Baby, I'm so sorry!"

She sniffed back the emotion and blinked her eyes closed, giving her head a little shake.

"Becca? Regrets?"

"No, that's not it. I was afraid I'd never feel that with you again."

"Aw, baby… I'm sorry for all my screwups."

"Me, too. But this time we have to talk about it, Denny. All of it."

He gave her a light kiss, but he couldn't bring himself to pull out of her. "We'll talk about everything, honey. I promise."

They vowed to talk about everything, but not right away. They held each other close, skin to skin, occasionally stroking and kissing, coming down to earth. And it was while they shared this intimate closeness that it struck Becca with utter clarity that before they fell apart three years ago, Denny had been more than a lover, he had been her best friend. Even though she was at USC and he was in San Diego, he was her ballast, her rudder. It grieved her that she obviously hadn't been that for him when he needed it, because she relied on him completely. She talked to him everyday; she told him everything, rarely making a decision without having a conversation with him first. Even those decisions that had little to do with him, like what subject to choose for a paper she was writing.

Then his mother became ill and he began to recede from her life until suddenly he was *gone*.

Now she wondered, had she been doing all the talking and too little listening?

"I can't believe you thought I had a girlfriend," Denny said. He was still in that perfect place inside her, though in his current condition he wasn't going to achieve much beyond the comfort of closeness.

"I can't believe you don't have one," she said. "In three years?"

He shook his head and nuzzled her neck. "You had boyfriends," he said.

"No," she corrected. "I hardly even went out. Then I met what's-his-name about a year ago."

"And you came up here?" Denny asked. "I guess, I don't get that part. . . ."

She gave a little huff of laughter. "More about all that when we're not all hooked up like this. I don't want anyone else in either of our heads." She ran her fingers over his beard-roughened cheek. "If we're going to try this again, you and me, we have to be more honest this time. About everything."

"Oh, we're going to try again," he said. "And this time we're going to get it right. I can't let you go now. And we're going to be more honest, but later." He ran his fingers through her hair. Then he moved his hips a little, growing inside her, filling her. He kissed the corner of her mouth, then the other corner, then her neck, then her breast. Then in a slightly desperate whisper, he said, "Please, tell me we can talk later. . . ."

She gasped as his lips closed around her nipple. When she let out her breath, all that came with it was her whisper. "Later works."

They only dozed through the night, their hands and lips rarely caught in slumber. When Denny wasn't making love to her, he was holding her close, whispering to her how much he loved her, wanted her, needed her in his life. Becca's deepest sleep came right before waking in the morning and it was in some surprise she found Denny sitting on the side of the bed, fully dressed, gently pushing her hair away from her face.

She opened her eyes slowly, yawned and purred.

"Tired, baby?" he asked.

"A little tired, but not sorry. I can sleep anytime."

His laugh was low and deep. He kissed her again. "I made you some coffee."

"Where are you going?" she asked.

"It's Monday morning and I have a job. It's probably a good thing, too—if I could stay in bed with you for a few days, I'd wear you out. But, after a week of having company and not spending any time at the farm, some of my work has piled up. Instead of staying out there for lunch, I'll meet you at Jack's. How's that?"

"That's perfect," she said. "Aren't *you* tired?"

"I've never felt better," he said with a smile. "About a week of this and I still won't be tired. But I might be dead." He grinned at her. "There's one thing you can tell me before I go, just to give me a little reassurance. Are you still on the pill?"

She nodded. "You're safe."

"I wouldn't mind, you know. But it's probably not a good idea to get ourselves knocked up," he teased. Then he grew serious. "Becca, is your leg okay? I didn't hurt you, did I?"

"I'm just fine. I go back to the doctor on Friday. I'm sure he'll release me to travel." A look crossed

Denny's face immediately and she interpreted it correctly. She put a hand over his. "That doesn't mean I have to pack up and go, Denny. I don't have a job waiting and I don't think I'm going to have much luck finding one while I'm on crutches. There's time."

He smiled at that and gave her yet another kiss. "God, I hate to leave you."

She laughed at him. "I guess this is why there are honeymoons. Go to work. I'll see you in a few hours."

Becca was tired enough to have slept, but she couldn't. There was something she knew she'd better do—call her mother. She might have said she'd call in a couple of days, but she had nearly hung up on her mother twice. She couldn't let this fester. She might not always agree with her mother, but she loved her. She brought a cup of coffee to the bedside table, plugged in the phone and dialed.

"Hi, Mom," she said. "I don't want hard feelings between us. Especially over a guy."

"Or guys," Beverly said.

"You're still angry with me," Becca said.

Beverly sighed deeply. "I'm disappointed. I'm afraid you've made a decision based purely on romance, or the idea of romance, when you should be thinking long term. Practically. Because romance doesn't last."

"Please don't be afraid, Mom. Honestly, I had

so many doubts about Doug, I ran for my life. I admire some of the things he's doing with his life, but I don't love him. And no matter how much sense it might make to you, I am not marrying a man I don't love."

Beverly sighed again. "Of course you shouldn't," she relented. "I just never saw a hint of this reaction from you. Not in a year. It came as a shock."

"I love you, Mom, but please trust me to know what's best for me. Think of it this way—if I screw up, at least it will be *my* screwup and not a mistake based on your advice."

In spite of herself, Beverly laughed. "Well, there's that. But can I just say this, Becca? Either way, based on my advice or your own instincts, all I ever wanted was your happiness. Please believe that."

"Thank you, Mom. That means a lot to me."

"I do wish your instincts matched my best advice a little better."

Becca laughed.

When Becca got to the bar for lunch, a glance around told her Denny wasn't there yet. She took her place up at the bar in front of a smiling Jack.

"What's your pleasure?" he asked.

"Diet cola?" she asked. "Denny's coming for lunch. I'll wait for him before ordering."

"You got it," he said. When he put the cola in

front of her, he tilted his head slightly, looked a little perplexed, and said, "What's different about you today? Something's different."

"Gosh, I don't know," she said. She ran a hand through her blond hair. "I didn't do anything differently."

He shook his head slightly. "No, something's different, I just can't… Ah! I know what it is! You're in love, that's what it is!"

She flushed.

Jack chuckled and gave the bar a wipe. "I'm teasing you. Denny stopped by the bar on his way out to Jillian's farm and he was grinning so damn big, I wouldn't let him off the hook till he told me what made him so happy. He said all it took was getting rid of his pals to get you two talking and it looked like maybe you could patch up any old differences and put your relationship back together. Got one over on you, didn't I?"

She couldn't help but smile at him. "You should be ashamed of yourself!" she said. "Weren't you afraid you might embarrass me?"

"Nah. My opinion of Denny is that a girl couldn't possibly do better. He's the salt of the earth. Very much admired around here."

"He fits in," she translated.

"Denny's special. But it doesn't take so much to fit in, Becca. People around here are pretty easy most of the time. Good neighbors, that's all."

"It's more than that, I think. Is it just that you don't get all that many visitors? Because everyone seems so welcoming. Eager to help each other."

"Oh, not everyone. We have our bad apples, just like any other town. We cut 'em a wide berth. But for the ones who want to get along, just about everyone's willing to go the extra mile. Most people are here for one of three reasons—either they grew up here and it never occurred to them to leave or they came here for a specific career like ranching, farming, maybe logging or government jobs like forestry or search-and-rescue. The rest seem to be a little like me—I just wanted to get out of the rat race. I was looking for good hunting and fishing and needed a way to make a living while I was doing that. Getting married and having a family never figured in my plans." He tilted his head and winked at her. "Good thing I can keep an open mind."

"Good thing," she said.

"There's an old saying around the mountains—if you last three years, you'll never leave."

"Why is that?"

Jack leaned on the bar. "It's not always an easy life. We're isolated here. It's a real pain just to get supplies, and if we have an emergency, we'd better be prepared to handle it. It's not a rich place, by any means—the average income is pretty low.

And nature has a heavy hand here—hard winters, forest fires, floods when the snowpack melts."

"What's so good about it?" she asked.

"Look around. Especially at night—look up. We have a pretty big sky. Lots more stars than in San Diego. The landscape is rich in natural resources and beauty. And we grow everything a little bigger. Even the marijuana."

"I heard about that," she said with a laugh.

"Virgin River isn't too accommodating to the growers. We like life as uncomplicated as possible."

The comment left Becca thinking about the complications in her life. She'd never been happier, but the issues were still there—no job, little money with an apartment in San Diego and the rent due, the love of her life living hundreds of miles away. And while he said he loved her, she knew he loved this town, too. In this town, he finally found what he'd always been looking for.

"A cloud just passed over you," Jack said.

"I think it was that word—*uncomplicated.* I have a broken ankle, no job to go home to and Denny lives here, while I live so far away…."

"Since those are things you can't do anything about today, try to enjoy the things that are going right," Jack said.

At that moment, the thing she enjoyed most about her present circumstances walked in the door. He dragged off his hat and as his eyes lit on her, he began to beam. *You're right,* she thought. And as he took the seat beside her, he dropped a possessive kiss on her cheek and grabbed her hand.

"Lunch?" Jack asked.

"Two," he said. "Thanks. What is it today?"

"Pulled-pork sandwiches. I'll get 'em. And then I'll leave you two alone."

Eleven

After lunch, Denny drove Becca down the street and carried her up the steep stairs, while she held on to the crutches. She could have stayed at Preacher's house and even napped there, but she chose instead to be out of the way for at least a couple of hours. And Denny was thrilled to get her alone in that little one-room apartment over the garage. He barely had the door closed before he pulled the crutches out of her grip, whirled her around and had her on the bed, his lips hot on hers. He rolled with her until he was lying beside her, snuggling her close. They didn't even have their jackets off before his breathing was coming hard and raspy.

"Don't you have to work?" she asked in a breathless whisper.

"I'm thinking of a leave of absence," he said,

pulling her shirt away from her neck so he could cover her with kisses.

"I remember this about you… You've always been so passionate. Is this normal?"

"I don't know, but I think you're going to be stuck with this now."

"Poor me…" she whispered, holding him close.

"Okay with you if I just chase you till you're about ninety?"

"Only ninety?"

"You don't know how hard it was to go to work this morning. How hard it is to think about going back this afternoon."

"I'll be here later, too." It didn't seem to be slowing him down. His hands were moving. "Go to work, Dennis."

"Ugh…"

"Do you think you'll ever have time to show me the place you work?" she asked.

He lifted his head from her neck. "Would you like to see it?"

"I would, if your boss wouldn't mind."

"She'd be thrilled. I'll take you tomorrow. Bring a book—after a tour, you'll have to wait for me to get my morning work done." He sat up reluctantly. "I'll go now, but I'll see you later." He closed his eyes briefly. "God, you smell good."

"You'd better leave before you change your mind again."

"Get a nap, Becca. Rest up." He put her crutches by the bed so she could reach them and headed for the door. "I kept you up half the night. Sleep."

That was exactly what she intended to do. She pulled the corner of the quilt over herself and with a smile on her face, she conked out immediately. When she woke, it was almost three in the afternoon. She pulled herself up, stretched and reached for the paperback that was sitting on the bedside table.

It didn't take her long to feel like getting out and the only thing she could think of was Jack's. By the time she got down the street, she noticed Danielle and Megan, walking into the church. Drawn to the kids, secretly hoping there was another activity she could help with, she followed them.

When she was inside the church doors, she heard voices. She had to manage a few stairs to get up to the sanctuary. There, at the front of the church, the pastor's wife was talking to the girls as they were taking off their coats. "Hey," Becca called to them.

"Becca!" they both said, beaming.

She made her way down the aisle. "More after-school projects?" she asked.

"I'm afraid not today," Ellie said. "The bus just dropped them off and I have work to do. I'm Noah's wife and the church secretary. While I finish up in the office, the girls are going to work on their homework in the conference room. Trevor and Jeremy are in the basement, hopefully staying out of trouble."

"I can help with homework," Becca said.

"We don't want to be any trouble, Becca," Ellie said. "You probably have better things to do."

Becca laughed. "Well, I was going to go skiing, but it's a little chilly for me."

"What about Denny?"

"Denny's working. I'll see him at dinnertime. Really, I'd be happy to help with homework. I'm great at math and spelling and reading. Almost as good as I am with crafts!"

Danielle smiled enthusiastically, but Megan's eyes shifted away and she looked unmistakably sad. Becca put a finger under her chin and drew her gaze back. "What? You don't feel like help?"

Megan shrugged. "I'm not so good, that's all."

"At what?" Becca urged.

"Just about anything. I'm not that smart."

"Well, I don't believe that for a second," she said sweetly. "If I help, maybe we'll figure out your best subjects. Almost everything gets easier with just a little coaching and practice!"

"I think that's a good idea," Ellie said. "Go on, girls. Show Becca to the conference room."

"Yay!" Becca said. "Let's play teacher and students!"

Once the girls got their homework spread out

and Becca had her leg propped up, it took her about ten minutes to see that Danielle was not just up to speed on her work but perhaps ahead of her class. Megan, a year younger and only in third grade, seemed to be struggling.

Becca tried to keep her attention fairly divided between the girls, but she really trotted out all her tricks to encourage Megan. She showed her a few simple exercises that would help her with the spelling words and her reading. "If you'll copy this word ten times, sounding it out in your head when you write it, I bet when I ask you to spell it, you'll get it perfect." And, "Most of this adding and subtracting is just practice and memorizing." And, "We'll read together for a while, sounding out the words, and it will get easier every day."

There was a problem, however. While Danielle was excited about performing for Becca, Megan was dropping little bombs that didn't bode well. She said she was going to flunk. "Of course you're not—you're doing quite well with this homework!" She said her teacher hated her. "I'm sure you're wrong about that. It would be impossible to hate you—you're so delightful!" Becca said. And the one that killed her—*I'm so stupid.*

At first, Becca suspected the parents or siblings. It happened—words like *dumb* and *stupid* were tossed around the home and it hammered little self-esteems. But then her mind was changed.

Becca asked if she could look at some of Megan's papers. She had a folder with at least a week's worth of work tucked inside. In fact, it was a great deal of work for an eight-year-old. She flipped through the pages and saw something she didn't like. On all the papers that weren't perfect, there were painfully negative remarks from the teacher. *You can do better than this! This needs work! Do this spelling test again! This is late!* Frowny faces!

And on the pages that were excellent, no comment at all. Just a letter grade. A. B. No pluses, no minuses. No stars, no happy faces, no praise. No effort anywhere to encourage the child when she'd done well. Zero positive reinforcement.

Becca had a sinking feeling in her gut. This was sadly familiar to her. For her, it was fifth grade, then again when she was a junior in high school. A couple of teachers who made their impact on her by being ruthlessly negative. The fifth-grade teacher kept telling her if she wanted to get to sixth grade, she'd better apply herself. It didn't take long before she believed there was a sound chance she wouldn't promote to the next level and her stomach hurt every morning before school. The high school English teacher, who seemed to favor the boys in the class, told Becca's parents that she "wasn't college material." The family joke was that it was lucky Beverly Timm hadn't been armed! Both teachers from hell; both enjoyed long careers even though they were mean as snakes and made no effort to help.

Both times, Becca had believed her teachers hated her. What she eventually learned was that she was right! But the teachers actually disliked almost all their students and they weren't crazy about teaching, either.

Once Becca was a teacher herself, she had a closer view. The great teachers outnumbered the bad, thankfully, but it was hard to get rid of the ones who hurt. Their negative impact was so subliminal, so pervasive. So *powerful*!

Fortunately for Becca, there had been a few teachers who made major changes in her life with their encouragement and positive reinforcement. At the end of the day, Becca graduated from high school with good grades, though she was nowhere near competing for valedictorian. She left college with a 3.2 GPA—a completely respectable performance.

She'd gotten very good reviews on her teaching, but the feedback that meant the most to her was from the kids, most of whom seemed to strive to impress her. And there were parents of second graders who thanked her. She took that very seriously.

The three of them worked on homework until Lorraine Thickson came to collect her kids. Her coat thrown over her pink waitress uniform, a great big purse hanging on her shoulder, she came into the conference room. "Ellie said you were working on homework," she said by way of greeting.

"That we are," Becca said. "What a smart girl you have here. We've hardly started on this week's work and she's almost ready for that spelling test!"

"Oh, that's so nice!" she said, holding her arms open to her daughter. She leaned down and said, "Go find your brother and get your coat, honey."

Once Megan had run off, Danielle following her, Becca faced Lorraine. "I'm going to ask Ellie if we can do homework together after school again. Would that be okay with you?"

A look of surprise and hesitation came over her face.

"I have nothing to do except elevate my leg," Becca said. "And they're such fun. I should probably ask Christopher if he wants to join us, too."

"That's awful nice of you," Lorraine said shyly. "The teacher keeps asking me to work with her, but it's almost impossible. I work five to five and—"

Becca's jaw dropped. "Five to five? A.M to P.M?"

"The overtime comes in handy. My husband had a job injury and he's home with the two little boys all during the day. By the time I get dinner and some chores done, Megan's off to bed. I know she needs the help and Frank just doesn't have the patience."

"She doesn't need that much help," Becca said, shaking her head. "She's smart. She just needs a little encouragement. I looked at her papers—she's doing fine. Nothing on her papers that would alert me to a learning problem, though I only saw about a week's worth."

"She's had a very hard year," Lorraine said.

"She told me about her dad. I'm sorry—it must be hard. I hope things will go better soon."

"Thanks," Lorraine said. "That's appreciated."

"So? Is it okay? Can we have a little homework club after school?"

"If it's okay with Ellie, I sure wouldn't mind. In fact, I'd be so grateful."

"I'll check that out. I have a feeling she'll be okay with it."

Becca met Denny for dinner at the bar. Since there were no real cooking facilities in his little efficiency and given the fact that he helped out at the bar on most of his evenings, it made sense he would take almost all his meals there. During Thanksgiving week, the place had been fairly quiet—townsfolk had family obligations. But on this Monday night after the holiday, there were quite a few of the locals. Mel was there; Becca learned that it was pretty common for Jack's wife and kids to have at least a couple of dinners a week there, often more. Jack's sister, Brie, and her husband, Mike, turned up with their little daughter, making it a family affair.

And there were others—Paul Haggerty and his family. Denny's landlady, Jo, and her husband. The preacher stopped by for a cup of coffee before heading home. Connie and Ron from the store across the street came out for dinner. Paige stole out of the kitchen with Dana and Chris to sit with their friends. There were a couple of ranchers who dropped by. The owner of a local orchard stopped in for a beer. The doctor Mel Sheridan worked with came over for a few minutes before going home for his dinner. Each time the door opened, Becca could see the gentle glow from the giant tree outside.

Becca met each one. When Denny introduced her as his girl, a teacher from San Diego, chatter started.

"We been trying to get a teacher around here for a long time," someone said.

"We?" Jack asked. "Old Hope McCrea was looking but I don't know that anyone else was, and Hope's gone now."

"Did she move?" Becca asked.

"In a manner of speaking," Jack said. "She's gone to the other side. Dead."

"Oh," Becca said. "I'm so sorry."

Becca could tell Denny was itching to get her back to the privacy of his little room, but she was learning a few things about this town and she couldn't be pried out of the bar. The children, even the first graders, were bussed to other towns to go to school. They all rode together, all ages. The driver dropped the youngest ones off first before going on to the middle school, then the high school. The ranchers and farmers from the outskirts of town drove their kids into Virgin River to catch the bus, which then took them to school, so for some of the kids it was at least an hour each way of travel. For kids like Megan, it could be a ten-hour day. And that for a child who wasn't having an easy time of it.

The folks around here put in long days, it seemed. Her first alert had been from Lorraine Thickson. Listening to the farmers and ranchers, they all started early, had very physical days and hit the sack early. Then there was Mel and the doctor, Cameron Michaels—they served the town and were on call 24/7. Jack was not to be left out. "Cry me a river," he said. "I get this place open by six and we never close before nine. Unless there's a snowstorm. I live for those snowstorms! The best ones last for days!"

"I don't live for them," Mel said. "Roughly nine months after a big storm, we have babies...*lots* of babies."

The bar was filled with laughter that verified she was accurate.

"I've been pushing for a school. At least for the little ones," Jo Fitch told Becca. "I know we're not a big enough town to rate our own high school, but I hate seeing those six-and seven-year-olds spending half the day on a bus."

"Does the county listen?" Becca asked.

"Sure," Jo said. "They gave us the bus. Molly's been driving that bus for thirty years."

"You're gonna want to stay out of her way, too," someone put in, and the whole gathering laughed.

"We could hire you, Becca," Jack said. "As Hope used to say when she was trolling for a midwife, then a town cop, 'Low pay, bad hours.' But at least you'd get to fight the snowdrifts and forest fires with the rest of us!"

She laughed at him along with everyone else—he was joking, of course. The beauty of these mountains was growing on her, but she couldn't imagine not living on the ocean. She'd been surfing and sailing since she was a child. In fact, that was about the only thing the thought of Cape Cod had going for it.

She was distracted yet again when she heard her name. "It was Becca's idea."

"What was my idea?" she asked.

"Watching all the holiday movies together," Mel said. "Once school is out for Christmas vacation and we have babysitters for the little ones, we're going to meet in Paige's great room. She's ordering the movies. I'll get the decorations for the bar out tomorrow—if you weren't on crutches, you could help. And this year, since we have a full-time preacher and full-time preacher's wife, we're getting together a children's pageant. They've already started lining up the characters."

"I can bring the sheep," Buck Anderson offered.

"Thanks, Buck," Jack said, "but we're in need of a few camels. Got any of those lying around?"

"We got us a bull, but he's on the mean side…."

While this big group of friends laughed, joked and planned, the bar began to fill up with people and Denny left her side to help serve and bus. Soon the place was packed.

"Wow," Becca said to Mel. "I had no idea the bar could get so busy. Last week, it was quiet."

"It's the tree," she said. "People come from miles to see the tree. Jack acts like he resents it—it's a lot of work putting it up and his hours are longer than ever during the season, but it's such a special tree and I know he's secretly proud of it. He says he expects the wise men to drop by any second. That star. Have you ever in your life seen a more amazing star?"

"The whole thing is amazing."

"This bar runs hot and cold. Jack built it mainly as a town watering hole and to serve as a place for hunters and fishermen, which is seasonal. Now he's adding Christmas to his busy seasons because of that awesome tree. So, are you going to be around for some of our holiday plans? Like movie day and the cookie exchange and maybe the children's pageant?"

She shrugged. "I'm not going anyplace fast. I don't see the doctor until Friday. I'm not going to be walking without crutches for another five weeks. Plus, I started a little homework club. I'm not good for too much, but I'm a whiz at helping with homework."

"Really? How'd that happen?"

"I was headed for the bar this afternoon, looking for something to do or some company, when I saw a couple of the little girls from our craft party going in the church. I followed them in. Ellie Kincaid told them to work on their homework while she finished up in the office, and I helped. We had a good time and decided to get together regularly. Every day till vacation, anyway."

"Aw, Becca. That's great. That's so generous of you."

"I used to stay late at school almost every day in San Diego. There were always a few kids who needed a little boost. But…" Her voice trailed off when she didn't continue.

"But what?" Mel asked.

"Well, I taught at a private school. I stayed late some days because I wanted to, but the families of most of my kids could afford tutors or shorter workweeks, so they had time to help their kids at home. The families around here seem to put in some long days and weeks…"

"Indeed," Mel said. "In this town, it really does take a village." Then she smiled. "We're so lucky to have so many on board with that notion."

Denny roused Becca early to give her time for her morning grooming and breakfast so he could get to the farm by eight. Even though Denny had made a pot of coffee, she was moving pretty slow until she got a cup of Jack's high octane in her. "How do you do it?" she asked Jack. "You had to stay late last night with all the people who came to town to see the tree and you're downright perky this morning!"

"I could comment on getting a good night's sleep, but I won't say anything about that…."

Becca looked at Denny and they both got a little rosy. Jack laughed. "I'll get your omelets. Today it's Spanish. One of my favorites."

She leaned closer to Denny. "Does everyone in town know we're doing it like bunnies all night?" she asked him.

"No, honey. They don't know. They assume. And they assume right…."

"Ew…"

"Ignore it. One of the things you'll find about this place—nothing goes unnoticed. Or unsaid!"

"Doesn't that bother you?" she asked.

He laughed. "You get used to it. In fact, you get to like it."

Becca contemplated this over breakfast. Then they drove out of town to his farm. She wasn't sure what she'd been expecting, but certainly not what she found. Denny drove up a long drive through the trees, toward an enormous old Victorian that was in pristine condition. The snow had been falling on and off for a few days but it was a light snow and melting off the roads quickly. "What is this?" she asked as they approached the house.

"Jilly's house," he said. "She bought it because of the acreage. It just has ten acres, but she's growing fancy heirloom fruits and vegetables—not a huge crop, but a unique crop. And it's only been in development a year and a half. We have greenhouses for winter plants and seedlings. Growing never stops around here, but it does go heavy and light."

"And who lives in the house?"

"Jillian and Colin—they're a couple. He's a painter. He used to be an Army helicopter pilot, but now he's retired and paints wildlife portraits. Jilly used to be a big-shot marketing exec. She escaped to Virgin River and started a garden. When she was a kid, her great-grandmother showed her how to grow rare and amazing things. I have no idea what she was like as an executive, but as a farmer she's miraculous."

"And she made you into a farmer?" Becca asked.

"A little bit at a time. I started out by helping with the heavy work around here, but every day she showed me something new and now I'm a junior partner in this place. She grows the stuff, ships some of it to high-end restaurants and the rest goes to the kitchen where her sister, a chef, manufactures relishes, sauces, salsas, chutneys… all kinds of stuff. The label is Jilly Farms." He pulled along the side of the house and parked. There was a golf cart with a flatbed back sitting in front of the back porch. "I don't know how far we'll get in the snow, but let's give it a try."

He carried her to the golf cart. As he was propping her in it, the back door opened and a couple came onto the porch.

"Hey there," the woman said. She was young and pretty, wearing overalls and boots with a ball cap on her head. Standing behind her with a hand on her shoulder was a very tall, handsome man.

"Jillian, Colin, meet Becca," Denny said. "Am I going to get very far in the gardenmobile?"

"I hope so," Colin said. "I fixed her up with some studded tires." Then he grinned. "Nice to see you again, Becca."

"Oh! It's you! From that first night we arrived!"

"It's me. You weren't on crutches then. How are you feeling?"

"Clumsy," she said with a laugh. "Thanks for letting Denny give me a tour."

"It's a pleasure. He knows how much we love showing off the farm," Jillian said. "After you've had a little twirl around the grounds, we'll show you the house—it's the most wonderful old house."

"I can't wait," she said. And the next thing she knew, the gardenmobile jerked into motion and Denny was driving her past a huge garden, through the trees and to more gardens and greenhouses that were warmed by smudge pots.

Becca was fascinated by the farm, by all that Denny knew about these fancy crops and the business of growing and marketing them. She was intrigued by the proud light in his eyes as he described their products and even showed her pictures of their rare fruits and vegetables. He was so at home with his fingers in the soft, dark soil, pulling out a delicate seedling for her to see. After they'd toured the greenhouses and grounds, he brought her back to the house. He stopped short of the porch and said, "Wait till you see this place in spring and summer. That entire wall of shrubs that's covered with snow—all flowers. There are a dozen apple trees along the front drive and a line of blackberry bushes dividing the front and back gardens. The bees around here get a little thick, but they're friendly. We're thinking of getting into honey—good money in honey!"

Becca thought, *Spring? Summer?*

And then she thought, *He's so proud of this!*

"Show me the house," she said.

He parked and lifted her out of the gardenmobile. He carried her into the kitchen and found her a chair, then went back for her crutches.

Jillian came out of a room off the kitchen with a laptop in her hands. "I thought you might like to see pictures Colin took of the grounds during summer. He had shots of some of our crop that I used for brochures." She put the laptop down in front of Becca and let her flip through the digital pictures.

"Gorgeous," she said of staged photos of bushels of tomatillo, tiny beets, peppers, tomatoes and brussels sprouts. There was a cart piled high with pumpkins, pictures of the grounds alive with flowers, even pictures of jars of relishes and sauces with their Jilly Farms label on them.

"This is some operation," she said.

"It's a commercial farm and processed food line," Jillian said proudly.

"Impressive," she said.

"I wish you weren't on crutches," Jillian said. "Colin's brother and wife and my sister and her husband are coming over later—we're going to cut down our Christmas trees. We've already picked them out—we have enough fir and pine still on the property to thin out to make room for gardens."

"She's not missing out, Jillian—we took her with us to find the town tree."

"I'm sorry I missed that," she said. "Are you going to take her around the rest of the house, Denny?"

"Yep," he said. Denny leaned the crutches against the wall and urged Becca up so he could piggyback her around the house and up the stairs. It was three stories, a spacious eleven-room house with high ceilings, five bedrooms, a huge sunroom that Colin used for his studio on one end and their family room with a TV on the other end. The only part of the house that Denny didn't think safe enough to carry her up to was the rooftop. "We can see all the gardens and greenhouses and over the treetops to neighboring farms and vineyards. When you're healed, I'll show you."

There it was again—a comment that sounded like they had a future in Virgin River.

"This house is wonderful. I wonder what it must be like to live in a house like this."

"One of the reasons I've been so long in Jo's efficiency is because it's practically free and I've been saving money for a house. A nice house. I have a little money from the sale of my mom's home, plus what I've earned. Jillian keeps increasing my pay, I have full benefits from her and she gave me a bonus at the end of last summer. Then I've been working at Jack's…."

"What *are* your hours at Jack's?" she asked. "It's kind of hard to tell."

He laughed as he piggybacked her to the kitchen. He put her on one of the kitchen chairs and propped her foot. "It's hard to tell because they're real irregular. I started helping out and refused to take his money. He gave me free room and board for a long time right after I got here—I have a lot to pay off. But it rankled him—he's proud. He's also generous. The only freebies he likes are the ones he gives. So he opened a savings account and put money in it. I'd usually just step up if I was there for dinner and the place got real busy, but then he had to call me to help a few times and he told me he'd been paying me all along whether I liked it or not, so I quit arguing. Besides, I've been saving for that house."

She thought of the way his arms felt around her, how it felt to have him say he loved her and she held her tongue. "What kind of a house do you think about, Denny?"

"There are lots of houses on big plots around here. But there's also the houses Paul Haggerty builds. I'll take you out to Jack and Mel's one of these days—they have an awesome house on a few acres, and from his front porch you can see forever. He helped build it. That kept the cost down. I'd like to do that—help build my house." He laughed. "I guess the answer is, I don't know. I haven't gotten serious about it yet. But you make me want to get serious."

Twelve

The homework club grew to seven kids, about three of whom could have led the class. Danielle, Christopher and Juliet were all ahead of their age groups. But Megan, Maron, Mary and Zoe needed a little extra help. Coincidentally, Megan and Maron were both in the same third-grade class and had the very same issues—very little encouragement, a lot of negative reinforcement, low self-esteem and little confidence.

Becca looked forward to their club every day.

Ellie asked her to help out with organizing the nativity pageant with the children for Christmas Eve, and they met on the weekend afternoons—Mary and Joseph, three shepherds, three wise men and a slew of little angels. She couldn't be sure she'd be available for more than one rehearsal, but she couldn't resist. Besides, Megan was going to be Mary! That in itself had done so much for the girl's confidence.

On Friday, the splint came off, the stitches came out and the splint was replaced with a soft, removable boot. "You can get the foot wet now," the doctor said. "But I discourage showers. If you lose your balance and put weight on the foot, you could be back where you started. And that's if you're lucky!"

He told her to move her ankle, though. No weight on it, but she was instructed to pretend to write the alphabet with her pointed big toe. A. B. C. And so on.

"That hurts!" she said.

"It's just stiff and sore. It'll loosen up. Do it five or six times a day. It'll save you a lot of heartache and physical therapy. Am I going to see you again or are you headed home to San Diego?"

She glanced at Denny. "I'm going to hang around. For a little while. Maybe another week, anyway. I'm helping with the Christmas pageant."

She couldn't miss the gleam in Denny's beautiful brown eyes.

Becca was making her way down to the church for Saturday-afternoon pageant rehearsal when she spotted a familiar car parked in front of the bar. A late-model BMW. Standing beside it was Doug. His hands were plunged into the pockets of his black London Fog dress coat. She could see his shiny black shoes, all mucked up from the mud and melting snow in the street. He wore a red turtleneck and gray wool slacks—he looked so classy and professional.

She slowly made her way to him. "Should I be surprised to see you?" she asked him.

"Let me take you home, Becca. We can talk on the drive. I'll stay in San Diego for a few days to give us time to sort things out."

She shook her head. "I'm not ready to go home, Doug. And there's nothing to sort out. I think what we have, if we want it, is a casual friendship."

"I'm not interested in that," he said. "We talked about marriage! We deserve another chance."

"It was the talk about marriage that forced my hand, Doug. I felt that coming. I knew I wasn't going to say yes. I had to figure out why."

"And did you?"

She nodded solemnly.

He grimaced and looked away. He looked back at her. "Have you been drugged or something? Because there was never a hint of this!"

"I think maybe there were lots of hints, but you were a little too busy making plans to notice. I'm sorry you came so far for nothing. Really. Sorry for all the inconvenience. And for your messed-up plans."

He shook his head. "You turned out to be so completely different than I thought you were."

"I did, didn't I? I'm not going to apologize for that." She backed away a little bit. "Drive very carefully down the mountain. The roads can be slick."

He stepped toward her and, in a purposely controlled and lowered voice, he said, "Becca, you can't really choose this hick dump over Cape Cod! Before you know it, you'll be wearing denim jackets, plaid skirts, combat boots and your hair in braids!"

She smiled tolerantly. "And you'd be embarrassed to take me with you to the Presidential Inauguration. I have to go, Doug. I'm on my way to the church to help them with the children's Christmas pageant."

With that, she began to move slowly toward the church. She heard him behind her as the car door opened and closed, the ignition turned and the car moved down the street.

She heard the thud of feet approach her and she looked over her shoulder to see Denny catching up to her. "That him?" he asked.

She nodded, then resumed walking.

"You sent him away?" he asked.

"Of course. That's over. Completely and totally. It wasn't that much to start with."

"He drove all the way up here to try to convince you it was something."

"He's used to having things go according to plan."

Denny was quiet for a moment. Then he said, "That's a helluva car."

"I know. But I'm pretty focused on who's in the car."

To Becca's great surprise, Megan didn't appear for homework club after school on Tuesday. Since Maron was in her class, she asked, "Was Megan sick today?"

"No," the little girl said. "She had a accident and her dad had to come and get her."

Becca gasped. "What kind of accident? Is she all right?"

"She just peed herself. But it made her cry a lot."

"Oh, no! Poor Megan! I think that happens to just about everyone. I think it happened to me when I was a little girl. I hope she won't be too upset."

Maron shrugged. "She was in the girl's line. But she kept wiggling, so Mrs. Anderson put her at the end of the line. Twice."

Becca felt her cheeks grow warm, then hot. Surely there was more to the story, she thought. As a second-grade teacher she had encountered that particular problem plenty of times. They kept spare underwear in the nurse's office for just such emergencies. Kids could lose all track of themselves or just get so caught up in their activities they waited too long. Just as often, someone would throw up with apparently no clue it was about to happen. It was the stuff of elementary school. And Megan was only eight.

Becca would never put a little girl who was waiting for the bathroom at the end of the line if she was wiggling! That's just asking for it! "Can't you excuse yourself to the bathroom whenever you need to?" Becca asked. "Raise your hand? Ask permission?"

Maron shrugged again. "Sort of."

"Sort of?"

She sighed. "We have bathroom breaks every hour. If you don't take the break when it's time to, you can color or paint or talk quietly, but then you have to wait for the next time. And then there's no talking, playing, pushing or laughing in line… or else. Megan kept saying she really had to go."

Becca raised her eyebrows. Nothing wrong with some rules; it was a good idea to help these little ones establish their own limits and boundaries. But dangling "playtime" if they pass on the bathroom break was too tempting.

"I bet Mrs. Anderson felt really bad about the accident."

"I think the whole class always makes her feel bad," Maron said. She shook her head, then went back to copying her spelling words.

Can't get much by kids, Becca thought. It seemed pretty obvious that this particular teacher was not a happy person.

After the children had gone home for the day, Becca made her way down to Denny's efficiency. Inside, she heard the shower running. She picked up the phone and called her mother.

"Remember that teacher I had in fifth grade?" she asked. "Was her name Mrs. Anderson?"

"No," Beverly said, laughing. "Johnson, I think. I'm not sure I remember, but I'll never forget her face."

"Me, either. One of my little girls has a teacher who sounds so much like that. Very punishing, very unhappy, thrilled when you screw up. Her teacher kept pushing her to the back of the bathroom line because she was wiggling too much and she had an accident."

Beverly gasped.

"This little girl has had such a hard year. Her dad was injured in a logging accident, lost his arm and his job, and the family is struggling. You'd think she could cut her a little slack."

"Is the little girl awfully upset?"

"She didn't come to our homework session so I guess the answer is probably yes. And you know what came to mind? I was in tears most of fifth grade, believing the teacher hated me, believing I'd never make it to sixth grade. I was miserable, and I didn't even have a troubled home life! I had every advantage, and I was destroyed."

"But here's what you did have, Becca—the best sixth-grade teacher in the world, Mrs. Dallas. We met with her before school started and explained how hard your fifth grade was. By the very look in her eyes, she wasn't surprised. Everyone knew that teacher was hard to survive, but there was nothing they could do. I think Mrs. Dallas made an extra effort for you. It was not the difficult teacher that made you want to teach, it was the wonderful teacher who inspired you!"

Denny came out of the bathroom, holding a towel around his waist. He blew her a kiss then proceeded to quietly dress.

"I think she saved me," Becca said. "You know, I've had some monumental *brats* in the past couple of years, but I wouldn't treat the worst kid so meanly!"

Beverly laughed. "You better not, Becca. A young teacher like you—it's so important that you focus on what you have, not on what you don't have."

"What does that mean?" she asked.

"You had a couple of crappy teachers, but you had way more wonderful, inspiring teachers. And if you look at your teaching career, young though it is, you'll see that it's been shaped by the excellent teachers. You've learned so much from them. You've become like them in so many ways. You haven't chosen teaching out of retaliation—you chose it to be as positive an influence as you can!"

"Oh, Mom," she said. "Thank you for saying that."

Beverly laughed. "Just because we've been known to disagree, doesn't mean I'm not proud of you, Becca. And I'm really starting to miss you, too."

"I'll see you soon," Becca promised. "I'll let you know when I'm headed that way."

"Be careful on the snow and ice!" Beverly said.

When she hung up the phone, she found that Denny was dressed and sitting in the chair, waiting for her.

"I wasn't eavesdropping," he said. "Not on purpose, anyway. But I'm sorry if you're missing your mom. If you need to go home, just tell me when. I can drive you."

"And then I'll miss you," she said. "It's no-win."

"We have to face it, honey," he said. "We've talked about everything but where we go from here."

She straightened and paid attention.

"I don't know what comes next for us, but whatever it is, it's got to be me and you. Together. Forever. I want to marry you, Becca. If you want that, too, we have some things to work out. We have a geographic situation. And I think we've both been putting off talking about it."

"I know," she said very softly.

"I have two jobs and a good opportunity here, Becca. Maybe you could give it a try, since you don't have a job to go back to in San Diego. You could probably find a good teaching job somewhere around here if you want to, but if not, I can support you. And since good jobs are real hard to find in this economy, I shouldn't give up two paychecks. Remember, I don't have a degree."

That made her almost gulp, thinking of what Doug had said and feeling angry all over again. "I might not have a job in San Diego, but my whole life is there." She shook her head. "I don't have anything here. I don't have anyone but you."

"You will have more good friends here," he promised. "Everyone loves you. This is a great place, once you get to know it. It's hard to explain, but everything is a team effort here. It gives a person an interesting kind of confidence, the way no one is ever left uncared for. If I needed something, I can name fifteen people who'd be right there lending a hand. And I can name twice as many people I'd be happy to help out. I've never had that before. It's more family than my family was."

"Oh," she said weakly.

"If you could just try," he repeated. "Give it a

chance. Consider it. See if it works out as well for you as it has for me. I mean, works out for us…"

"Denny, we talked about what happened to you when your mom died, when we broke up and you went to Afghanistan, but we haven't talked about what happened to me, and we should. It was horrible. I didn't eat or sleep, I was depressed, my grades dropped and it was a struggle to graduate. I'm scared, Denny. What if I give this place a chance and you change your mind again? What if I leave everything I know and love to be here with you and you come up with some profound reason why it's better for us to split up, like before?"

"Whoa, honey, I won't, I swear to God. I always knew that was a stupid mistake. I regretted it right away. I learned from that. You can trust me. I love you so much."

"I do trust you," she said. "And I love you, too. But it's going to take time for me to feel a little more secure about that. I want to go home. Think things through. Everything and everybody I love is there…everyone but you."

"Okay," he said. He said it quietly and smiled, but it was a weak smile. "Let's plan next week, after I get Jilly's farm caught up and you're done with all the stuff you have planned with the women and the kids. You have your pageant practice on Saturday and some hen party on Sunday, right?

I'll get you home in plenty of time for Christmas. Will that work?"

"Thank you," she said. But she was afraid to ask if he would stay.

Becca and Denny went to Jack's for dinner and sat up at the bar. It was easier now that she could dangle her injured leg. As soon as they'd eaten, Denny started helping out behind the bar, in the kitchen, around the tables. The place was packed. Mel had kept her word and brought out the Christmas decorations. There were pine boughs heaped on the mantel and twinkling lights everywhere.

"I love that tree outside," Jack told Becca. "But I probably shouldn't have let Melinda talk me into it."

"Why?" she asked.

"Look at this place," he said. "Tuesday night and it's standing room only. We never had crowds like this around the holidays until that tree started lighting their way into town. A lot of these folks have military backgrounds—they come to see the red-white-and-blue tree, leave unit patches to be added next year."

She looked around. "They all look pretty happy. And it must be a few extra bucks in the Christmas kitty. Huh?"

"Can't complain about the business," he said.

"Just the hours. We've got stuff to do. Like the Christmas baskets."

"Ah. Would that include the 'town turkeys'?"

"Huh?"

"One of the little girls in my homework group indicated her dad resented what he called the 'town turkey.' You probably know him—lost his arm in a logging accident?"

"Yeah, that's Frank. He's a real sourpuss. Too bad—he wasn't before the accident. Used to be a sweetheart. Lots of fun. But now? Not so much. He's just a young guy with a young family. I bet he's thirty-two."

"I think I saw him in here once. And I met his wife. Frankly, I thought she was a bit older."

"We'd all be a bit older if we worked twelve-hour days in a truck stop," Jack said. "Frank can resent the town turkey, as he calls it, all he wants, but I bet his kids don't. He'll be getting a real nice Christmas package."

"Do you do a lot of that sort of thing?"

Jack shrugged. "We help out where we can. There's enough to keep us all busy around here. But we only do the baskets at Thanksgiving and Christmas. We got together with Noah, the preacher, and started a list of people who needed a hand. No one is better equipped to put names on that list than the pastor, the town doctor and my wife." He rubbed his chin. "Bothers me that there are probably more folks out there in need that we just don't know about. I worry about the elderly. There are some folks around the mountains who have been here fifty years or more and most of 'em just don't take to charity. If they get sick, they'll just hunker down till they either feel better or drop dead."

"Ew. What a creepy thought."

He grinned at her. Then the grin faded. "And the children—I always worry about the kids. While the elderly won't ask for help, the kids can't. We keep our eyes open and do the best we can."

She smiled and said, "And yet, even with all that, people seem to find this place enchanting."

"Enchanting? I don't know about that." He leaned on the bar. "I can't speak for anyone else, but I feel useful here. Needed. I'm appreciated for what I can contribute and people let me know that. In a lot of other places, I could disappear and barely be missed."

"Aw, I can't believe that."

"Accurate or not, I *know* I'm counted on here." He glanced down the bar to see a patron with his hand up, beckoning him. "Excuse me a minute."

While he moved down the bar to serve a drink, she caught sight of Denny bringing food from the kitchen to a table full of people. Locals, she presumed, because they all laughed with him, joking around with him, and he was giving it right back, as if they'd all been friends forever.

That's what Denny meant. He felt useful; he knew he was needed. Back in San Diego, he must never have been sure of that.

Because the bar was so busy, Denny wanted to help out until closing, despite the fact that both Jack and Preacher told him to take off, spend time with his girl. He took a fifteen-minute break to walk Becca home and make sure she got up those stairs safely. "I hope you don't mind too much, I'm going to be another hour, maybe hour and a half. The guys told me to call it quits, but Paige is busy with the kids and I can help while you use the time to get ready for bed, call your mom or maybe read for a while."

"Thanks. I don't feel like sitting around a packed bar."

"Whew, we hardly ever see it that busy. Maybe at the peak of hunting season. Or if we have a fire and the firefighters are passing through on their way in and out of the mountains. Jack takes real good care of those boys."

"Takes care of them?"

"Anyone who looks after the needs of the town, he serves for free. That includes law enforcement, firefighters, doctors, et cetera. He says it keeps things in balance."

"How?"

"It's what he has to offer," Denny said with a shrug. "And they give back what they have to offer."

"To him? Like free law enforcement or firefighting? Because that comes out of taxes, right? We don't actually get a bill."

Denny laughed softly. "There was a big fire in these mountains a few years ago—it came real close to town. The bar is still standing. That would've been a big bill." He pulled on one of her arms so they would stop walking. He slowly turned her around and they looked back down the street at the Christmas tree. The lights around the tree reflected under the black sky, while the star on top lit a path down the street. "Look at that thing," he said. "Kind of amazing that a bunch of guys from town can make that whole thing happen."

Becca noticed that in addition to the tree, the houses lining the street were decked out in their decorations, lights lining the eaves of houses, trees glittering in the living rooms behind picture windows, wreaths on doors, smoke curling from chimneys. This wasn't a quaint Thomas Kincade village, that was for sure. Rather, it was an old town that had endured, a town whose character showed in its wrinkles and cracks. The homes were well used and some more well kept than others, but the street was wide, the trees tall and the dark mountains rose majestically beyond.

There was the roar of an engine and the jingling of bells that brought to mind Santa's sleigh, and Denny quickly pulled her out of the way just in time for a tractor-drawn wagon to come around the corner and pass. It was covered in hay and loaded with laughing kids and a few adults.

"Hey, Denny!" someone yelled.

He raised a hand in return and watched them drive by. Then he turned Becca and walked beside her down the street.

"Who was that?" she asked.

"One of the local farmers. He's got grandkids, so he's always giving sleigh rides. Or I should say wagon rides." When they got to the foot of the stairs, he lifted her into his arms and carried her the rest of the way up. Once inside the efficiency, he gave her a kiss. "I won't be too long. I won't hang around the bar, that's for sure."

"Take your time," she said, watching him leave.

The door closed behind him and she just stood there for a moment. Then, even though she had time for a leisurely bath and relaxation before he returned, she went to the phone and called her mother. "Mom, tell me the story of when you fell in love with Dad…"

Beverly fell in love with Alex Timm when she was twenty-one. She was at an Army-Navy game in Philly. She was a senior at George Washington

University and it was a big game. Beverly's dad had been Navy, so she was tied to that team and had driven from Virginia with a bunch of girlfriends.

"Your dad's ship was dry-docked in Baltimore and he was at the game in uniform—those beautiful Navy whites. I know I shouldn't tell this to my daughter, especially since I keep advising you to stop being so ridiculously romantic and use your head, but I think I fell in love with him the second I saw him. I was certainly down for the count when he and his friends took me and my girlfriends out after the game. I'd just never met anyone like him. He was…how can I put it? Gallant. Funny. Handsome. And on shore leave for a few weeks."

"But you knew right away?"

"I thought I did," she said. "But after a few weeks, he shipped out and we were separated on and off for the next two years. A long-distance relationship."

"When did he ask you to marry him?" Becca asked.

"When he was stationed in San Diego. He flew out to Virginia. He only had a few days of leave. He told me then that he didn't want to be away from me any longer and he'd tried his best to get assigned to Virginia. But it didn't work out, and there was nothing he could do but beg me to marry him. By that time, I'd graduated and had a pretty stable job at a newspaper. And we lived on different coasts. So he asked me to take a chance on him and come back to San Diego with him."

"And you did."

"Not immediately. I had to think about it. I was born in Virginia! And my parents were completely opposed to the idea—they were old-fashioned. There's a courtship, a ring and a wedding first. It wasn't a hard decision, it was a terrifying one."

"How long did it take you to decide?" Becca asked, even though she'd heard the story a few dozen times.

"Three weeks," Beverly said. Then she laughed. "I guess that shows you that at twenty-three I didn't have a whole lot of willpower. And when I packed to leave, my father said, 'Make no mistake, you do this against my approval.'"

"Wasn't it hard for you to make such a big change?"

"Of course," Beverly said. "And it was a huge adjustment. San Diego was nothing like Virginia. I had to make all new friends, your father's friends. I planned a wedding without my parents. In fact, my father was so opposed to the idea of me living with my fiancé, he refused to help pay for the wedding." She laughed a little. "For a while, he said he wouldn't even attend unless it was in Virginia, but my mother put her foot down. It was a wonderful and scary time."

Her mother stopped talking and silence enveloped them both. Wonderful and scary, thought Becca. That just about summed it up.

When Denny entered his apartment, only the bathroom light was on. Becca was curled onto her side, snuggled into the quilts, her hair fanned out over the pillow.

He ran his cold hands under hot water in the bathroom, stripped and crawled in beside her, spooning around her back. He slid an arm over her waist and pulled her against him. "Sorry I'm late," he whispered. "Those people didn't want to leave."

"Hmm," she murmured.

"Are you asleep?"

"Yes," she whispered back, wriggling against him. "Shh."

He lay still and quiet for a while, his face against her hair, inhaling her sweet scent. Minutes passed before he whispered, "You awake?"

"Barely," she said.

"I think I forgot to do something..."

She rolled onto her back. "Are you leaving again?"

He grinned down at her and shook his head.

"What did you forget to do?"

"I forgot to make love to you." Just pressing up

against her, even against those boring flannel pajamas, he was already aroused.

"Are you really waking me up for sex?" she asked him.

He grinned as he nodded, looking down at her beautiful face. He covered those soft, pink lips with a searching kiss. "I need you," he said. "I want to be inside you." He had never wanted anyone the way he wanted her. In fact, he had never wanted anyone else. "If I say *please?*" he whispered against her cheek.

"I can hardly say no, since you're so polite…."

"Good, I'll remember that. I'll mind my manners at all times. For the rest of my life." And then he stopped talking, kissing her while he made those pajamas go away….

"Mom?" Becca said into the phone the next day. "When you went to San Diego to be with Daddy, did you ever wonder if you'd made a terrible mistake? Even though you loved him?"

"Did I cry for my mom and dad? Was I sometimes real lonely without my girlfriends? The answer is yes. I told you, it wasn't easy."

"How did you do it? How did you make that decision and then stick to it?"

"Well, it's been so long…but there was the story of Ruth from the Bible. My dad was real big on the Bible sometimes. Ruth left the family she knew and went with her new husband. She said, 'Your people shall be my people.' I know that's supposed to be biblical, but I actually found it romantic. Of course, at the time, I didn't realize your Dad's people would include the beer-drinking champion of the Naval base, a few fellow football fanatics he couldn't be away from if there was a game playing anywhere in the universe, a bowling team and a very sour-smelling fishing buddy who might show up for a meal once a week."

Becca laughed softly.

"A Navy second lieutenant's pay was pretty small, I didn't have a job in San Diego and my parents lived on the opposite coast. Leaving them for the man of my choice meant not seeing them for a long time—air travel was pricey, there wasn't email and long-distance phone calls were expensive." Beverly paused. "What's happening, Becca?"

"Oh…just pondering… Denny so loves this town…."

"I suppose you think I was born yesterday," Beverly said. "Becca, I haven't made it any secret that I wanted a different partner for you. One who was going to be successful enough to take you to Europe and the kids to Disney once a year. But I'd be less than honest if I didn't admit I followed my heart. Besides, you can't cry alone at chick flicks for the rest of your life. I might not like it, but I understand you have to confront it."

"I don't cry alone at chick flicks!"

"Yes, you do. Maybe you can bring him home. This was his home once, after all," Beverly said.

"You were so angry with me for coming up here and now it sounds like you might actually understand!"

"Tell him we're having ham and turkey for Christmas," Beverly said.

Although Becca laughed, a few tears slid down her cheeks.

Thirteen

Becca had hoped to see Megan the day after her "accident" but she didn't show up at the church for homework. Since her little brother also hung out at the pastor's house or around the church, she asked Jeremy where she was. "Home, coughing," he said.

"Oh, no. She's sick?"

He shrugged. "Sorta. She barks like a dog."

"Not good," Becca agreed.

When Lorraine came to pick up Jeremy on her way home from her job, Becca was able to ask after Megan. Lorraine was keeping her home, giving her cough syrup and Tylenol and shoveling chicken soup into her. "Her biggest worry is that if she has to miss the pageant practice on Saturday afternoon, she won't get to be Mary!"

"If she were one of the singing angels, missing practice could be dicey," Becca said. "But Mary doesn't have to do anything but sit beside the manger. I'll double check with Ellie and Jo, but I think her role is safe even if she misses Saturday, as long as she's not contagious. And please, don't let her talk you into letting her come to practice until she's better. Whatever she's got? No one wants to share it!"

"Whew! This is about the most special thing she's had going on in such a long time. I'd hate to tell her she has to give it up."

"Nah, don't tell her that. Tell her she has to rest and eat chicken soup."

Friday was the last day of school before the holiday vacation and Saturday afternoon there was a rehearsal at the church for the Christmas Eve Nativity Pageant. On Sunday, some of the women got together to watch those Christmas movies at Paige's house. When Becca passed through the bar's kitchen to enter their quarters, she was stopped short by the accumulation of tons and tons of food. "Wow, preparing for a flood?"

"Christmas boxes," Preacher said. "We used to do it out in the bar where we had more room, but since the tree made us famous and we have so many visitors in town, we're doing it in the kitchen and in our serving room."

"When do they go out?"

"Christmas Eve is next Friday—but we'll start delivering tomorrow. It's almost all nonperishable so people can save it or eat it right away. That was Mel's idea—she said if we're bringing food to people who are hungry, let 'em eat!"

"I thought you gave turkeys?"

"Some, about a dozen. But canned hams work well, too. We don't want to deliver birds to anyone who might have oven issues—as in no gas. There are people around who make due on fireplace heat."

"Do you put them all together before delivering?"

"Nope. We deliver 'em as they're ready. We have a lot of people volunteering. We'll be at it most of the mornings this week, I imagine. Paige insists on making more cookies—there are families with kids."

We're so lucky, Becca thought. *When I get home, I'm going to be better about volunteering.*

Mel had a babysitter with her little ones and the town doctor was in charge of his three-year-old twins so his wife, Abby, could attend the hen party. Jack's sister, Brie, came for a couple of hours and Jo and Ellie stopped by. Jo brought some pageant costumes with her, along with a sewing box, enlisting help in hemming angel's robes.

Everyone had a pageant costume in their laps, there were Christmas cookies, coffee, tea and punch on the dining table and the first movie of the day was *It's a Wonderful Life.* There was a little light chatter, voices low so as not to disturb the movie too much.

"Jack said he can't understand why we're going to so much trouble for this pageant. He was a shepherd when he was seven and he wore his father's bathrobe."

"Did he tell you he wore that old plaid bathrobe till he was thirteen?" Brie whispered. "When he wasn't a shepherd, he was a Jedi warrior."

"Ellie and I made all these costumes loose, with wide seams and huge hems so they can be altered if necessary and used year after year for kids of all sizes," Jo said. "Oh! Shh! No talking while Clarence, the angel, arrives!"

Everyone was obediently quiet. Then soft talking resumed until the part in the movie when George begins to see how life in the town would be had he never been born.

"I actually believe all this," Ellie said. "The smallest act is part of the whole universal scheme of things and everything is altered. Take away one good deed and everything changes. Add a good deed and there's a ripple effect."

"Every time we watch this movie together, my mom says that same thing," Becca said. "I think I believe it, too."

"Like making a cake," Paige said. "Leave out one ingredient and it just won't be the same. Becca, I bet you miss your mom so much by now."

"I talk to her every day, just like when I lived in my own apartment in San Diego." She laughed. "Who am I kidding, I talk to her twice a day!"

"I hope we meet her soon," Mel said.

Becca cleared her throat. "Well, you should know… I asked Denny to take me home before Christmas. I hate that I'll miss the pageant, but I want to be with my family for the holidays. Though it's hard to imagine, I miss Rich, too."

"Perfectly understandable," Mel said. "How long will you be gone?"

She cleared her throat again. "Maybe I'll be back for a visit…"

The only sound in the room came from the television. The complete absence of the women's voices was heavy. Finally, Paige asked, "Are we losing Denny?"

"Probably not," she said, lifting her chin and trying to be brave. "He loves it here so much…."

"But I thought…" Paige began.

Mel touched her hand to stop her. "I'm not going to kid you, Becca—I would have been so happy if you chose our town. We all would. But there's nothing mysterious about wanting to live near family. Sometimes I miss my sister in Colorado so much."

Before long, the movie was ending. Jimmy Stewart was united with all his family, friends and neighbors, Clarence had earned his wings and Becca was sobbing. "This movie always makes me cry."

"Wait till you get to *White Christmas...*" someone said right before she blew her nose.

The Sunday night before Christmas, the bar was busier than other Sunday nights. People from the lower elevations drove up to see the spectacular tree with the amazing star, and since there was a bar and grill right there, stopped in for food and drinks. It seemed many hands were called upon to help. Brie's husband brought their toddler daughter to her so he could help behind the bar; Denny shoveled his dinner in his mouth and then began helping Paige serve and bus while also fetching ice, bringing clean glasses from the kitchen and sometimes taking orders. Becca sat at an out-of-the-way corner table with Brie and the little girl. Denny occasionally brushed his lips against her cheek as he passed.

Once he stopped and whispered, "Everything all right, honey?"

"Sure, fine. Why?"

"I don't know, you seem a little down."

"Oh, I love those holiday movies, but they make me cry! Then it takes me a couple of hours to recover."

"Then why do you women watch them?" he asked, looking between Brie and Becca.

"Because they're so wonderful," they both said at once.

He just frowned for a second, then said, "Right."

There was so much he really didn't understand about women, he thought. They were an eternal mystery. Did they actually *like* to cry?

But there was one thing he understood perfectly—Becca needed to go home soon. She was moody. A little bummed out.

When he saw Brie stand up and start helping her toddler into her jacket, Denny glanced at his watch. Seven-thirty. He went to their table. "Want me to get you home, honey?" he asked. "I can help out for another couple of hours and then I'll be down."

"That would be good," she said. "I'm ready." She stood on one leg, put the knee of the vulnerable leg on her chair for balance and pulled on her jacket. She leaned on her crutches and made her way out the door with him.

"There aren't any stars tonight," she said.

"I think it's going to snow," Denny told her. "I don't think I'll be at Jack's late—it's Sunday night, people work tomorrow. And with snow forecast, those out-of-towners are going to head down the mountain early."

"Take your time. I'll be fine."

"Are you still sad about the movies?"

"No," she said with a laugh. "I'm fine. I'm going to get a hot bath, put on my ugly pajamas and crawl into bed with my book."

He carried her up the stairs and into his little room. "I'll see you in a little while. And if you forget the pajamas, I'm okay with that."

Denny's prediction was right—it was only another hour before the crowd in the bar was down to just a few people. "Go ahead, Denny," Jack said. "You wanna get back to your girl."

Denny walked around the bar and jumped up on a stool facing Jack. "But I wanted to talk to you first," he said.

Jack tilted his head. "Something wrong?"

"Yes and no. Been a while since we had a shot together. Tonight might be a good night for it."

Jack pulled down a bottle and two glasses. He poured a couple of shots and raised his glass. "What are we drinking to?"

"I got things all worked out with Becca."

Jack grinned. "Well, here's to you!"

They drank, then put their glasses down. "Thing is, it's not going to work here, Jack. I'm leaving with her. She wants to be near her family and the only home she's known. I asked her to give us a chance here because I love it. I've never had such great jobs and friends. But the bottom line is she's real close to everyone down there, and she just can't see making this big a change."

"Yeah," Jack said slowly. "It's not for everyone."

"I can't let her get away again…."

Jack's hand came down on his shoulder. "I know, Denny. I understand. I've been there."

"Yeah?"

"Oh, yeah. Mel talked about leaving Virgin River from the day she got here. One thing or another held her here for a while. Six months later, I had her knocked up—"

Denny's eyebrows shot up. He didn't know that.

Jack cleared his throat. "Yeah, she was pregnant, and I wasn't letting her leave me behind, so I told her I'd go anywhere she needed to go, but I had to be with *her.*"

"How'd you get her to stay?"

"There's the thing—I didn't. She made the decision by herself. I didn't have anything to do with it. Seriously, I would have been disappointed to leave, but I would have gone anywhere I had to go. There was a lot at stake. Kid, much as I hate to see you go, you have to put your life together the way it works best for you. For you and Becca, if she's what you want."

"No question about that, Jack. I love her," he said. "But I kind of saw myself growing that farm with Jillian and growing a family in a safe, quiet place like this."

"Remember, son, the safest place for a family is under the umbrella of a happy marriage. That's going to take compromise." He smiled. "You'll visit. This is a great place to visit. My whole family, except Brie, are city people. I can hardly keep them away."

"I'm going to visit," Denny promised.

"When are you out of here?"

"I hate to do this to you, Jack. I'm going to tell Jillian tomorrow, offer her some suggestions for help, but she won't be in a real fix till spring. Then I'm going to pack up my stuff and my girl and head south. We'll leave first thing Tuesday morning. I thought about taking her home for Christmas and then coming back to tie up my loose ends, but I don't have that much. Better to come back in spring if I can, to visit and check out the farm. But I'm leaving you high and dry during a busy time and I'm sorry. I know you were counting on me."

Jack was shaking his head. "Nothing to worry about, son. We can always get a little help around here." He laughed a little. "Cheaper than you, as a matter of fact."

"Hey," Denny said, smiling back. "I didn't set any salary! You did that all on your own."

He chuckled. "If we get a crowd, I can always call Mike V., Walt Booth, Paul Haggerty. As for Jillian, she's got Colin and Luke if she needs anything in a hurry. And plenty of time to look over prospective assistants before spring planting. Does Becca know this? That you're taking her home?"

"Sure," he said. "We talked about it last week and I said I'd get her home in time for Christmas."

"Hmm," Jack hummed, scratching his chin. "Shouldn't she be a lot happier about it? If that's what she wants?"

"That could be my fault," Denny said. "I'm pretty sure she still doubts me. When I asked her to give Virgin River a try, she asked me, what if all she had here was me and I decided we should break up. 'Course, I know I'd never be that stupid twice, but you can't blame her for wondering if I'd let her down again. So I told her I'd get her home before Christmas. Suppose she wonders if I'll keep my word?"

"Then I guess the best thing to do is get on down the street, boy. Reassure your girl that if she throws her lot in with you, she's gonna be safe." He stuck out his hand. "I'll see you tomorrow sometime. I'll tell Preacher to cook up something you like."

"That would be great."

"And, Denny? If the idea of leaving this little town gets you down, just stop and think about why you're leaving. It's worth it, son, if you found the woman you love. You're lucky. You found her young. Got a lot of years to look forward to."

"Yeah," he said with a smile. "Thanks, Jack."

Denny turned and left the bar.

Jack poured himself another shot, though it was early for him to do that. He lifted his glass to the closed bar door and said, "No. Thank *you*."

* * *

There was a soft and gentle snow falling when Denny walked back to his apartment. The town Christmas tree was going to look fantastic with the lights twinkling behind a fresh layer of lacy snow. Last year, they had to knock the snow off the branches to make sure they retrieved all the unit patches when they were ready to take the tree down. Mel counted and cataloged them afterward; to miss one felt almost personal.

He kicked the snow off his boots on the top step, then took them off before stepping into the room.

Becca was sitting up in the bed, leaning back against the pillows, one knee drawn up and circled with her arms. He leaned against the closed door, still holding his boots. She was so beautiful. Her face was shiny from being scrubbed free of makeup before bed—she was squeaky clean and would smell of soap and lotion and taste minty fresh from her toothpaste. Though they'd been intimate when they were together years ago and had managed a night together here and there, they'd never actually lived together before. He was surprised by how much he loved sharing these little rituals with her; their routine brought him such a feeling of comfort and stability.

He couldn't figure out how he got so lucky, to have her love him. It was even harder to figure out how he'd been insane enough to let her get away once.

He put his boots down on the towel just inside the door and took off his jacket, hung it on the peg and headed for the bathroom. "Be right with you, honey."

He washed his face, brushed his teeth and ran hot water over his hands to warm them. He got down to his boxers and T-shirt and left his folded jeans and shirt on top of his trunk. Then he sat cross-legged on the bed, facing her. "How about if we pack up tomorrow and head for San Diego Tuesday morning?" he asked.

"That would be wonderful, Denny. Thank you."

"I'll go out to Jilly Farms first thing in the morning to tell her I'm leaving."

Becca frowned. "You haven't told her yet? You told me last week you'd take me home by Christmas."

"You had your own obligations around town and to be honest, I had to figure a few things out about leaving. There's a lot of stuff to do in the greenhouses when the temperature drops like this. And Jack's…well, the bar has been so busy with people driving up here to get a look at that tree, I wondered how he was going to get by without my help. But Jack's the greatest. He totally understands. He said if he needs help he can always call on some of his friends, like Brie's husband, Mike.

He even joked that his friends are a lot cheaper than I am."

"What if Jillian says she just can't manage without your help?"

"She's got Colin and Luke Riordan if she needs something in a hurry," he said. "I got as much done out there as I could after we decided to head for San Diego. The only big worries for her right now are snow related. The passages from the house and sheds to the gardens have to be plowed and those greenhouses can't withstand snow on the roofs—they could collapse. But just like with Jack at the bar, if she needs an extra hand or two, there are friends around."

"You know, I could always catch a flight," she said. "I mean, if you're needed here. I know you have commitments..."

He put his hand against her cheek. "Do I look crazy? You're my primary commitment."

"I wouldn't hold you to it, Denny."

He leaned toward her to place a gentle kiss on her lips. "You'd better hold me to it. I'm counting on that. Now I have a question for you. I know you have your own apartment. Are you going to let me move in with you? Will that freak out your parents?"

"Huh?"

"I could stay with Rich," he said. "But really, Becca. I just don't want to let you too far out of my sight. I scared myself good the last time we got too far apart. Will your parents get all upset about that? If we live together? Because it's going to take a while to find a job down there. Don't worry, I have some money saved that we can put toward rent, but—"

"*Live* with me?" she asked. "You're *staying*?"

"Where would I go?" he asked, completely confused.

"I thought you were just going to drive me home and come back here!"

"What gave you an idea like that?"

"I don't know. Because you said how much you loved it here, because you wanted me to try it, because...because you didn't say you were *moving*! You said you would take me home for Christmas."

He stared at her for a moment. "Listen, if you're not ready to take this to the next level, if you need a little more time before we start planning a whole lifetime together, I can just ask Rich if I can have his couch. But seriously, the way we can't seem to keep our hands off each other, I bet I end up staying over at your—"

A squeal of laughter erupted from her and she threw her arms around his neck. Then she planted a kiss on him that quickly melted into a deeper, more demanding kiss. Their heads tilted, mouths opened, tongues dueled. Denny moved to embrace her; his hands slipped under her pajamas to stroke her naked back.

When their kiss finally broke, she laughed.

"See what I mean?" he asked. "We might just as well share the rent, since there's no question we're going to share the bed."

She giggled.

"And this is funny, how?" he asked.

She shook her head. "I didn't get it," she said. "I thought asking to go home was something you were going to do for me. I thought… We're going to have to work on our communication."

"Well, I thought I might have to come back up here after Christmas for a few days to pack up and at least get Jillian on stable ground so she could manage without me. Those were a couple of the details I was trying to get organized in my head while you were finishing up your homework club, pageant practice and stuff. But when you get down to it, I don't have that much to pack. And you came up here with one suitcase. Bottom line is, I can't stand the idea of even spending a few days away from you if I don't have to."

"Good, because neither can I!"

"So here we are, two jobless people—ought to be interesting. I've saved money since living here—when you live in one furnished room and work two jobs, it's not that hard. And there's that money from the sale of my mom's house when she died—that was going to go toward a house of my own. Now it will be a house of our own, but it might not come as fast, honey. With neither of us working yet and real estate so much more expensive in San Diego—"

"I don't care," she said. "I have a cute apartment. And I'll get a job. I'll do whatever I have to if I don't get a teaching job. I have office experience, waitress experience—"

He stroked her pretty blond hair. "You should be with kids. I've seen you with them. There's no question that's were you belong."

"I will be, but if it takes a while to find a teaching job, I'll just work somewhere else while I'm looking."

"You're unbelievable, you know that?" he said. "I wondered why you weren't all jazzed about going home. Crap, once again it was me—just because I didn't say the right things!"

"Or I didn't ask the right things," she said. "I have to be honest, I was afraid to ask. I didn't want to cry when you told me you just couldn't come with me."

"Listen, you're first, Becca. I'm going to teach you to trust me again somehow. Right now, just remember you're first. What you need is the top of the list. Always." Then he laughed. "That Jack, sometimes the guy is brilliant, you know? I was telling him tonight that I was leaving—saying goodbye, really—and I told him that I had kind of liked the idea of growing a family in a place as clean and safe as this. He told me to remember that the safest place to grow a family is in a happy marriage. I'm going to make you happy, Becca, because I love you. You're what keeps my heart beating."

"Denny," she said, her eyes welling up with happy tears.

He rubbed a thumb under one eye. "You didn't want to cry, remember?"

"Then don't be so wonderful all the time." She sniffed. "Now what?"

His eyes took on a naughty gleam. "Well, the plans are set. The schedule is set." He started unbuttoning her pajama top. "I guess I'll just have to work you out for a while. In fact," he said, putting his big hands on her small butt, "if you just climb up on my lap, you wouldn't be putting any weight on that ankle…"

Fourteen

The routine of having Denny get up in the early morning, make her coffee and leave her curled up under the down quilt while he went off to work was an easy thing to adjust to. When the phone rang beside her bed, she eyed the clock as she rolled over. It was eight-thirty. She was surprised she'd slept so late, as excited as she was to pack up to leave. She reached for the phone and said hello.

"Becca," Jack said. "Are you awake?"

"Sure," she said.

Jack laughed. "No, you weren't. Have you looked outside yet?"

"Why?" she asked, sitting up in bed.

"We had heavy snowfall during the night. I'm going to come down there and clean off the steps and salt them. When you're ready to leave the apartment, you have to call me. The street is under almost two feet of snow. So, it's nonnegotiable—you could break your other leg and your neck."

She thought about that for a second. "What are you going to do?"

"I'm going to drive down there in Preacher's truck to pick you up—Denny took mine out to the farm. When you get up, you'll see a mound in the driveway—that's Denny's little truck. I'll drive you to the bar or wherever you want to go. And dress warm. We have more snow forecast."

"Why is Denny in your truck?"

"That Nissan of his wasn't gonna make it all the way out there, even with chains. We're not a priority for plowing—we generally do our own."

"When will you be down here?" she asked.

"Ten minutes. It'll take me twenty to clean off and salt your steps. You can go back to sleep, if you want to—I just didn't want the noise to scare you."

"Thirty minutes gives me plenty of time to dress and be ready to leave. But take your time. I don't want you to have to wait for me."

As Jack carried Becca down the snow-crusted stairs a half-hour later, she saw the mound of snow that had been Denny's truck. A lot was going to have to happen to transform that igloo into a moving vehicle.

In all her trips to ski slopes, Becca had never seen anything quite like this. Even in the heaviest of snowfall in the mountains, this was her first time in a tiny town that was buried by snow. People were shoveling and snowblowing their way out of the homes and driveways, standing on ladders to shovel and scrape some of the weight off roofs. Kids were throwing snowballs, building forts and snowmen. Dogs were rollicking in the snow. There was exactly one narrow lane plowed down the street—just enough room for a vehicle, one at a time.

Becca couldn't suppress a brief fantasy about being completely snowed in with Denny. Not in their little room above the garage, but in a house with a fireplace and a nice, functional kitchen. She'd be more than happy to lose a few days that way....

Jack drove her to the bar. Rather than parking in the back as usual, he pulled through two feet of snow to take a narrow space in the front and left the truck running. Preacher, all bundled up, was shoveling off the stairs and a path to the street.

As Jack carried her past, Preacher said, "Help yourself in the kitchen, Becca. I'm going to be tied up awhile."

"Thanks," she said with a laugh.

When Jack put her down right inside the door, she found an unexpected flurry of activity there. There were canned goods, bags of nonperishables and miscellanea lined up on the bar and on tables. Mel and Paige stood behind the bar, sorting and creating piles. Their four kids were coloring at a table in front of the fire. Jack went immediately to a stack of unconstructed boxes and began to fold them into shape and tape them.

"Hi," Becca said to the women. "Getting those Christmas boxes ready?"

"We have to try to get them all delivered right away," Paige said. "We have more weather on the way."

"It would be awful if people didn't get them before Christmas," Becca said.

"It would be awful if they didn't get them," Mel said. "Some of these people need them. They might be hungry even as we speak, and if they're also snowed in, have no way to get food. If we wait even a day and can't get down some of those back country roads…" She shuddered. "One of the local farmers is plowing a lane out to Cameron's house. He's got the Hummer—our ambulance. He has to be able to get to town to the clinic. It's heart-attack season, not to mention slips on ice, broken bones, strained muscles, cars sliding off roads, et cetera."

"Heart-attack *season*?" Becca asked.

"First dramatic snowfall of the year," Mel said while making groupings of foods for care boxes. "Shoveling and heart attacks. All the warnings in the world just don't seem to help. During an ice storm a couple of years ago, we had a school bus go off the road. Jack and some of the guys rappeled down the hill to them. First responders had to carry the kids up one at a time. Fortunately no one was seriously hurt, but it could've been disastrous. Three years ago, we had a teenager lost and half the town went in search. Oh, Jack!" she said, turning her attention to her husband. "Paul Haggerty called—he's plowing the stretch from 36 into town so if we have to get to the hospital, we can. And once he has access, he'll bring some heavy equipment into town along with the construction company's fuel truck."

"Good. We could get gas out at Buck Anderson's ranch—he keeps a good supply for his equipment—but getting there could be a problem."

Becca felt a sudden surge of panic. "Is there any way to check and be sure Denny got out to the farm all right?"

"I'm sure he did or Jillian would have called asking after him," Mel said. "But go in the kitchen and use the phone. Her number will be in the listing by the phone. Matlock. Jillian Matlock. And then get yourself something to eat—I bet you haven't had breakfast."

Becca worked those crutches very quickly.

"Yes," Jillian said. "Denny and Colin are out clearing, plowing and removing snow from the roofs of the greenhouses. Most of it melted from smudge pots warming the inside, but sometime in the night, the snow and cold overwhelmed us and covered our paths to the greenhouses. How are things in town?"

"Very active," she said. "Everyone seems to be very busy."

Jillian laughed into the phone. "Yes, when Mother Nature pulls one of her tricks, the town rallies to make sure everyone has what they need. In big cities, you have whole agencies on the job, but out here, the wait could be a little too long. And there's no agency to dig out my greenhouses or make paths to them for the gardenmobile! Luke and his helper, Art, are coming out to help as soon as the road to his house and cabin is cleared. He's got a plow attachment for his truck. Slow going, but effective."

"So you guys are okay out there?"

"Oh, yes," Jillian said. "I have a major snowball fight scheduled for later today. Hey, Denny tells me you guys are heading south to begin whole new lives together. I hate to lose him, but congratulations, Becca! Even though you're taking my best guy away from me, I wish you endless happiness."

"Thanks," she said somewhat meekly. She was taking the favorite son away. She felt kind of bad about that.

"I'll get him out of here as quickly as possible so you can gather up your stuff and be ready to get on the road before this storm gets any worse.

At least once you get off the mountain, you won't have any more trouble. Just maybe a lot of rain…."

Except that the little truck is buried, she thought.

"Be sure you get that last ounce of help out of him," Becca said.

Jillian laughed. "You're a sport. Just so you know, I made Denny promise that you guys would be up for a visit. Many visits!"

"Sure we will. Tell Denny to drive back here real careful!"

"Oh, he'll be careful," Jillian said. "There's no other option."

Back in the bar, the television mounted high in the corner was turned on to the weather station and the volume was up. The blast of snow had hit the northwest, and the worst was in the mountains. The Sierras were socked in. South of town was rain and the inevitable flooding and mud, all the way to Southern California.

Becca heard a banging sound and looked out one of the bar windows. Preacher's truck was backed up to the wood pile and, with Jack's help, they were filling the back of the truck with split logs.

"What are they doing?" she asked the women.

"They'll take firewood with them wherever they go today. The people around here have good survival instincts, but Jack likes to make sure they have wood on hand in case the heater fails or they run out of propane."

Becca leaned heavily on her crutches, her bad leg lifted. This was driving her crazy! She wanted to be a part of this. "I want to help," she said. "Tell me what I can do."

Paige and Mel both stopped what they were doing and looked at her. "Well," Mel finally said. "I guess you could color with the kids…"

"I'd be happy to, but they don't need me. *You* need me. There must be *something* I can do."

There was a moment of silent indecision between the women. "Do you cook?" Paige asked.

"A little bit, I guess."

"Any favorite dishes you like to make? Can you follow a recipe? We're not going to have a crowd tonight, but whoever is here is going to have to eat."

"We might have to stay in town tonight," Mel said. "I don't want to risk not being able to get to the clinic. I've got a couple of women in advanced pregnancy." She laughed suddenly. "And nine months from tonight, I'm going to have plenty ready to pop. People can only think of so many ways to entertain themselves during a snowstorm."

"I can get food together," Becca said. "I can help in the kitchen."

"Good," Paige said. "Because John isn't going to have a lot of time to cook if he's delivering food and firewood. And I have to get these care boxes fixed up before I can get in there. Let me get you set up."

Becca found thawed ground beef in the refrigerator. She boiled potatoes and shredded cheddar for her favorite potato casserole. She found Preacher's recipe for meat loaf—simple enough. There were frozen and canned vegetables from the local farmers and gardens. She found green beans and thought, if needed, she could throw together a green-bean casserole. Paige promised to help her with desserts after she finished with the care boxes.

Becca began to realize there were a number of things she could have provided—spaghetti and meatballs, homemade mac and cheese, lasagna, stroganoff and noodles…

Every time she heard an increase in noise, talking or laughter in the bar, she pushed open the door to see who had arrived. Ellie and Noah Kincaid came to help; Jo and Nick Fitch arrived. Next, she found Paul Haggerty in the bar, cheeks and nose pink and a big smile on his face, brushing snow off his hands and shoulders. "You're plowed through to 36," he announced. "Gimme some hot coffee and I'll clear the rest of this street for you."

A while later, she stuck her head into the bar to see a few men she didn't know laughing and warming up with coffee before getting back out into the weather. Then Jack and Preacher were there, carrying care boxes out to the truck. At almost noon, Denny arrived. He came right in the kitchen, all grins, and swept her up in his cold arms, burying his icy nose in her neck, causing her to *eeek!* loudly while he laughed.

He set her free. "I'm going to start digging out the car and put chains on the tires. We're going to have to try to get out of here, get south today. There's more weather due tonight and if we don't go now—"

"I can't," she said instantly. "I'm busy. If I don't cook for these people, who knows if they'll have time to get a meal together!"

"They'll be fine, honey. Wrap it up and I'll get you down to the apartment to pack up."

The phone rang and she automatically reached for it. "I think I have to take a chance on the weather," she said. Then into the phone, she said, "Jack's."

"Hey, Becca, it's Jack. Get Mel to the phone, will you, sweetheart?"

"Sure, hang on." She crutched over to the swinging door. "Mel? Jack's on the phone. He needs you."

She gave her attention back to Denny. "We might not get on the road exactly when we planned, but it doesn't matter as long as we get on the road eventually. Right? What if there's another heavy snowfall and Jillian needs you?"

"I've got her squared away. She's called in her troops to stand by if she needs them. Think about this, Becca, because you said you wanted to be home before Christmas. Christmas Eve is Friday."

"I bought a couple of presents before Thanksgiving, but other than those, I don't have a thing," she said, thinking aloud. "I don't have anything for you and I'd like it to be a special Christmas."

He grinned. "You think it won't be? You don't need to put a bow on it, baby."

And then she heard Mel say, "Oh, for Pete's sake, they should know better than to worry about money when something like this happens! I'll get right out there." There was a pause. "No, I'm not waiting for you to come and get me. Cameron and I will come together in the Hummer. Paige will mind the kids. Tell them to get the heat turned up, get the worst one in the steam and I'll be right there."

Mel hung up and looked at Denny and Becca. "I'm on my way out to the Thicksons'. They have sick kids with coughs, sore throats and fevers. I hope they didn't let it go too long."

"I'm going with you," Becca said. "That's little Megan's house."

"You can't, Becca," Denny said. "You're on

crutches. If there's a problem, like if Mel got stuck in the snow or something, you'd be a liability."

"He's probably right, Becca," Mel said while she dialed. She spoke quickly to Cameron Michaels, instructing him to pull the Hummer up to the bar so they could go to the Thicksons' together.

"Then you take me," she said to Denny. "I need to go. I can't leave without telling Megan goodbye, anyway. Please?"

"We should get on the road..." he said again.

Becca went to the pantry and pulled out cans of chicken soup. The supply must be something that Preacher kept on hand for the kids. She put six cans on the work island, then transferred them into a bag. She pushed the bag toward Denny. "We'll get on the road in plenty of time. First things first. We have things to do."

Becca turned off the stove and preheating oven, slipped her bowl of shredded potatoes into the refrigerator and crutched her way out of the kitchen.

"Denny," she said over her shoulder. "Come on!"

He followed, pulling his stocking cap back on his head. "Yes, sir!"

Jack hung up the phone and looked at Lorraine. "Where's Frank? We'll go help him out."

"He went out to the shed quite a while back.

He said he'd have to get the snow off the roof and bring in firewood."

"Let's do it," Jack said to Preacher. They pulled their hoods up and tromped out of the house, following footsteps through the deep snow around to the back, where a shed sat next to an abandoned outhouse.

Frank was up on a ladder, using a shovel with his only arm to clear the roof of the rickety shed. He was leaning precariously to one side. Progress was extremely slow.

Jack stood at the bottom of the ladder with hands on hips. "Frank, man, you need to learn to ask for a hand. You could fall and break the only arm you have left."

"What's the difference?" he grumbled.

"Well," Preacher said, scratching his head. "About one…"

Frank looked down at them. "I ain't much good to anyone as it is," he said. "I tried like hell to get this shed reinforced before snow, and look how far I got."

"You need another arm," Jack said.

"No shit?" Frank laughed bitterly.

"Shouldn't you be getting a prosthetic limb?"

"There's a waiting list. You oughta know that. By the time they get around to me, I won't need it anymore."

"And why's that? You fixin' to grow one?"

"Funny. Don't be an asshole."

"Listen, two of my closest friends have artificial legs. They didn't like the process that much, but one of 'em can run on his now. The other one, Ricky, I figure he'll be able to run on his once he makes up his mind to. If you had another arm, you'd get a lot more done. You'd probably land a job if you had two arms and weren't such a miserable cuss. Now, get off that goddamn ladder. We'll clean off the roof and bring in the wood. I don't have all day!"

Frank swore, but he left the shovel lying on the roof of the shed and started down. "That shed's a piece of crap, but I can't do without it. Stores half my tools and there ain't no room in the house for that."

"I'll get the snow off," Jack said. "And I'll tell Mel you need an arm. Maybe she can find you one. Or at least get you moved up on the list."

"She can't do that."

"Technically, she probably can't. But she's annoying as all hell and when she starts making phone calls, people tend to do what she wants just to get rid of her." Jack smiled proudly. Then he opened the door to the shed and peered inside at an impressive stack of split logs. "Holy crap, you do all that? With one hand?"

"Took a while," Frank said.

Jack scratched his head. "How the hell did you do all that?"

"Took a while," he repeated.

Jack laughed in spite of himself. "Frank, if you'd drop the poor-me attitude, you'd probably be a whole circus act. Now, let's get over it, man. I grant you, a logger losing an arm is a lot to handle, but seriously, there's work here and there. You want a little help looking, I'll be glad to help you put out feelers. You're just going to be twice as good at everything once you get that prosthetic arm."

"Yeah. Sure," he grumbled.

Denny and Becca talked in circles on the way to the Thicksons' house. *We should go. We should stay through this emergency. We'll end up going late. Late is better than too soon...* The unexpected twist was that Becca was arguing for staying and Denny for leaving.

They pulled up to the house right next to the Hummer. The Thicksons lived on a big piece of property on the outskirts of town. A little house was burrowed into a large copse of trees at the end of a long drive that had been recently plowed. Preacher's truck was still there, which meant that Jack and Preacher were still there.

Denny deposited her along with her crutches onto the narrow porch and went back for the bag of canned soup. She gave two knocks and opened the door. Right inside the door was a little living room/dining room/kitchen—one room. Just a quick glance told her the Thicksons were poor—the floors were scarred wood, covered by a threadbare rug, a lamp without a shade sat atop a barrel covered by cloth, the appliances were very dated. Mel was kneeling on the floor beside Megan, who was using a small, sagging couch as her bed.

"I'm mostly well," she was telling Mel.

"Just let me be sure, while Doctor Michaels checks your brothers. Open your mouth and let me have a look. Say 'ahhh.' Throat's a little red, but not scary." She ran the temperature sensor across Megan's forehead and read it. "Normal. You're right—mostly well."

Then Megan coughed. It sounded like a seal barking.

"Well, you could use some help with that," Mel said.

"Where's Jack?" Denny asked. He put the bag of canned soup on the table next to the big box Jack had delivered.

"Out back, helping Frank with something," Mel said.

"I'll go see if he needs me," Denny said, disappearing at once.

Becca stood, waiting, balanced on her crutches, while Mel checked Megan, listening to her chest, looking in her ears. A few moments passed, then Dr. Michaels poked his head into the living room. "I need you in here," he said to Mel.

When Mel went into the bedroom, Megan noticed Becca and her little face lit up. "Mama said I probably wouldn't see you again!"

"I still haven't left," she said, moving closer. "How are you feeling?"

"I'm mostly well," she said. "But I think I gave it to the little boys. I tried not to!"

"Megan, you might have all caught it at the same time. You never know where germs come from." She lowered herself carefully to the edge of the sofa. "You still have a cough."

"If I'm Mary, I promise not to cough!"

"Hmm," Becca said, thinking. "Mary was sitting outside in a stable. Chances are she had a cough. Or at least a sniffle. What do you think?"

"Maybe. Will you stay for the pageant?"

She shook her head. "I'm sure we'll be on our way by then. We were planning to leave by tomorrow morning, but weather reports aren't good. We might be stuck another day. But I'm planning on getting home by Christmas to be with my mom and dad."

"You know what I wish?" Megan said. "I wish you lived here."

Becca smiled and brushed the little girl's hair

back from her brow. "I'm so glad I got to meet you. I'm just visiting, but I'll visit again. Promise."

"I know, but…"

Mel came back into the room. She handed a couple of bottles to Becca. "Tylenol for fevers, cough syrup as directed." Then she leaned down. "Megan, we're going to take Jeffie and Stevie to the hospital for X-rays and medicine. Your mom is coming. Jeremy will be here with you and your dad. Probably the little boys will be back home tomorrow, the next day at the latest. They're going to be fine—it's for precaution. I don't want them stuck out here, caught in the snowstorm if their fevers and congestion gets worse. You understand?"

Megan nodded, but her eyes were a little scared. Becca squeezed her hand.

"Everything is going to be fine. Jack and everyone will stay till they're completely sure you have all the firewood and food you need, okay? And your mom will call you from the hospital to let you know the little boys are just fine. Okay?"

Again she nodded.

"Becca, hang out with the kids until Frank is briefed. Give him the medicine. Make sure these little ones are getting what they need. Tell him Jeremy has been dosed and should stay in bed. He gets more Tylenol and cough syrup in four hours. And try not to breathe the air if you can help it. No kissing sick kids, no matter how tempting!"

"Right," Becca said, thinking that all she wanted to do was pull Megan onto her lap and cuddle her, reassure her.

Mel disappeared into the bedroom. In just seconds, Cameron Michaels came through the living room, carrying a child wrapped in a blanket. Right on his heels came Mel, also carrying a little boy. Behind them came Lorraine, her coat hanging open, carrying two doctors' bags. She leaned down and kissed Megan's forehead. "Tell Daddy I'll call home as soon as we know what the chest X-rays say. Can you remember that?"

Megan nodded.

"It's going to be just fine, Megan," Lorraine said. "Dr. Michaels and Mel know exactly what to do."

"I know...."

Becca watched Lorraine quickly race out the door, closing it.

She was filled with emotions she couldn't quite label, but one of them was a fierce longing. She wanted to throw down the crutches and walk; she wanted to carry one of these children to safety.

She patted Megan's hand. "I brought some soup. I'm going to warm it for you."

Fifteen

Denny stood back and watched as Jack, up on a ladder at the Thicksons' shed, dumped a pile of snow on top of Preacher's head as Preacher was backing out of the same shed, his arms laden with firewood.

"Hey! Watch it!"

"Sorry, Preach."

"Like the three stooges," Frank Thickson muttered.

Preacher filled Denny's arms with the firewood. "Here. Make yourself useful."

"Gimme a load," Frank said.

"Since we're here and willing to help, why don't you go back to the house and check on the family. We'll bring your wood."

"I don't like being done for," he said.

"Get over yourself," Jack said from up on his

ladder. And then he scooped another pile of snow on his cook's head. He grinned. "Sorry, Preach."

"Come down here and do wood!" Preacher commanded. "I'll clean the roof!"

"That's okay, buddy," Jack said. "I got it."

"You're gonna get it!" the big man threatened.

Denny chuckled and started moving toward the house with his load of wood. Frank followed and Denny slowed. "Say, Frank, you have a lot of property out here. You ever keep a garden?"

"Summertime," he grunted.

"There's a reason I'm asking. I'm leaving my job out at Jilly Farms. You know, it used to be Hope McCrea's place and Jillian Matlock has been farming it. Very interesting work. They're going to be looking for someone—"

"Someone with one arm or two?" he asked.

"Jack's right, you should get over yourself. I served two tours in the sandbox with the Marines—I know an unfortunate number of guys with missing limbs. I know it's a struggle, but the crankier you are, the bigger your load is gonna be. You seem to do okay with one arm and you're probably due to get a prosthesis before too long. You could at least talk to Jilly. You could at least try."

Frank stopped walking. "You think I don't *try*?"

Denny stopped. "I couldn't say for sure whether you try or not. I can say for sure that it would all be a lot easier if you weren't so angry and a little more grateful for what you've got instead of all pissed off about what you're missing."

"Oh, yeah? And what is it I'm supposed to be grateful for, Mr. Know-It-All?"

Denny lifted both brows. "Let's see. A brain that works, eyes that see, ears that hear, two legs and one arm, for starters. Then there's the wife, four good-looking, smart kids and a roof over your head. A lot of people would give their right arm for that." Then he walked to the house and deposited the wood on the porch. He walked right past Frank on his way back to get another load.

Denny heard a sound and turned to look back. He saw Dr. Michaels and Mel hustling out to the Hummer, carrying small children. He moved back toward the house and Frank.

"What are they doing here?" Frank asked.

The doctor lifted his bundle into the back of the Hummer before he addressed Frank. "I think they're going to be just fine, Frank, but they have to go to the hospital. They both need X-rays and antibiotic therapy. We have to be sure it's not pneumonia. If this has settled into their chests, and it sounds like it has, they'll just get worse out here without the right medicine—and there's another storm on the way."

"I can't afford no hospital!"

"If you can't afford it, they'll still be treated.

Mel can help you with some paperwork for assistance—that can be done later," Cameron said.

"They'll just heap the bills on me—they'll get their pound of flesh eventually. I'll never get on my feet this way!"

"Well, Frank, I believe the price of not taking these little ones to Valley Hospital could be a lot higher than that. I aim to get 'em taken care of so they can get well."

Then, ignoring any further argument, Cameron got behind the wheel of the Hummer.

Lorraine Thickson hurried out the door and across the porch, carrying two doctors' bags. "Frank, please watch over Megan and Jeremy. I imagine I'll stay the night with the boys. I'll call you later to tell you how they are."

She climbed in the back with Mel and the little ones, the hatch closed and the Hummer backed away. Frank tromped up the porch step and into the house.

Knowing Becca was in there with Megan, Denny abandoned the idea of another load of wood and jogged through the deep snow to the house. He kicked the snow off his boots before opening the door, just in time to hear Frank angrily bellow, "I don't need no goddamn charity!" With a swipe of his arm, he knocked the care box off the table and sent the food scattering across the floor.

The frozen turkey bounced twice; canned goods rolled around.

Becca was supported by her crutches at the stove, a pan steaming and a spoon in her hand. Her eyes were round with fear. Megan sat straight up on the sofa and screamed, "Daddy!" Then she covered her mouth and began to cry.

Denny took two giant steps into the house and grabbed Frank by the front of his jacket and with a snarl, pulled him right out the front door. He closed the door and pushed Frank right up against it. Denny's face felt purple with rage and Frank had the intelligence to look a little intimidated, if not scared.

"Listen to me, Frank. *Listen!* You ever shout at my girl again, I swear to God you'll be sorry! She is nothing but kindness! I doubt she gives a crap about your sorry ass, but she insisted on coming out here because she loves your little girl." Frank's jacket still in his fist, he gave him a little shake and pushed him against the door again. "How can you do something like that in front of that little girl? She loves you! You'd turn your anger on a child of your own, who loves you? Who's counting on you? What's she going to think? That it would be wrong for her to eat that food because it makes you so angry? She's *sick*!"

Frank's eyes glittered with unshed tears. "Mind your own business."

"It *is* my business! When you turn on my woman and a young innocent child I make it my business! Now, we're going in there. We're picking up the groceries and I want you to tell your child you're sorry you shouted. If you don't want to eat, I don't care. But you tell that sick child that you want her to eat. And if you don't, we're going to come back out here and rehearse it again!" They stared at each other a moment and Denny said, "You hearing me, Frank? Because I am not fooling around with you."

"I hear."

In a quieter voice, Denny said, "You're wrong to make the whole world around you suffer because you're angry. Especially the world your kids live in."

Frank just looked down.

Denny let go of his jacket. "Let's go inside and make peace. You were wrong. When you're wrong, you make amends. It's not complicated." He opened the door for Frank to enter.

They went quietly about the business of picking up the scattered food. Denny stored the frozen turkey in the refrigerator, where it would slowly thaw, while Frank picked up canned goods one at a time and tossed them, catching them in between the stump of his missing forearm and his body so he could carry more. This caused Denny to stop and watch; the man had definitely learned some compensating moves! If he'd just get an attitude adjustment, he'd probably make it just fine.

When the kitchen was straightened again, Frank went the few steps to the couch where Becca huddled next to Megan.

"Miss, I apologize for my temper. It's been a hard winter so far. Megan, honey, let's eat us some of that soup."

"It's okay, Daddy. I don't need it." Then she covered her mouth and coughed.

"Come on, baby, I need some. Will you sit with me?"

"Okay," she said meekly. "The little boys went to the hospital, Daddy."

"I know, honey. That was smart of the doctor. Mama will be there. She'll call us tonight." He looked at Becca. "Will you stay and have some soup with us?"

"I would," she said, getting up and positioning her crutches. "But I'm going to do a little cooking at the bar because Paige and Preacher are running all over the mountain trying to be sure everyone has what they need before another big storm hits. I'm not much of a cook, but I'm doing what I can. I brought enough soup so even if you don't feel like messing around in the kitchen too much tonight, you and the kids will have that."

"I'd gladly pay for the soup," he said.

She smiled warmly. "No need, Mr. Thickson.

It's all good." She bent and kissed Megan's head, against medical advice. "I want you to get better, little girl!"

Denny and Becca sat in Jack's truck in front of the Thickson house, waiting for Preacher and Jack to finish up. "I think it's best to get out of their hair," Becca said. "And just hope Mr. Thickson can mend some fences with little Megan, the poor darling."

"I was hard on him, Becca, probably too hard. No one understands better than me how overpowering self-pity can be."

She grabbed his hand and gave it a squeeze. "We've both come a long way."

"We have to make a decision now. When do you want to leave?"

"I want to leave right now, but I'm not going to. I'm going to go back to Jack's and make sure everyone who's shoveling, plowing, delivering and helping get fed tonight. They're all throwing themselves into the care of this town and they've been awful good to me. The least I can do is return the favor."

"We might not get down the mountain tomorrow, you know."

"Then we'll get down the next day. Or the next. It doesn't matter—we'll get there. The important thing to me right now is that we're both moving in the same direction."

When Jack and Preacher delivered the last of their wood to the Thicksons' front porch, Jack transferred two care boxes to Denny and Becca and gave them the names and directions for delivery. Because Becca was on crutches, these boxes were not going to the country, but rather the edge of town, where most of the streets were passable.

They pulled up to a small house, the street numbers hanging kind of drunkenly from the nails that held them next to a warped front door that didn't look strong enough to keep the wind out. Even though Becca had to contend with her crutches, she was determined to see who lived in this ramshackle little place. She turned herself around and lowered herself carefully to the ground on one foot, holding her lame foot above the snow. The walk was covered with a little more than a foot of snow, less than on the street because of the huge trees that formed a protective canopy. She made her way carefully to the front door while Denny came behind her with a big box.

The woman who opened the door was young, maybe early twenties. She was thin and a little pale. She held a baby in her arms with a coarse Army blanket covering her shoulders and the baby. Hiding behind her and hanging on her leg was a little one, perhaps two years old.

"Mrs. Crane?" Becca asked.

The woman pushed her hair back over one ear. "I'm Nora Crane. Who are you?"

"My name is Becca Timm. We brought you a Christmas box. This is Denny—he can carry it into the kitchen for you if you want."

A huff of embarrassed laughter escaped her and she stood aside, pulling the two-year-old with her. The toddler peeked out from behind her mother, a thumb in her mouth. Becca stood back so Denny could enter, but then Becca stepped inside the doorway and saw the reason for the woman's laughter. It was just one room; there was a broken-down couch, a table with two mismatched chairs and while there was a stove, there was no refrigerator.

"Would you like us to put some of this stuff away somewhere for you?" Becca asked.

"You can just leave it." Then she brushed impatiently at a tear.

"If you don't mind me asking, how do you keep food without a refrigerator?"

"There's just milk to worry about—I keep it right outside the back door." She gave a limp shrug. "I don't guess we'll be here too long."

"Oh. How old is the baby?"

"About six weeks now. Who sent this food?"

"Well, there's a group of folks from the church

and Jack's Bar. Will someone clear the walk for you?"

"Don't matter much," she said. "I don't think we'll be going outside."

"Nora, do you need a few things? Clothes for the kids? Blankets?" She looked around. "How are you keeping warm?"

"I run the oven now and then. Tell them thanks, whoever sent this over. I didn't think anyone knew I was here."

"Someone knew. I'm going to tell the pastor you could use some sweaters and blankets. Maybe he knows where we can find some things to help get you through the winter."

Her lip quivered slightly and she nodded once, but said nothing.

"Do you have any family?"

"Not anymore," she said. "I had a…" She straightened, trying to find some pride. "There's no one anymore."

"I think you could use a hand," Becca said. "I'll talk to Pastor Kincaid or Jack—maybe someone can help."

"For the kids," she said.

"There's a can opener in the box, along with some plastic bowls, spoons, a couple of knives."

She nodded again.

"Bye, then," Becca said. She moved out the door right behind Denny and heard it close behind her.

Denny positioned himself in front of Becca, took her crutches and bent slightly at the waist. "Come on, gimpy," he said gently.

She looped her arms around his neck, bent her knees to lift her feet out of the snow and he piggybacked her to the truck. Once there, he helped lift her inside. He went around to the driver's side and jumped in.

She faced him, pale and stricken. "Denny," she said, her voice just a squeak of emotion.

"We'll get her some help," he said, starting the truck. "Looks like the next house is just a few doors down. You going in this one with me?"

"Yes. Yes, I have to. I had no idea this town was so poor!"

"This town is like all towns, Becca—there's a little of everything. And there are some folks real hard on their luck, but the people who can help, do. That's worth a lot." He pulled down the block, past three houses. "Here we are. There's a porch—let me get you on the porch and come back for the box."

Becca thought this house looked to be in better shape, though it could sure use some paint and repair. This time when the occupant answered the door, Becca breathed a sigh of relief. It was an elderly woman, and she might not be robust but she didn't look thin and ill. She was dressed for the cold and had a shawl thrown over her shoulders.

Her house was not rich but contained plenty of substantial furniture and the doors and windows appeared to have a good seal against the cold, at least on first glance. "Mrs. Clemens?"

"Yes, hello," she said, and smiled with warmth. "Did the pastor send you?"

"Yes, ma'am. We have a box of goodies for you," Becca said. "Merry Christmas."

"Thank you, child. I'm happy to take that off your hands—my social security just doesn't go that far, especially with my prescriptions! But girl, I'm worried about that young woman down the street! Did Pastor send something to her?" She stepped aside so Denny could enter with the box.

"What's her name?" Becca hedged. "I'll be glad to check."

"It's Crane. I don't know the first name, but she's in a terrible way!"

The difference between this house and the last was shocking. Mrs. Clemens's furniture was dated and worn in places, but there were homey touches, as well—doilies spread over the arms of chairs, a tablecloth, bric-a-brac, a nice big area rug that was a bit worn but still perfectly functional.

"That poor girl down there. I saw them move in when she had that brand-new baby and not long after, that young man moved out with a trailer and took everything with him. Everything! Furniture and rugs and even the refrigerator. I spoke to him, asked him what he was leaving his poor wife and he shouted at me to mind my own business or I'd be sorry." She *tsked* and shook her head. "The shame! I told Pastor there was a young woman in need and I saw him write down her name. I'm so glad she got a box! She did get a box, didn't she?"

"Yes, ma'am," Becca said.

"I'm so glad! I look forward to the Thanksgiving and Christmas boxes all year long. But did she get a turkey? Because I don't think they have enough to get by on down there, and there's small children..."

"It's going to be taken care of, Mrs. Clemens," Denny said with authority.

The little woman grabbed Denny's forearm in a vice-grip. "It's gotta be taken care of right away," she said emphatically. "I'm afraid they'll freeze to death. I worry about that baby!"

"Right away," Denny confirmed, patting her hand. "Right away."

She let out a sigh of relief. Then she let go of his arm and gave it a pat. "That's good," she said. Then she turned away and began to pick through her care box. "I do look forward to this all year," she repeated. "The dollar just doesn't stretch as far as it used to."

When they were back in the truck, Becca said, "That was a big promise."

"I'll find someone to pull together something

or I'll borrow this truck for a run to Target. They need to be fed and warm. I wonder if there's formula and diapers..."

Becca gasped. "How dense am I? I never even thought of that!"

"I helped out last Christmas. Mel was the one who knew about the need for formula and diapers and which boxes should include them. She might be the one to talk to about this. But if she's too busy, I'll get to the store before we have more snow."

"They have to be warm and full tonight, Denny," Becca said.

"They will be warm and full, honey. I promise."

Becca was back at the bar by three. With Denny close at her side, she explained about Nora Crane and her dire needs. Paige tried putting a call in to Mel at Valley Hospital, but she wasn't answering her page, which meant she was probably on her way back to Virgin River.

"If Jack can manage without his truck awhile longer, I can go to Fortuna and pick up some things—diapers, formula, maybe a space heater. That baby's real little, Paige. Can you write down what I'll need?" Denny asked.

"You don't have to go to Fortuna," Paige said. "There's formula and diapers at the clinic and we have an emergency closet here in town—used clothing, blankets, jackets, that sort of thing, though they do tend to run a little low during the holidays. Does she have a fireplace?"

Denny shook his head.

"Hmm. Maybe one of the guys can do something about the doors and windows. I'll call Paul—he might be able to send over one of his crew who can nail down a proper strip for a seal. At this stage, even some good duct tape would help around the windows. And we can loan her a cooler with ice for her perishables—she shouldn't be opening and closing the back door in the dead of winter. I'll go dig out some of Dana's old bottles and sippy cups. You know what? I bet I have some clothes just ready to be given to the shelter—how big is the toddler?"

"A little smaller than Dana," Becca said. "But it's the baby I'm worried about most. That woman doesn't have the means to wash clothes, and it's cold in that house. If you had any infant wear that's nice and warm…"

"Oh, I have lots. Denny, mind the bar while I gather up some things. And for the woman?" she asked.

Becca shrugged. "I have no idea what she has. She was wearing jeans and had a scratchy old Army blanket around her shoulders, covering herself and the baby with it."

"We can't have that," Paige said, wandering off toward the kitchen.

A feeling of satisfaction grew in Becca's chest. She thought how much like a successful day with a struggling second grader it felt. One stop at one unfortunate house and an opportunity to find some help for them… It almost felt as though her whole journey to this little town had been justified.

She followed Paige back to the kitchen, ready to finish the meal she'd begun. She found the sink was full of dishes. While Paige talked to Paul Haggerty on the phone about emergency repairs on a poor woman's house, Becca went about the business of cleaning up. Leaning against the counter and with the dishwasher opened, she began to rinse and load the lunch dishes. She heard Paige give Paul the address and thank him—it brought a smile to Becca's lips. Then she turned the oven back on and pulled out everything she had stored in the refrigerator.

Becca had no experience cooking for a large crowd but she noticed that Preacher's meat loaf recipe was four loaves for forty people. She put more potatoes in the pot to boil, increasing her potato casserole recipe. She filled a colander with frozen green beans and thawed them under cold water. By the time she'd patted four meat loaves into shape, Paige came back into the kitchen, her arms heavily laden with clothes, towels and a couple of blankets. She was smiling.

"I think this will do, at least for a few days. I found an old space heater, too. It hasn't been used in forever—I don't need it back. We'll have to get Mel to take over formula and diapers, of course. And if Mel takes them, she'll have a chance to make sure they're all right at the same time. And Mel has supplements for adults on hand, as well—Ensure and that sort of thing. Something fortifying for Mommy."

"Thank you," Becca said gratefully.

"No, thank *you*! We can't be everywhere at once!"

"Paige, what time should this meat loaf be ready?" she asked.

Paige glanced over her big pile of clothing at her watch. "Put it in now, Becca. We should be ready for an early crowd at five, though I can't imagine who will brave the elements tonight. The rest of us will eat much later. Keep what we don't serve in the warmer."

As Paige left, Denny came into the kitchen. "Need me for anything, babe?" he asked.

"I don't think so. I have it handled."

"Good for you. I'm going with one of Paul's men over to the Crane house to seal some doors and windows. I'll put a note on the clinic door for Mel about what we need and the address."

"Is it snowing yet?" she asked.

"Just a little. The big stuff will probably come later."

And for some reason, that news made her grin like a fool.

"That shouldn't make you smile," Denny said.

"I think we're stuck another night."

"Most definitely," he said. "And my truck is getting more buried by the minute." He turned to leave, but had a second thought and turned back to her, snatching her up in his arms and planting a giant kiss on her, momentarily taking her breath away. "I'm okay with being stuck another night," he whispered, running a knuckle over her cheek. "It's nice and warm under the quilt." And then he was gone.

Becca went to the phone and dialed her mother. "Hey, Mom. What's going on?"

"Just leaving work, honey," she said. "I've been watching the weather. It looks pretty serious up there."

"It's serious, all right. We're pretty much snowed in. We've been so busy getting ready for a big storm. You have no idea all there is to do around here. First of all, it was important to get the Christmas food boxes delivered—there are people who will really need them and more snow could prevent getting them out. And, Mom, I helped deliver and I saw some need in this little town that just can't go unnoticed." She described the young woman with the baby and toddler, the elderly woman who was concerned for her and little Megan, whose brothers had to go to the hospital and whose father was out of work due to his amputation.

She told her mom about cooking for whoever might show up at the bar that night because the cook and his wife were busy making sure anyone who was cold or hungry or in any way needy was being taken care of.

"Meat loaf for forty?" her mother asked. "My goodness, Becca! Have you ever cooked for that many?"

She laughed and said, "I might've ordered pizza for about half that many. No—I've never been responsible for this many people. Mel and Jack and their kids will probably stay in town tonight rather than going home—she's the midwife and has a couple of women in advanced pregnancy and can't risk getting snowed in out at her house. The clinic is across the street from Jack's. And right now one of their friends, the builder who made sure all the streets were plowed, sent someone from his crew over to the young mother's house to seal up the doors and windows so they don't freeze to death tonight. Paige had a space heater for them—God, I hope it works. I think I'll be worried about them all night."

"It sounds like you should've gotten out of there first thing this morning!" Beverly Timm said.

"Oh, Mom, I couldn't have," Becca said. "It's just…you just can't imagine… Mom, I'm so glad I was here to help. It's a little like sandbagging in a flood or hosing down a fire!"

"Is that so?" Beverly asked. "As serious as that?"

"At least as serious as that! I just had to be a part of it."

"Is that little town growing on you?"

Becca laughed. "I got pretty caught up in the action."

"Well, as long as you get home for Christmas…"

"Oh, I'll get—" She stopped. Her voice caught. "I'm sure I'll be home for Christmas," she said, but she said it very softly. And what she couldn't add was, *But home might not be in San Diego.*

Sixteen

Becca cursed those crutches that got in her way! She found she could manage in the kitchen pretty well, with countertops to lean on, but she couldn't serve or bus tables. She longed to be on the move! Fortunately Denny was back at the bar by five and could help. He pulled out the heavy trays of meat loaf and lifted the hot potato casseroles onto the work station. Becca was able to handle the beans and warm the dinner rolls—she felt like a wimp.

A thick, swirling snow began to fall in earnest. There were only a few people in the bar at five o'clock and when she had some plates prepared, Denny delivered them. He also fed the fire, served drinks and cocoa and turned the lights on the Christmas tree, as much to brighten the street as to provide holiday decoration. He helped Paige make sure the little kids were all eating their dinner and cleared away dirty dishes.

Of course, it was dark by five and Becca began to worry about their other friends. Preacher and Jack were not back; Mel hadn't reported in. Noah and Ellie Kincaid stopped by after their boxes were delivered. "The church will be unlocked," he told Paige. "It always is, but if anyone needs refuge, it's available. Ellie put out some blankets in the basement and there's a full working kitchen."

The wind picked up and really began to howl outside. Denny swore their young mother was in far better shape than they had found her, but Becca worried about Megan's family.

It was seven by the time Mel returned to the bar and right behind her came Jack and Preacher. With the weather bearing down on them, no one else was out, but the noise in the bar rose with their presence. Although they were all frosty and rosy-cheeked, with snowflakes clinging to their caps and shoulders, Mel instantly cuddled two-year-old Emma, Jack tossed David in the air, making him screech, and Preacher ran his cold hands up Paige's back, enjoying her protests.

"Set us up a couple of shots, Paige," Jack said. "I don't think even Jack Frost is going to drag us out again tonight!"

"Unless someone goes into labor," Mel said.

"You're going to need Santa and his eight reindeer for that one," Preacher told her.

"Is everyone safe?" Becca asked. "All tucked in?"

"Everyone we know about, anyway," Jack said.

"But what if there are others out there like Mrs. Crane?" she asked.

Jack no doubt saw her concern and draped an arm around her shoulders. "It's a small town, honey. It isn't often someone like that gets by us. It happens, but not often. People around here are real nosy."

She leaned against him. "Man, I'm worn-out!"

"Worked hard, did you?"

"I'm worn-out from worrying about everyone! How about the Thicksons?"

"As soon as the roads are cleared tomorrow, Cameron is going to drive Lorraine and the little boys home from the hospital," Mel said. "He's doing rounds at the hospital as early as he can get there in the morning and the boys are in pretty good shape, despite some bronchitis and ugly throats."

"But what about Mr. Thickson, at home with Megan and Jeremy?" she asked. "He was in a real mood."

"More bluster than anything," Jack said. "He loves his kids. If it'll make you feel better, I'll call and check on him."

She looked at him with wide, pleading eyes. "Please?"

"Sure," he said, heading for the kitchen.

Denny quickly filled the empty space Jack had

left, putting his arm around her. "Come on, honey. I think you should sit down, put your feet up and take a breather."

"I can't!" she said. "I made meat loaf for forty!"

The place fell suddenly quiet. Finally Preacher said, "Forty?"

"That's what your recipe said."

"Hmm. What's Jack gonna eat?"

Becca just groaned and allowed herself to drop into a chair, while everyone around her seemed amused, chuckling.

"Everyone is fine out at the Thicksons," Jack said as he returned to the bar from the kitchen. "Megan is bouncing back and Jeremy's fever is gone. Something sure smells good in that kitchen. Whatcha got going in there, Paige?"

"Not me," she said, getting down the bottles requested by Jack and Preacher. "Becca made meat loaf. I was busy all day!"

"Thank you, Becca," Jack said. "I didn't know you could cook!"

"You haven't tasted it yet," she warned wearily.

"It could taste like a cow patty and I wouldn't know," Preacher said, tossing back a shot to warm his bones. "I'm half frozen and half dead."

Denny went behind the bar and poured Becca a short snifter of brandy, pressing it into her hand. Then he sat real close while everyone in the bar talked about their adventures. Jack and Preacher had shoveled, plowed, chopped, stacked, carried logs, rounded up animals, carried old women and old men, emptied portable indoor latrines, cleaned the snow off roofs, pulled a car out of a ditch, jump-started a battery…

"Preacher damn near stuck to the seat in an outhouse," Jack reported, bringing laughter out of the entire group.

"Jack had to be rescued off the top of a porch when he let the ladder get away," Preacher said. "Crossed my mind to leave him up there. He was a pain in my ass all day long."

"Mel, you have a hard day?" Paige asked.

"Nah," she said. "Two bronchitis, one strep, one false labor—or at least, false so far—and a little home health nursing." She looked at Becca and smiled. "The woman and children you found are doing well, Becca. The baby is perfectly healthy. They're all fixed up with what they need, they're warm and safe, and I'll check on them in a couple of days. Thank you."

"I didn't do anything. I mean, I just went with Denny to deliver the box."

"She asked me to tell you she's very grateful," Mel added.

"It was nothing," she said in a small attack of shyness. Then she sighed. "Oh, God, I'm so relieved!"

"Time to hunker down with some of that meat loaf!" Preacher nearly roared.

And with that, people started heading for the kitchen to serve their own plates. Denny followed the band. Becca just let out a breath and stayed where she was, sipping a little brandy. She was exhausted. In short order Paige brought out a tray of cookies and milk for the kids, while the adults returned to the bar with their plates laden with food. Denny brought two—one for her and one for him.

As they dug in, they praised her work, pronouncing the meal to be delicious. There was lots of "oohing" and "aahing" and lip smacking.

Becca leaned against Denny's shoulder and said, "I get it."

"Huh?"

"I get it," she repeated softly. "How you feel. How it's like being part of the team. How you know you're really necessary. Needed. I get it." She smiled at him. "I like it."

Becca kind of hated to see the evening end. The Sheridans and Middletons were going to be having a pajama party. They had put the kids to bed at Preacher's house and were all enjoying the warm fire in the bar, talking about the town, their friends, the people who weren't friends… It wasn't yet nine, but Denny said, "If we're going back down the street, we'd better get going."

"Don't walk," Jack said. "Take the truck."

"I'm afraid I'll end up parking it in the middle of the street."

"Doesn't matter," Jack said with a shrug. "The Virgin River snowplows won't be out until I call Paul. But go. I'm tired and the snow could get wilder. If you're going, go now. I'm not pulling my boots back on to dig you out."

"All right, old man," Denny said. He pulled Jack's keys out of his pocket.

"Wait," Paige said. "There's no telling what we'll find in the morning. I'm going to fix you a little care package in case you don't feel like coming down here for breakfast. Think you can manage on venison salami, cheese, crackers and biscuits?"

"Throw some peanut butter in, will you?"

Paige gave a nod and dashed off to the kitchen. In what seemed like seconds, she was back with a big bag for them to take home.

After helping Becca into her jacket and taking her crutches from her, he crouched so she could climb on his back.

Once in the truck, she said, "I can't see anything."

"Awful, isn't it? I can barely see, either," he said. He turned into what he believed was the driveway and pulled slowly forward into the flurries.

He stopped with a thunk. "There. See that? That was the Nissan."

"Oh, God, I hope you didn't hurt Jack's truck!"

"Becca, I didn't hurt Jack's truck. I hurt the Nissan!"

"Oh," she said, laughing. "How are we going to get up the stairs?"

"Slowly. Very, very slowly."

He came around for her, carried her up the stairs, deposited her on one leg in the apartment and went back for the crutches. Momentarily he was back, crutches in hand. He leaned them against the wall, pushed back his hood and eyed her with glittering eyes.

"Denny?" she asked, tilting her head.

One side of his mouth lifted. Then he charged her, tackling her around the waist. She squealed and found herself pinned beneath him on the bed. He held her hands over her head and covered her mouth in a searing kiss. His intentions were already obvious, straining against the zipper of his jeans, pushing against her. He released her lips, but barely. "I have some ideas about how to spend the snowstorm."

"Oh?" she asked.

"For starters, naked. Then after I do all your favorite things, I think we should do all my favorite things. Then new things. Then things we never thought of but can dream up. Then if I'm not dead, we can start over. How about we start with me tasting every inch of your naked body…"

"Aren't you tired?" she asked him.

"I'm *hard*," he pointed out to her with a little hip movement. "And hungry. For your body…"

Yes, this was what she wanted, she thought. Her man back; the one who couldn't get enough of her. The one who always put her first.

"I have another idea," he said. "Let's not reserve this for blizzards. Let's plan on nights like this regularly, for the rest of our lives. How's that?"

"That's going to work," she said, pulling his lips down to hers.

The snow continued through most of Tuesday, dumping another two feet. Paul plowed again, leaving five- and six-foot berms along the streets. Denny joined Jack and Preacher when they helped people dig out, get their cars and trucks started, delivered supplies. Becca spent most of the day helping Paige in the kitchen; they baked bread and pies and prepared a hearty stew for dinner.

The Sheridans spent another night in town because more snow was predicted for Wednesday morning, but it was supposed to be clear on Thursday.

"If we leave early on Thursday, we can be in San Diego by the evening," Denny said to Becca. "In time for Christmas Eve on Friday."

"All I have to do is close my suitcase," Becca said. "What can I do to help you get ready?"

"I'm as good as ready," he said.

When they weren't holed up in their little room above the garage they were at Jack's, where, despite the weather, there were always a few people. It was the gathering place for the town and the best spot to get the latest information.

On Wednesday night, Becca and Denny were having yet another farewell dinner. By her calculation, this was their third. She was sitting up at the bar, talking to Jack, while Denny was out gassing up Jack's truck.

"Tomorrow it will be clear," Becca said to Jack. "You'll have your life back."

He gave a nod. "Not quite. My family is due tomorrow. And we'll also run around checking on people. We've been lucky—no power loss. I'm assuming we'll find that everyone is fine. We could still get more snow before spring—an outrageous amount this winter. You know what that means? When the snowpack melts in the spring, we could have floods."

"Here? In town?"

"Virgin River doesn't usually have a real bad time, being at this elevation. But there are areas around that will have issues. But down the mountain could be a challenge. A few years ago, our friends in Grace Valley were just about wiped out. We helped where we could."

"You *always* help where you can," she said. "I can see why Denny has become so attached to this place."

Jack grew suddenly serious. "Becca, I hope you know I support Denny in his decision to leave, to go to a place he can have a life and family with you."

"I know," she said. "I appreciate that. Where will you go tomorrow? To check on people?"

He thought for a moment. "Mel will go out to the Thicksons and check on the kids. She'll check on the young mother. Noah will see about some of his elderly congregation. Me and Preacher, we're kind of in charge of the outlying areas. There are folks out on the ridge and up the mountain a ways that need help digging out. Thank God no one got out on a trail and lost!"

"Has that happened?" she asked, sitting straighter.

"It's happened in good weather! This is no place to wander if you don't know where you're going. Becca, you haven't seen the half of Virgin River."

She laughed. "I'm going to miss this place."

"And this place will miss you. You were a huge, one-legged help." She just laughed at him. "Seriously," he said. "Terrific meat loaf and potatoes. And there will be terrific meat-loaf sandwiches for a long time!"

"Thanks. Although I don't have a future in a

bar and grill kitchen, I'm finding it kind of hard to leave...."

"Is that so?"

She shrugged. "A couple of weeks ago I was feeling like I'd been real lucky to meet such nice people. By now I feel like you people are the closest friends I've had in a while."

He laughed. "That kind of happens here. We get bonded real easy when we pull together for a cause. A big snowstorm is a cause."

"I was scared to death," she said, but her smile was huge. "I had fun."

Jack stilled. "Let me get this right..."

"Yeah, scared to death *and* fun. It's kind of a pattern. I've always been like that. My mom always said I just didn't like things easy. She's the mother of the century, you know—managed the perfect home. Everything was always stable, secure, perfect. I mean, she wasn't the kind of mother people write bad mother novels about—she really is awesome. So what did I always need? I needed to jump out of airplanes or surf the biggest waves or barrel race on horseback. Anything with a rush."

He grinned largely. "My wife's the same," he said. "Mel's a longtime adrenaline junkie. She spent ten years in an inner-city E.R. If it wasn't scary and risky, she was unenthused."

"I get that." Becca laughed. "Yet Denny is the one who went to war. Twice."

"Totally different," Jack said. "He's a trained Marine. He's not looking for war, he's responding. You and my wife? You like the edge."

She laughed happily. She felt so understood. "Mel doesn't seem like that now," she said.

"She'll be like that forever. She holds the health of this town in her hands—a very big job. They depend on her completely. We have a good doctor, but Mel is still delivering a lot of the babies, sometimes under adverse conditions, getting financial assistance, writing grants, you name it. Before we were married, she let a pot grower take her out to a grow site to deliver a woman in big medical trouble. I found out later that he took her at gunpoint. I almost lost my fucking mind... Sorry.

"It's okay," she said. "She did? She did that?"

He grew serious. "That was not smart—adrenaline junkie or not."

"Of course," she said. "Not smart."

He relaxed. "Thing is, life around here seems balanced against two extremes. Calm and challenging. That's why we stick together. When you get down to it, that's the only option. Fortunately, it's calm and beautiful most of the time. It's also a frontier."

"Denny's right about one thing—it would be a

good place to raise a family. Too bad I don't have a job here."

"That job thing? I could make that happen," he said.

She leaned an elbow on the bar. "And how are you going to do that? I don't think you need another cook or waitress."

"A school. We've been wanting a school. At least, for the little kids."

"Don't tempt me," she said.

He turned away from her briefly, just long enough to pour her a glass of the white wine she seemed to enjoy. He put it in front of her. "Would tempting you work?"

"Ha ha. You don't happen to have a school."

"I could have one in a matter of weeks. Remember my friend Paul? He could throw up a prefab modular building in no time at all. The construction would insult him—he's very proud of his work and never cuts corners. But the price and speed would fit right into this town's needs."

"Where would you put it?" she asked.

"I don't know. Probably down the street—there's a lot of available land between the most populated part of town and Noah's house. For that matter, I think the church basement is mostly available. But the town should have an elementary school."

"How many teachers do you plan on luring here?" she asked, sipping her wine.

"I was thinking one. One teacher. And probably teacher's helpers. It would be good if, for starters, the little kids didn't have to ride that bus into the valley. When you add up all the kindergarten, first, second and third graders, there aren't all that many…"

"Oh, stop," she said, putting down her wine and covering her ears.

He pulled a hand off her ear. "It could happen."

She stared into his eyes. Hard. "My *family* is in San Diego!"

"You've been away from them for a month, I know," Jack said. "You've probably never been separated that long before."

But of course she had. "College," she said. "But it was in L.A. and I went home almost every weekend." At least, when she could see Denny. When Denny was in Iraq, she went home once a month, if that.

"You must be missing them a lot right about now. After a whole month."

Oh, and what a month! A beautiful month of reunion with the love of her life. Better than she had dared dream. "I have a nice, furnished, two-bedroom apartment in San Diego," she said. "Denny has one room over a garage."

"Easy-peasy," he said.

"Don't!" she warned.

"Rick Sutter's house is on this block. Two bedrooms. Small and cute. Empty. He might get back here in a couple of years. I hope so, anyway—he grew up here. He's in college in Oregon and has his grandma in a nursing home up there so he can visit her often. But he hasn't talked about selling the house so I think he's hoping to come back. He might end up working with Paul." He poured himself a cup of coffee. "The kids would love it. Having you for a teacher. Right now, the people who can afford it are carpooling their kids all the way into the valley for private preschool. We ought to have one of those, too. Even if there aren't more than a dozen preschoolers. Mel says the kids who miss that have a disadvantage."

"I think you're the sneakiest man I've ever known in my life," she said.

"Yeah, so I've been told a time or two. But you have your plans. It was just a thought. I know better," he said. "Too bad you have to miss the pageant, though, after all the time you put in helping."

Ha! The pageant was just one thing! There were other, far more exciting things to her. Spending her days with children who were just learning to learn. Helping them construct art projects that showed their imaginations. Having learning games that were fun and funny. And field trips—she *loved* field trips! The parents of her kids were always running for their lives and hiding under beds to avoid being chaperones, and Becca *loved* field trips.

"You couldn't do it," she said to Jack. "You have to have it certified—the whole school. That's the only way you get funding. You'd need a school board. You'd have to form a PTA."

"Hey, if we can pull a bunch of church deacons out of this run-down, sinful town, we can manage a school board and PTA." He grinned.

A bunch of guys came into the bar, all rosy-cheeked and laughing. Jack excused himself and set them up a few drinks, absorbed the latest news and left Becca alone to think. She had a good ten minutes before he was back. He wiped off the bar in front of her.

He studied her for a moment. Then he said, "If I screwed up your last night in town by tossing out crazy ideas, I'll have to apologize."

She turned those crystal-blue eyes up at him. "I kind of miss my mom," she said. "She wasn't exactly supportive of me coming up here." She shrugged. "It wasn't as last minute as I said. I was sort of plotting it…."

He turned a fake shocked expression on her. "No way."

She smirked. "I really had no idea what I was walking into. It was quite a gamble. After all, Denny could have been committed." She lifted one shoulder in a half shrug. "It's not as though that's the kind of thing he'd be likely to tell Rich."

"It worked out for you, Becca. And I'm glad."

"Thanks. He's a really special guy."

"You're a special young woman." He leaned on the bar. "Tell me something. Aside from Denny, who is now your slave till the end of time, what do *you* really want? What's your big dream?"

She shrugged again. "It's totally crazy," she said, staring into her wineglass.

"Come on," he urged. "Lay it on me."

She looked up. She took a steadying breath. "When I was a little girl, I had a couple of teachers who were so awesome, I sometimes liked to pretend they were my big sister or aunt or even my mother. We had one of them to dinner once—Miss Tindle. She was young and sweet and made me love school. Then there was Mrs. Dallas—she helped me love school again after an awful teacher just traumatized me. I had a teacher in junior high, Mr. Hutchins… I loved that man. I had such a hard time in his math class and he still managed to make me feel smart. He was so funny, so patient, so *there* for every one of his kids." She blinked. "That's what I want. I want to be that teacher to some kids. I want some twenty-five-year-olds or forty-year-olds to say, 'I'll never forget Miss Timm—without her, I'd probably be nowhere.'"

He covered her hand with his big paw. "I have a feeling about you, Becca. I have a feeling you already are that teacher."

She smiled. Then she said, "Are you serious about that prefab modular school?"

He gave a nod. "As a heart attack."

"I think you might've just totally screwed up my plans for Christmas...."

Seventeen

Becca begged a moment of privacy in the Middletons' house to call her mother. "You were right," Becca said. "I was taking a big chance coming up here like I did."

"Oh, honey," Beverly said. "This doesn't sound good. What happened?"

"What happened is, I fell totally in love. With Denny, of course, but also with the kids. With the bartender and his wife. With the town. Denny wants to live here and..." She took a breath. "And I have a job offer. Jack offered to put up a schoolhouse for me. So I can teach the little kids."

"You can't be serious," Beverly said.

"I am totally serious."

"Then why do you sound down?"

"Well, there's only one thing wrong with it. It's much too far from one of my best friends." She felt her throat thicken even as her vision blurred with tears. "We don't agree that often, Mom, but at the end of the day, you're always on my side."

"Oh, Becca," Beverly said. "Best friends are never very far apart. The job sounds great, but what I really want to know is, have you made the right decision about Denny?"

"Oh, yes. He is the man I missed so much, the man I fell in love with such a long time ago, before I was ready for it. Before *he* was ready for it. I wish you could see him here, with the people of this town. He takes such good care of his friends. He looks after people he doesn't even know. And, Mom, he takes such good care of me. Even though this place is the best thing that's ever happened to him, he never hesitated for a second in saying he'd move back to San Diego to be with me. Anything that would make me happy, he would do it. I love him so much. Mom, it's right. It's completely right with Denny. I'm going to marry him."

"Please, please don't rush," Beverly pleaded. "At least give yourself time to think, to be sure. Besides, I want to be the mother of the bride!"

She laughed through her tears. "Of course, Mom. Do I have your blessing?"

"Becca, a very long time ago I had to leave my parents to start a new life with your dad. It was one of the hardest things I ever did. Sometimes I was so lonely. But nothing helped me grow up faster than taking that new direction and building my own family. I've watched you the past few years. Much as I wanted you to, you never let go of Denny. He was always the love of your life. I'm only going to ask you one more time—are you sure? Of him?"

"I'm sure," she said. "I've never been more sure. Mom? Will you be very disappointed if I don't live in San Diego?"

"I might become an expert on flight schedules," she said with a laugh.

"This is the first year I wasn't there to help get out all the decorations and ornaments," Becca said. "Like the really old ones from your grandmother. When I was little, it was a very big deal to peel back the tissue paper and discover some of those precious holiday things…the crystal balls, the crewel tree skirt, the nativity scene that Great-Grandpa carved."

"I'm sure we'll have many holidays together in the future," Beverly said. "I'll miss you the rest of the time, but what I want for you is much bigger than our friendship and our holidays together. It's time for you to build your own family. I can't be so selfish that I'd put restrictions on how you do that."

Becca cried. "You are the best mother. If I can be half as good a mother as you…"

"I have no doubt you'll show me up! Now, when are you coming home?"

She sniffed back her tears. "I'm going to stay long enough to see the pageant I helped with and to tell the kids and my friends that I'm coming back. Will you be terribly hurt if I don't get home until late on Christmas day?"

"I'll hold dinner," she said. "Just don't rush. Drive carefully and safely."

"We'll leave extra, extra early. The weather will be good. We'll make good time. I'll stay home a week—long enough to pack, close up the apartment and spend some time with you and Dad. And Jack, the guy who owns the bar, he's going to fix us up with a little two-bedroom house in town rather than that one room over the garage. Denny's been saving for a house. In a couple of years…"

"Are *you* going to be all right if you're not here for Christmas Eve?" Beverly asked.

"The little girl I told you about? The one who's playing Mary in the pageant? She reminds me of me. Oh, her life is much more difficult than mine ever was, but if anyone could use a champion, it's that kid. I'm going to watch her do her part, tell her that I'm going to be around to make sure she gets smiley faces on her good papers, and then we'll get a little sleep so we can start the drive home real early."

"I can't wait to see you, sweetheart," she said.

"Me, too. Thank you, Mom. Thank you for believing in me. Thank you for trusting me to know what I want."

"Becca, my sweet girl, this is far easier than watching you bungee jump or poised at the top of a thirty-foot wave. And tell our sweet Denny that if he ever hurts you like that again, he'll answer to *me*!"

She laughed through her tears. "I'll tell him. But I bet he already knows."

It was during dinner at the bar with the Sheridans and the Middletons that Becca made her announcement. She hadn't even told Denny in private first. She said, "Jack and I came up with an arrangement that works for me and for Virgin River. He's going to put up a schoolhouse and I'm going to be the teacher. We have lots of details to work out, but that's the gist. I called home and told my mom. I told her I'd just be coming home for Christmas dinner—and to pack up my apartment."

Denny was frozen. He had a spoonful of stew halfway to his mouth and he dropped it.

She hooked her gaze into his and said, "I hope you can get your job back with Jilly Farms, because I made a commitment."

"You told your mother this?" he asked.

"Yes," she said. She lifted her chin and a tear slid down her cheek. "She said you better be very nice to me."

He smiled and, cradling her jaw in his hand, he kissed the corner of her mouth. Then the other corner. And then he said, "Okay."

There was a dress rehearsal for the pageant at noon on Christmas Eve and when the kids saw Becca crutch her way into the church, they all squealed and broke ranks to run to her. When she told them she was going home to San Diego to pack up her things and come back as their full-time teacher, cheers and tears surrounded her. Megan Thickson clung to her and wouldn't let go.

"This is the best Christmas ever," she said.

The pageant began at 7:00 p.m. sharp. The church was completely full. The entire Sheridan clan from out of town attended. Jillian and her sister and the Riordan clan were there. Everyone Becca had ever met and many she hadn't—a real community affair.

Becca's role was behind the scenes, telling Mary and Joseph when to walk down the aisle toward the manger at the apex of the church. Then she pushed off the wise men one at a time and finally the shepherds. Ellie Kincaid directed the angels from the door that led to the church office and their voices were never more angelic. Christopher read the story of the birth of Christ and finally the congregation joined the angels in singing a couple of carols.

Then the lights in the church came up and many congratulations were exchanged before the entire gathering moved to the church basement, where cookies, coffee and punch were waiting. Becca received what seemed like a hundred hugs and offers of help in setting up a school. There were dozens of congratulations to the announcement that Denny and Becca would marry, hopefully in summer.

Then Preacher cut his way through the crowd. He was wearing his jacket and carrying a box. "This came to the bar right before the pageant started," he said. "It was expressed—and it's addressed to you, Becca."

"What in the world," she said, taking the box. "It's from my mother!"

She put the box on a nearby table and opened it. She peeled back the tissue paper to reveal the beautiful crewel tree skirt her great-grandmother had made, that had been passed down to her mother along with so many other precious decorations. There was a note on top in her mother's hand.

Time to start your own traditions.
Love, Mom

* * * * *

Return to Thunder Point with
#1 *New York Times* bestselling author

ROBYN CARR

and discover a town where hard work and determination make dreams come true.

Professional triathlete Blake Smiley has traveled the world, but Thunder Point has what he needs to put down roots. There he can focus on his training without distractions. That is, until he meets his new neighbors.

Lin Su Simmons and her teenage son, Charlie, are fixtures at Winnie Banks's house as Lin Su nurses Winnie through the realities of ALS. A single mother, Lin Su is proud of taking charge and never showing weakness. But she has her hands full coping with a job, debt and Charlie's health issues.

When Charlie enlists Blake's help to escape his overprotective mother, Lin Su resents the interference in her life. But Blake is certain he can break through her barriers and be the man she and Charlie need. Slowly, Lin Su realizes Blake just might be the man of her dreams.

Available now, wherever books are sold!

Be sure to connect with us at:

Harlequin.com/Newsletters

Facebook.com/HarlequinBooks

Twitter.com/HarlequinBooks

www.MIRABooks.com

MRC1749